BECO

Chris Ord

For Brian Hannaford

Carpe diem

'The old world is dying away, and the new world struggles to come forth. Now is the time of monsters.'
(Antonio Gramsci)

1

Gaia was desperate to escape, but there were the creatures. At night there were often noises, chilling, high-pitched shrieks that curdled the blood. Shadows moved, the glimmer of a tail, or the arch of a back as something swept through the waves. They were black, the merest hint, a flicker, never more. There was something in the water. She looked out over the sea, and across to the mainland. It was inviting her. The journey was not far, the stretch of water was narrow, maybe a mile. The waters were not deep, but the currents were treacherous, and the dark shadows were waiting. The creatures and the narrow stretch of water were all that lay between her and a new future, of answers and truth, her answers and truth, not the community's.

Gaia crouched on the beach, combing the grey sand with her blue marble eyes and soft fingertips. Caressing the sand, her long, red plaited hair swept over her shoulder, piercing eyes looking for the beads. The small, fossilised shells, that had washed up on this beach on the island for centuries. This beach alone. Each had a distinct conical shape, flat not pointed, a small hole ran through the centre. She collected them, and had throughout her time on the island, threading them in fishing line, making necklaces and bracelets. This was strictly forbidden. It was wasteful, only constructive tasks allowed. She would be punished if caught, and that meant isolation at the far end of the island. Locked in the space beyond the walls where few went, and even fewer returned. Those that did never spoke of what they saw, or what they endured. No-one spoke of what they had experienced. The past meant nothing to the community. There was only their present and their future, designed by them, determined by them, for the greater good. The individual was nothing, the community was everything.

She had heard whispers of the fossils, once called 'St Cuthbert's beads'. A name from the old religion, the old ways, those none spoke of anymore. Only the whispers remained. The ruins of the abbey stood not far from the shoreline, dominating the skyline. They were an echo of what may have been before, a question, not a reminder, there was nothing to be reminded of. All history of the abbey had been destroyed. The bold, imposing castle watched over them from the mount of rock at the southernmost point of the island. It was still intact, well preserved, but deserted. Some spoke of spirits there, ghosts, voices heard, and shadows seen. There'd been no attempt to destroy it, only to demolish all memory of its past. It was there, but no longer existed.

Both the abbey and castle had been built by Holy People. They had settled on the island many years ago, seeking sanctuary from those that looked to persecute them. Those that would destroy simply for who they were and what they believed. The island had provided safety, a haven. It was a place to build a new community around the old ways. St. Cuthbert was one of the Holy People, one of the founders of that religion. The island had once been named 'Holy Island' or 'Lindisfarne.'

This was all before her, and the time of the new community. The island still provided sanctuary, but now it was for the new ways, after the poison.

The beach was Gaia's refuge, the place she came to be alone, to wonder and question, to collect and create. Much of her free time was spent making the necklaces and bracelets. Once finished they would be concealed in a hole at the far end of the beach, a secret only she knew, the place of her findings, her treasure, her rebellion. These were her links to the past, one imagined but never known.

The beads were her oldest objects. She did not know what they were, but suspected they were ancient. There were other things too: ornate shells; shimmering stones; shards of frosted glass smooth from decades of churning waves. There were also fragments of the recent past: splinters of wood; flotsam; gnarled pieces of rope; junk; chunks of plastic decorated with letters and words. There were her magical finds, her special treasures like her yellow, plastic duck which squeaked when squeezed. Where had it come from? How had it found its way to her? There was also the small, bright orange ball, made of rubber, soft and squishy like sponge. There was her prized possession, bobbing in the water by the shoreline, nodding, waiting to be rescued. It was an old, brown bottle with a cork in, a piece of paper concealed within. On it was a hand-written message, faded, short and simple:

'All is not what it seems. Seek the truth.'

Gaia would often sit and read the blurred words and wonder who had written them, feeling sure she was meant to find it. If not her, someone like her, someone who questioned, who wanted to know more. Escape would be difficult, though there were rumours of those that had made it. No-one knew for sure. Gaia was determined she would be the one, and this is what drove her, kept her alive. Escape was her reason for being, and it was only a matter of time. When the moment was right. She would know when. The bottle and the message were a sign, telling her, calling her to find the truth.

A bell clanged. Free time was over, and it was time to return. Gaia stood, shook herself down, and removed the sand from her canvas trousers and navy shirt. Looking across the water one more time, the waves rolling and tumbling she saw it. It could have been a mistake, but no, there it was again. This was no trick of light or wave. It was real, a flash of something moving just below the surface. It left a splash in its wake. It was a considerable size, and it was fast. She scoured the waters, but it was gone, a shiver running down her spine. Composing herself, Gaia made her way back up the dunes towards the Dome. Others were emerging and making their way from their own private refuges. Scurrying from their own special places with their own thoughts and treasures, and making their own secrets. The bell rang for a second time, and she picked up her pace. From the dunes beyond the beach something stirred, someone. They were watching.

2

The dome was a huge green marquee. Never intended as permanent, it was the best they could do. It was all they would allow given the limited resources, and the lessons they had learnt from before. Inside the floor had been lined with a fixed wooden base. A central pole towered overhead around which stood a raised platform with stairs leading to it. There were large cushions everywhere, each grey and numbered. Every member of the community had a number and a cushion. They were known by that number. Names were tolerated and used, but only amongst the young.

On the platform more cushions encircled the central pole. This was where the twenty leaders sat. They had names not numbers. They were meant to be equal, no single leader dominant. The community knew different though. There were those that had more power and presence, and one at the very top, the leader of leaders.

The young filed in and sat in their places. The leaders watched over them as they assembled. Once they were assured all were there the bell rang three times in quick succession. There was silence, and everyone waited. All the leaders sat bar one. She stood at the head of the platform as the other leaders sat and waited.

Kali paced around the edge of the platform, her head bowed and hands clasped behind her back. She wore green canvas trousers, and a navy shirt. On her feet were light sandals, no socks. Her hair was short, almost shaven to her skull, her eyes the brightest blue. Her skin was light, not yet wrinkled, but scarred and worn. Kali was one of the elders, maybe in her forties. No-one knew for sure. All the leaders were fit and agile, at their physical and mental peak. Every now and then a leader would disappear and be replaced. No-one knew why. Being a leader was a privilege and a position of note. All contributions to the community were deemed equal, but everyone knew the leaders were special and held above all else. At the end of your becoming you were designated a role, and being a leader was the pinnacle. All the young wanted to be leaders. All except Gaia. Kali addressed the group.

'Community. Welcome. Once again we gather together to share our reflections, learn from each other, and discuss how we can progress. This is an important time for us all, as the time of your becoming will soon be here. In a few weeks you'll ascend to the next phase of your journey where you'll make your greatest contribution, and be given your role. This will determine how you help to shape the community. It'll give you the opportunity to apply all you've learned so far, all your specialist knowledge and skills. You'll leave the island and move to new settlements, some of you to the haven. These are exciting times.

In a moment you'll break into your groups and go to your areas to share and discuss your reflections. But first I'd like to invite one of you to join me on the platform to give today's reading.'

The tension in the room mounted as they waited for the announcement. Most heads were bowed, hoping to avoid eye contact. Not that it mattered, as the decision had been made. Kali was silent as she paced back and forth, her hands still behind her back. She stopped and stared straight at Gaia. There was a pause as their eyes locked, Kali uttered the dreaded words.

'Thirty seven.'

Gaia sighed. This was her seventh occasion. It confirmed to her she was being singled out. Making her way between the others towards the steps, there was relief as their anticipation and fear dissolved. This would soon be replaced by glazed eyes and creeping boredom. For Gaia this was all part of the game, being who they wanted and expected. Painting her face with the appropriate expression, she would deliver what was asked.

Gaia climbed the steps, and neared Kali who was waiting, her arms held forward holding an open book. Gaia kept her head bowed, and did not notice the wry smile on Kali's face, or the brief flash in her eye and flare of the nostrils. Taking the book she turned to face the others. It was a circular room, and the drill was to move around the platform, ensuring all members of the community saw you. Everyone had to feel as though they were being addressed, that the words were meant for them all.

Gaia examined the page, and scanned the words laid out before her. Each was waiting to be brought to life by the caress of her voice, to sail through the air, leap from ear to ear, and worm into their minds. Every letter had a function, every word a meaning, something to open and absorb, to poke, prod and unpick. Every paragraph could be played with, given new light and twisted interpretations. Every page could illuminate, inspire, and enthuse. There before her were the still and lifeless words. She focused on them, and spoke, her voice crisp and clear.

'The stag story. One day a hunter hears a knock at the door. He opens it to find another hunter.

'Today I'm going to hunt a stag,' the hunter at the door says.

'I cannot do it on my own, but together we may be successful.'

'What is in this for me?' The other hunter asks.

'An equal share of the deer,' he replies.

'On your own you are only likely to catch a far smaller animal, but a deer is a large catch with fine meat. It will last us both through the winter.'

The hunter thinks about it and they agree to work together as a team.'

Gaia moved around the platform, absorbing the words and projecting them, reaching out to each section of audience. Her words washed over them, some listened, but most let them drift past, their minds shutting down. She continued.

'The hunters go out together into the forest and separate, watching and waiting for any sign of a deer. Suddenly, one of the hunters sees a hare run past him. It is close by and would be easy prey. However, he doesn't want to divert from the task of hunting the deer. Killing the hare would break the deal, and it would let the other hunter down. The hunter is torn. Here is an easy kill, and there is no guarantee they will find a deer. They could waste the day and find nothing. The deer would be a better catch, but it is a big risk. The hunter has a dilemma. Why work together when there is an opportunity to work alone? What should he do?'

Gaia stopped, closed the book and looked up. Kali approached and took the book from her.

'Thank you thirty seven. Please return to your place.'

Gaia climbed down the steps and made her way to her cushion while Kali watched and waited, and addressed them all.

'You've heard the story of the stag hunters. It's a simple story, but within it lies a powerful dilemma, one we all face. It is about a contract between people, a social contract, something that binds them to work together for the greater good, something powerful, a sense of obligation, a realisation that you are stronger together than alone.'

From beyond the dome the clanging bell sounded again. This time it rang repeatedly in a wild frenzy. This was the alarm. They were under attack. It was the rats. Everyone sprung to their feet. They were calm, assured, showing no signs of outward panic. They had been here many times before. Everyone was trained and well drilled, all forming into orderly lines. The leaders brought large wooden boxes from the central platform, and made their way to the head of each line. They opened the boxes and handed out weapons: spears; daggers; scythes; small axes. All simple, but effective in the right hands, and all of the young knew how to use them. Some, like Gaia, were expert killers and fighters. This was their specialism. Each line now had a leader, and they all took their weapons and made their way to one of the exits.

The warning from those on lookout always gave plenty time to gather, to prepare, and wait. The numbers of rats varied, and of late the attacks had been heavy, brutal, and the numbers had risen. They were large, the size of a dog, quick, and ferocious. They hunted in packs, and were savage killers. They roamed the island, most often sticking to more remote parts away from the community. They were the products of what came before, of the poison. At first they were a myth. Then there were sightings and as they grew in numbers they were seen much more. For a long time they had been satisfied with feeding on scraps and hunting other animals. When they were desperate they would feed on the weak within their own. At first the attacks were random, isolated, always on lone community members. A body would be found, mauled and shredded, the distinctive tooth offering a clue. Then came the offerings. The community began to collect waste food and dump it on the far side of the island, to satisfy their hunger, to keep them at bay, and alleviate the attacks. It worked for a while, but they came again, and grew in number and ferocity. The island was limited, prey was becoming scarce. The rats were now more desperate and there were far more of them, too many. The island was a place of finite resources. From scavenger they became hunter. They adapted and became more organised. They attacked in larger packs, more and more, wave upon wave, growing in confidence, fueled by hunger and desire. It was hunt and kill or starve and perish, and the community was now their prime target.

Everyone filed out and moved towards their sections, each headed by a leader. Gaia's group was led by Kali. They took a position to the far left of the dome, on the edge of the dwellings, in the dunes. It was a raised position, protected by the long sharp grass sprouting from the sand. Their role was to wait until the rats moved towards the front line of defence, they would then sweep down and attack them from behind. There would be the element of surprise. The rats would be sandwiched, having to attack two lines front and rear.

Gaia crouched low in the grass, well hidden, a good vantage point with a clear view of their attackers as they swarmed forward. They would see their numbers, the ferocity of the onslaught, and have time to prepare. It was worse for the front-line, as they saw them much later, often only as they were upon them. They had to be instinctive and make the right calls. The front line tended to be the older and better trained. Gaia was never part of the frontline which puzzled her and others. She excelled in combat and was one of the most effective killers, yet was always in a rearguard position, and led by Kali.

Everyone waited and listened. They always heard them first. There was the scurrying sound, like the rattle of snare drum, faint at first, but growing louder and louder. As the rats approached and sensed their prey drawing near they would screech. It was a jarring, high pitched noise that pierced the ears, clawed at the skin, and gnawed at the bones. That was when the heart raced, when the adrenalin shot through the veins, when each felt the urge to jump up and pounce, to scream, to attack. They had to resist though, as it could be fatal. The community were trained to be composed, to contain the electricity, the wave of excitement, to harness it. To react and bolt would mean death.

There was silence. The bell had stopped. All that could be heard was the whispering of the wind between the dune grass. Gaia listened, but still there was nothing. To her right was a young girl, about six feet away hugging the sandy floor. She was shaking, beads of sweat dripping from her forehead. Her face was white and her eyes flared with terror. Gaia shuffled across and held her. Looking down at her, Gaia smiled and whispered.

'Don't worry. I know it's scary, but remember your training. Try to stay calm. I'm here if anything goes wrong. I'll watch your back.'

The shivering eased, and the girl looked at Gaia, a smile crept on her lips, but it was awkward and forced. She still looked petrified.

'Thanks. This is my first attack. I'm scared.'

'It's OK. Stay focused and you'll get through it.'

They lay together, waiting. Gaia could feel the girl's tension, her stiff body gripped with fear, her frantic breathing. Then it came, the sound of the low rattle, rising as they neared. There was something different to the sound though. It was broader, more intense than usual. It could mean only one thing. The shrieking came, like none Gaia had heard before. It was deafening, chilling, blood curdling. The girl began to shake. She was curled into a ball and covering her ears, pushing Gaia, fighting her, struggling to break free. Gaia held her tight, wrestled with her, pinned her to the floor. Breaking ranks would make her prey. The rats would see her, sense the vulnerability, weakness, and would attack. Gaia whispered.

'Try to be calm.'

The girl began to scream, a loud, wailing cry, a siren. Gaia placed her hand over the girl's mouth and tried to muffle the cries, but she continued to wail, fight and kick. The moment came, the trigger, the turning point. The girl bit Gaia's hand. Gaia pulled her arm away in shock as the girl flung her off, jumped to her feet, and hurtled down the dune towards the beach. Gaia lurched forward, and went to make after her, but something clicked, took over, stopping and composing herself. Gaia wanted to follow her, save her, but something prevented her. She froze, as though a switch had been flipped. Her mind was racing, willing her to move, but she could not. Everything told her to stay with the others, focus on the task. A voice inside was barking at her. They were a team. They were stronger together. It pounded like a drum inside, the rhythm of all their training, their programming. This voice, the belief, it was the difference between living or dying. If Gaia tried to save the girl, she would die. Heroes were noble fools. They died. That is what defined them. Gaia ducked back down in the grassy dunes, and watched as the girl fled alone.

The rats were lightning quick. In a split second a group saw their victim, broke out, pursued her, and pounced. The leader lunged towards her jugular like an arrow. Its dripping jaws, and razor sharp teeth exposed. Ready to plunge into the neck and rip her throat. The rats' jaws hit their target, and with one flick of the neck severed the artery and tore away a chunk of flesh. Blood spurted from the wound, the shock rendering the girl helpless. She fell to the ground, writhing in agony. The rat was upon her. Its long, fleshy tail flapping. Its head ripping and wrestling with her throat.

That was the signal. The others smothered her body in seconds, tearing it to shreds in a series of frantic bites. The creatures were swift and surgical, with seldom time to feast, little window for them to savour, knowing an attack would be upon them soon. The rodents exploited vulnerability, but were at their weakest as they fed. There was a flurry of frenetic bites as they seared her warm flesh, clutching the few seconds available to ease their hunger. These were the brief flashes of savagery, before the rats would move onto their next victim. The next piece of prey felled by one of their own. They too were stronger together.

It was all over in an instant, and the rats moved on, back towards the front line where the main attack had begun. The girl lay in a heap. Only her bloodied, dismembered torso remained. The flesh from her front had been stripped, leaving bone and entrails. Gaia turned away in disgust and shame. It was over. It was done. The girl was weak. There was no way to save her. Any attempt would have killed them both. The girl panicked, broke free, and paid the ultimate price. Staring at the crimson remains, a shiver of horror and sorrow ran through Gaia's body. She had done the right thing, but hated herself for it.

Gaia focused back on the main onslaught. Watching and waiting, looking for where and when, ready for the moment of their attack. Kali would give the signal. It was always the same cry. Kali looked for the point where the frontline were struggling, where they needed help to bolster numbers and split the rat lines. Either that or wait for a moment of weakness, the point at which the rats were suffering heavy losses, when they were faltering.

The swarms of rats were met by each frontline team, where they were slaughtered and eliminated. The teams worked together as one. Everything ran as planned, as taught, drilled, and programmed. Each plunged spears into the creatures, severed throats with knives, thrust axes into skulls, and crushed them with hammers. The central lines, where the main onslaught was taking place were coping well. They were the primary line of defence, with the bulk of the young. The rats were drawn towards them, to the critical mass, but this was where the creatures were weak.

The rats saw food, but what waited were skilled assassins. The rodents had become hunters through necessity, but were still scavengers by skill. The creatures had speed, but were crude, impulsive, and lacked stamina and resilience. They were desperate, not courageous, and would retreat as soon as there was a sign of danger or defeat, or they were slain in any numbers. There was always a tipping point. Hunger drove them to attack, but the instinct was to run. The community knew this, and that they had to hit them with intensity and ferocity. Both the leaders and young people were brutal, slaying without prejudice, without thought, without emotion. They were a unit, a killing machine. Their aim was to bludgeon the creatures with an onslaught of terror forcing the rats to crumble and flee.

Gaia noticed something from the corner of her eye. So focused on the main onslaught, and death of the girl she had not seen them coming. There was another wave, fewer than the first, but still significant in number. This had never happened before. Either the creatures were becoming braver, or more desperate. The rats were learning from the mistakes of previous attacks, and their confidence was building.

The second wave swept over the corpses of the first. Almost all the dead were rats. A few of the community had bites and lacerations, but none were down or dead. None except the girl. The teams met the second wave, but they were tiring and surprised by the fresh onslaught. Now was the moment. It had to be. Kali must respond soon. Gaia waited. The tension and anticipation smothered her. Her chest was pumping and her heart pounding. The speed and frenzy of the carnage below seemed to be in slow motion. There was the flailing of arms, the hurtling of spears, and the flash of daggers. Black lurching bodies leapt and were flung away, the blood of the slain rats splattering on clothes and faces. It was a quilt of crimson death, spreading across their bodies like a disease, staining them in its fleeting warmth. Gaia and the others on the dune were locked in limbo, hanging, waiting. They were like a coil ready to spring, a bullet about to be fired, a wild cat waiting to pounce. They were locked on their target, their eyes fixed and ready, waiting for Kali's cry.

It came. Without a thought Gaia and the others leapt to their feet and cascaded down the dune. Kali was at the front, followed by Gaia. Kali leapt forward like a panther and in an instant she had reached them, the others close behind. They had caught them off-guard. The element of surprise had worked. Kali took the first kill. She was cold and clinical, deadly, plunging her spear into its back, then her dagger through its head. Without hesitation or thought Gaia moved onto her next victim. With two movements it was all over, then another, and another. One by one they were butchered. Instinctive and unrelenting, without any emotion, leaving a trail of carnage in her wake.

Gaia mirrored Kali, and launched herself at them. The first was a straight kill through the head with her dagger, the second crush of the skull with a hammer. Blood shot from her victim and sprayed across her face, feeling its warmth as it touched her lips. The tumbling onslaught continued. Rat upon rat, victim after victim. Together Kali and Gaia swept through the sea of rodents, each slain in swift succession. They were like a dancing duet, choreographed in a ballet of brutality, smooth and sweeping. The rearguard attack was proving decisive, and the second wave of rats were being swept aside. One by one they fell, but did not crumble, nor flee. Instead, the creatures fought on in an attack that was intense and relentless, the most vicious to date. The rats were different, more of a match and threat. They were growing stronger.

Gaia saw someone struggling, a boy, a few feet to her right. He had fallen, knocked off his feet by the force of an attack. Seeing the opportunity, a couple of rats had moved in for the kill. He was managing to fend them off, but wouldn't hold out much longer. Gaia hurtled across to save him, diving at one of the rodents, and with one swift movement slitting its throat. Casting it aside, she launched a fierce blow to the head of the other. Stunned, it rolled over, as her knife plunged in its chest twisting, jerking, and removing the blade. The boy jumped to his feet, his face smothered in blood, eyes ablaze, a mixture of fear and relief. He staggered backwards.

'Thanks! I owe you.'

'Don't mention it.'

Gaia recognised him, had noticed him before. It was number eighty four, Aran. His face lit up with alarm.

'Look out!'

Aran grabbed a spear and hurled it over her shoulder. Gaia turned and rolled away, looking back to where the rat lay impaled by the spear. Its dark body was still writhing, clamouring to reach them, its jaws slavering in desperation. The same jaws that had been aimed at her throat, and within a second would have reached her. It fought and flailed, struggling in the last moments of imminent death. Dark blood oozed from the fatal wound. The spear had penetrated its heart, ripped through its soft flesh, the spear that had saved her.

'Now we're even. Let's see if we can break them.'

'Do you think we can hold out?'

'They'll crumble and turn. They always do. Come on.'

Aran reached out his hand and helped Gaia to her feet. His blue eyes caught hers, the sun flashing through her red hair. For a moment there was a connection, brief and awkward, but enough. They both looked away. He was tall, fair haired, attractive. His grip firm and arm strong as he pulled her up from the ground. Like all on the island he had been bred and nurtured to be trim and athletic. Gaia noted his sparkling eyes and the faintest hint of a grin. Eyes which had been admired by her before.

They fought on together, despite being weary and jaded. After several more decisive kills the rats broke ranks and began to flee. One after another they turned and scurried away, their coarse, black hairs stained with the fresh blood of the others. The creatures scattered and fled into the fields beyond, but the community knew the rodents would be back. Next time they would be bolder and stronger again. For now the victory belonged to the community. They would savour it. For now the community remained safe and intact.

Gaia looked around, the boy still by her side, sitting, head in hands, exhausted. It was all sinking in now, how close they had been to death. They were alive, and that was all the mattered for now. Gaia surveyed the carnage, the festering aftermath. There were corpses everywhere, mostly black and red, steaming rodents, their thick hair and long pink tails soaked in death. Most lay still, but some still heaved, death not yet upon them. The leaders and young people each made their way through the remains and finished off the near dead. Nine, maybe ten of the community were injured. They were tended to by the medical specialists. Two lay dead. Two, in addition to the girl who still lay away from the main group, alone on the edge of the dunes. Kali crouched next to one of the slain, head bowed in honour and respect. Her hands reached down and closed their eyelids one by one, lifeless eyes now locked beneath.

Gaia moved back to where Aran was resting. She sat down, and put her arm around him, a gesture only, there were no words. He knew what was meant, and appreciated it. For a moment they sat together, sharing a rare moment of tenderness and warmth. Something they both needed, a reminder of their humanity, a reassurance of life. He tilted his head towards her and whispered.

'Thanks again.'

'It was nothing. We got through it, and we're still here. That's all that matters.'

They sat for a while, wrapped in the blanket of each other's warmth, their thoughts locked together. Gaia was not accustomed to this. She had little interest in boys, at least not in the way that some of the others did. To her they were shallow and childish, trying to impress with their lame jokes, and puerile shows of physical prowess. The boys in the community all looked and acted the same. Most of the other girls seemed to disagree. They would roll their eyes, and let out giddy laughter, flick their hair and flirt. Each loved to play the fool to attract the boy's attention, but not Gaia.

Physical liaisons were frowned upon, but it happened. There were attempts to conceal them, but with little success. It was tolerated by the leaders, monitored and contained. As long as it was discreet the young on the island were fine. Open shows of affection or contact were forbidden. This was never a concern for Gaia. Her icy disdain was apparent, and boys made no attempt to thaw her. However, Aran was different. She had noticed him before and made a point of finding out about him. This boy did not act the same as the others. There were no jokes, no attempts to show off. He was quiet, shy, kept to himself. There was a distance from the others, and most left him alone. Aran was on the fringes, much like Gaia, respected for his skill, but not courted. There was a mystery, something compelling, and for some reason Gaia had been drawn to him. There was a story with Aran, something more. He intrigued her, made her want to find out more.

Aran and Gaia rested for a while, drifting in the comedown, the aftermath. The community would regroup soon and consider the attack together, looking at lessons for the next time. The rats would return, and the community must be ready.

3

Gaia lay in her bed staring at the base of the bunk above. The wire supports stretched across the metal frame bulged and creaked. She had looked at them a thousand times, studied every detail, reached up and traced the weaving line as it spread across the divide. Hooking her fingers under each, Gaia would allow the wire to take the weight of her arm. She had threaded string through to create ornate patterns, turning the cold, grey metalwork into a sea of colour, like an exotic snake. This was her nightly view, her routine and shell. This was Gaia's moment alone, her time to think.

It was a large dormitory with twenty bunks, filled with thirty nine girls. The room was dark and silent, oozing a damp and musty odour. The building was made of timber, and had a varnished, wooden floor and high pitched ceiling. Each bed had a table next to it and a wardrobe at its base. Clothes and belongings were few, so their was ample room for storage. The dorm had been an outward bound centre in the old days. The island was popular with holiday makers. They would come in organised packs, tribes of young people in uniforms and ties, singing bizarre songs, and performing strange rituals. Gaia had found a magazine behind one of the wardrobes and read about the world before, the now lost and distant past. The dorm had toilets and shower rooms at one end. At the other was a doorway to the entrance hall, and a room where the leader slept.

Gaia was having trouble sleeping. This was not unusual. Her mind would not shut down, often bursting alive in the last few hours of the day. In that time just before sleeping when you are meant to unwind, a charge would shoot through her, like an electric current. Thoughts would race through her head, pounding from all angles. She would try and catch them, order and contain them, make some sense of them. Sometimes there would be moments of perfect clarity, where the light would blaze, and everything would slot into place. Those rarest of moments when everything would make sense. More often there would be the demons and darkness, the anger and hatred, the hunger and thirst for revenge. There were often thoughts of conflict, a longing to strike out against those that wronged, controlled, and oppressed her. Gaia longed to destroy the ones that prevented her from breaking free. There were often visions of the pain she would bring upon those who stopped her from finding herself, and the parents never known. She often thought of killing.

Most of the mental venom was thrust towards Kali. The one that pushed her, ordered her, commanded her, dictated to her, and abused her. It was often the smallest of things, the looks, the things said and even unsaid, the body language. Gaia knew Kali hated her, and always had to put in extra effort to impress her, never managing to. At least Kali never acknowledged it. The day the rats attacked, Gaia had killed far more than the others, and had saved Aran from certain injury and possible death. She had fought as hard as ever, maybe harder. Kali wandered around in the aftermath, and laid reassuring hands on weary heads and shoulders. There were whispered words of comfort, and thanks. Yet when Kali came to Gaia all she could ask was what had happened with the young girl, the one who Gaia had allowed to die.

Gaia explained everything, but it was not enough for Kali who moved on. There was no comfort or reassurance, no thanks or commendation for the bravery Gaia had shown. All Kali said was that they needed to talk, and that Gaia was to go and see her tomorrow. This was Kali through and through. Plant the dagger, then twist and watch you wince and writhe.

There were several incidents that had nurtured Gaia's hatred. Instances when Kali would show her power and dominance, her willingness to inflict the severest pain. The first time was when Kali made Gaia stand in the snow in only a T-shirt and shorts until close to dying. All because Gaia had questioned her in front of the others. Soon after on construction duty Kali made Gaia drag the heaviest logs alone through thick mud. One by one, through the driving wind and rain. Worst of all were the quarantines. This was time in the shed where community members would be locked in solitary confinement for acts of disobedience. Kali had sent Gaia there more than anyone. One instance was during a sweltering summer when Gaia was locked inside for days without food and just enough water to survive. She was half-dead when Kali released her.

When Gaia was not hating Kali her thoughts were locked on Aran, his smile, his blue eyes. Such thinking was discouraged. The phases of their lives were functional, each with a purpose. The leaders had a role, and their ultimate goal was to shape the community, to turn them into productive members, to be the best that they could be. There was no room for sentiment, emotion, or shows of affection. Each stage of Gaia's life had felt like a cold, relentless march towards a manufactured outcome. The community had moved away from machines, but had become a machine itself. It was little more than a piece of engineering, an engine, a factory. The young were treated like parts within it, the cogs, the pistons, and the fuel. When they had become each would be given a separate role and function. Each would be honed and shaped, polished and finely tuned. Each would be necessary to the overall functioning of the machine. Emotion clouded rational thought and function, it was water in the oil. It served no purpose, but to complicate and confuse. There was something missing for Gaia.

The moments spent with Aran had stirred something inside her. Feelings she had not felt before, feelings that confused and frightened her. She wanted them to go away, tried to smother them, but could not. They kept returning. Gaia needed to control these emotions, but all thoughts kept returning to his smile, and they would churn and flare up inside her. The acid in her stomach would rage and spit as though it were about to erupt from her throat. She tossed and turned with the tingling and burning, the warmth for Aran, and burning hatred of Kali.

There was a tap at the window behind her. Gaia sat up and turned. There it was again, a gentle rap, maybe nothing. It came again, faint, not wanting to be heard. She stood, pulled back the corner of the curtain and peered out. The night was black, but for the soft light from the thinnest of crescent moons. Gaia peered over the ledge and saw Aran, his back pressed against the timber wall of the building. He peeked out and cast the briefest look up at her, pointed to the window, and gestured to her to open it. Gaia waved her hand at him to leave, but he twisted his face and shook his head, repeating the mime with more urgency. She mouthed the words 'No. Go away!' There was a silent plea, a begging look, and a pause. Aran shrugged his shoulders and shook his head, miming a sigh, and folding his arms.

Determined to end the charade, Gaia frowned and loosened the old iron latch. It was tight and almost rusted on. There was a creak as it came free. There was a pause as Gaia listened, fearing someone might stir. Sure there was nothing but silence she opened the window, just enough to speak through it. Lowering herself to the crack Gaia spat at him in an angry whisper.

'What are you doing here? You know what'll happen if we're caught!'

'I need to speak with you. It's important. Can we talk?'

'Are you mad? You're taking a big enough risk just being here. Get back to your dorm before you get us both thrown in the shed.'

Gaia tried to close the window, but Aran grabbed it. The whisper was louder, his voice becoming more desperate.

'Look, I wouldn't do this unless I had to. It isn't safe to speak in the day. You're being watched. Please Gaia. It's important.'

'What could be that important at this time of night?'

'It's about escaping the island.'

Gaia struggled to breath. This was not what she had expected at all. To meet Aran was risky and complicated, but this was too intriguing. She had to hear him out at least. Gaia's mind raced, thinking of all the complications, the possible dangers. There was the leader's room at the end of the dorm. She would need to get past that and out of the door without being heard. The door would be locked. There would be serious consequences if they were found. Then there were the night birds. These were large, shadowy creatures that patrolled the skies at night. Some said they had once been bats, and the poison had changed them, deformed them like the rats. Others claimed to have seen them, but sightings were rare and unreliable. There was very little light on the island after dark, as the old streetlights in the deserted village no longer worked, and there was no mains electricity. All power came from generators using fuel which was rationed, and it was considered wasteful to use it on night lights. Some thought the night birds a myth, something spread by the leaders to control them, to instill fear and stop them from leaving at night. At first Gaia preferred to believe this, as it made more sense to her, but there were the noises. Lying awake at night, her mind churning, she had heard things outside, flapping sounds, along with a strange clicking. These were rapid and loud at times. Gaia was convinced there was something sinister out there, creatures in the pitch black of the night skies, waiting for them. Gaia feared the night, the darkness, and the night birds. Aran reached up his hand and passed something through the window. It was a key.

'Here. This'll get you out of the dorm. I won't keep you long I promise. Just hear me out. Please.'

Gaia hesitated, but took the key and closed the window. She could regret this, but something urged her on. Perhaps this was the mystery, the story he was hiding. Aran had said she was being watched. What did he mean? Gaia had to find out.

Gaia dressed and reached under the bed for her boots, carrying them to the door, tiptoeing past the other bunks. She paused, grabbed the handle and eased the door open. There was a faint creak, but no-one stirred. When there was just enough room, Gaia squeezed through into the passage. Her leader was Hakan who was not as strict as the others, but would still see an attempt to leave as a serious offence. Her best chance was that he was preoccupied and distracted. It was often so. There was much talk about Hakan, along with some of the other male leaders, whispers of their behaviour with and power over some of the girls. Gaia knew it happened. They all did. She had heard girls creeping out of the dorm at night. They would leave when they thought the rest were sleeping, and return just before dawn. Everyone knew where they were going and why. It was another of the things unspoken. They were all targets and potential victims. If you were chosen there was little you could do to avoid it. There was a conspiracy of silence, a layer of hypocrisy that drew a veil over the unsavoury and unforgivable. It was the darkest of secrets, smothered to maintain a fractured veneer of honour and respectability. A bridge of lies between the adult world and the young, between those that had, and those that were yet to become. The becoming was the time the young would cross the bridge to be one of them, when they would discover their world of deceit. Gaia hated the leaders, feared them, but she was at their mercy, like all the others.

Gaia crept through the hall to the door. It was locked, as expected. She placed the key in the lock and turned, easing the mechanism. There was a slight kick, and a clicking noise that echoed in the empty hall. She paused, stopped breathing and listened. There were noises from Hakan's room, mumbled words, a faint laugh. Gaia waited to be sure, opened the door and slipped outside, closing the door without locking it. There was a noise in the trees. Aran stepped forward from the shadows. The crescent moon was hanging in the sky, a thin curved arc of light smiling, and providing just enough light to cast playful shadows. He gestured to follow him, and she made her way across the patch of grass to the trees. As Gaia approached the trees something flew across the beams of moonlight. It was something dark, just a shadow. Neither of them noticed it, but there was another, along with a clicking sound, and the faintest echo of flapping.

Aran welcomed Gaia with a delicate touch of her arm. There were no words as he led her through the trees. They veered right towards what looked like a dead end. It was pitch black under the canopy. She stayed close. He stopped before a bush and pulled back some branches. The blanket of foliage concealed a narrow passage, an archway was formed by the bending boughs. Aran lit a candle and gestured through. They moved a short way into a snug inner chamber covered by a ceiling of branches. It was high enough to stand in, and there was ample room for three or four people to sit. The candlelight cast a feeble glow, just enough to see the few logs scattered on the ground.

Aran sat on one of the logs and Gaia took another. They waited within the wall of silence. Gaia was convinced there were footsteps outside, that they had been followed. Despite the chill in the air, beads of sweat trickled down her forehead. Her heart raced, and she could taste the staleness of her breath. She could wait no longer, and broke the silence in a low whisper, her voice still bold and commanding.

'Let's get this over with so we can get back.'

'I'm going to escape the island and I want you to come with me.'

There was a gasp.

'Are you mad?'

Part of Aran's face was lit by the faint flicker of the candlelight, but most was cast in shadow. There was the slightest glimmer in his eyes.

'I've seen you on the beach. Watched you in tasks and discussions. You're angry and restless, I can tell. You don't want to be here any more than I do. You do know they're watching you? I don't know why, but they're keeping a close eye on you for some reason.'

She felt a mixture of anger and alarm.

'So you've been spying on me, but expect me to escape the island with you? Why should I trust you?'

'Look I'm sorry. I know this is a shock. But I only followed you when I was convinced you might be up for this. I could see you were pissed off with the leaders, but I couldn't be sure. You and Kali clearly have some issues.'

The fury was now bubbling up and boiling inside. Gaia wanted to slap his face, but she needed to remain calm, and find out more.

'Let's suppose I overlooked your snooping about, and we assume I did want to escape the island. It's near impossible to get off here. So come on, humour me. What's the big plan?'

Aran laid the candle on the floor between them. There was just enough light to highlight part of their faces, while shadows danced upon the rest. She could see his sharp features wrapped in the soft golden glow. He looked down at the floor, playing with his hands, then stared at her, an intense look on his face.

'Everyone thinks the only way on and off the island is by boat. It's an island, of course and we're surrounded by sea. Why would you question that? Well, it's not the only way. For the most part we're cut off, but not always.'

Gaia was alert now, a tingle of excitement rippled through her. She had always assumed that escaping the island would mean stealing a boat. Swimming would be treacherous, suicidal. There were strong currents, the creatures in the water. Gaia had been developing wild and creative alternative ways of escaping for some time, but she knew most were fanciful. Her plans had reached a dead end, and as the becoming neared she was resigned to her fate. This had stirred the excitement again.

'Go on then. Tell me.'

'On the far side of the island there's a causeway. It's why we're restricted from going there. At low tide you can see it. It's only there for a few hours until the tide rises. It's narrow, and is about a mile long. It was built in the old days, for vehicles. It's just a road really, lined with rocks, but it's pretty solid still. It was the main means of getting to and from the island in the past. Now, it's a weakness and the best means of escape. They don't want us to know about it.'

'So how did you find out about it?'

'A couple of years ago, I became friends with an older boy. He told me he was planning an escape, and asked me to go with him. I reacted just like you, but he told me about the causeway. I was tempted, but I wasn't ready. I was too young and scared.'

Aran paused. They both listened to the silence beyond the leafy walls of the lair. They were both nervous, still checking they were alone.

'Let's just say I've had enough now. I need to get out of here. The boy told me there's a community in the hills, and that the rumours were true. He had proof and was going to find them.'

Gaia could feel the heavy thud of her beating heart. Her voice remained just a whisper.

'So what happened to him?'

'He and another boy took off, but I never heard from them again. I've no idea if they made it, but they never came back and there was never any mention of them here, or of their escape. You might remember them disappearing when we first arrived from the mainland.'

Gaia had a vague recollection of something. There were rumours all the time about young people going missing. Some would say they had tried to escape, others suggested more sinister things. She tended to ignore them, as the possibilities were too disturbing.

'So you don't actually know if this causeway exists or not? You've only got his word for it.'

'No. I was curious about it, and wanted to see it for myself, so one afternoon, in free time I ran across the island to find it. I followed the beach. It was a bit of a hike and it was a tight thing getting there and back in time. I only just made it. I was sure they'd rumble me, but I got away with it.'

'So you saw it and it's possible to cross?'

'Yes. From this side getting across doesn't look too bad. It's all about the timing cos of the tides. We'd need to make sure we have enough of a head start. The last thing we want is the leaders finding out we're missing before we reach the mainland. Once we're across and the tide is in again we'd have a good lead on them. The plan is to make for a river and follow it upstream to the hills.'

Aran paused again, and gave her time to take it in. Gaia was cooling now, and heartened that he had chosen her. That he trusted her. He continued.

'If we get to the hills there's a chance the other community hiding there will find us. It's risky, I know, but there's a chance. What's the other option? If we stay here we'll spend the rest of our lives under their control. Who knows what'll happen when they ship us off to the haven. If we make it we get a chance to build our own lives.'

Gaia put her head in her hands. This was a lot to process and her brain was burning with energy and excitement. For a long time her plans had been just dreams, and of late they had been crumbling in despair. This changed everything.

'OK, so you know there's a causeway. It sounds as though we've got a chance if we can get there. But I can still pick a load of holes in your plan. I mean there's how and when we get away from here, making sure we don't get found before the tide is in. It needs a lot of thinking through. This causeway. Why didn't they use it to get us here? I can remember the journey from the schools on the mainland. We reached the island in a boat. I'm sure of it.'

'How do you know?'

'You could tell. You could feel it.'

'Exactly. They had to do that so no-one realised. The best way of keeping us here is for us to think there's no way to escape. This whole place is a lie built to control us. The causeway is just another part of it.'

Something else was troubling Gaia.

'This other community in the hills. How can you be so sure they exist? We've all heard the tales about the place, but it could be just wishful thinking. What if we get all the way there and there's nothing?'

There was a long pause, then Aran leant forward close to her face.

'I know it exists. I've seen proof.'

Gaia was struggling to contain herself now. A midnight candlelit conversation in a hidden camp in the woods was turning her world upside down. All she had hoped might be possible was becoming real. She tried to keep her voice down and suppress her emotion.

'So show me!'

'When I knew the boy was planning to escape I followed him here to the camp. I came back when he wasn't here, and found some stuff hidden. There were some papers, maps, letters. One of the letters was from the community. I've still got it here. Look.'

Aran stood and moved to the back of the camp. The candle was still flickering by Gaia's feet, casting the same discerning glow. She was nervous and excited, trying to process all that had been thrown at her. There was some shuffling, a pause, then Aran appeared and sat in front. There was something in his hands which he handed to her. As Gaia moved it into the glow of the candle she saw a small piece of folded paper. It looked grubby, and felt damp. Aran spoke.

'Go on. Read it.'

Gaia unfolded it, struggling to see in the dim light. The hand-writing was rough, difficult to read, the letters were large and flowery, ornate. She tilted the letter further towards the light, her eyes squinting:

Dear Savas

Hopefully you will get this letter. Everything is in place as planned. We are waiting for you. Just head to the hills and we will find you.

Good luck

M'

Gaia read it again, her heart fluttering and hands trembling. She paused, took a deep breath, attempted to compose herself, needing to think this through. This was all that she had dreamt of, but this needed to time. There were many risks to consider.

'I guess it looks genuine. I assume Savas was the boy you spoke of.'

'Yes. I don't know how he was communicating with them, or how he got the letter.'

'Let's say this all stacks up. We've got the causeway as an escape route. If that comes off, and it's still a big if, then we have to find our way across the mainland, somewhere we know next to nothing about. We have to find a river, follow it to the hills, and hope this community will find us. All on the strength of a note for someone else that's now a few years old. And you can guarantee the leaders will send out a pursuit party with dogs to track us down. Not to mention any other delights waiting out there to surprise us. And there'll only be the two of us! As plans go, it doesn't sound the best, does it?'

'Look I know it's a long shot, but there won't be just the two of us.'

Gaia twisted her face, leant forward, drawing closer.

'There are more?'

'Yes. I've asked a few others.'

She snarled, spitting the words out.

'How many? Who?'

'If they all agree, there'll be four of us. I'm not saying who though. I want to protect everyone. I'm the one taking the risk at the moment. If we're found out before we manage to get away I don't want to drag others into it. This is the best way. Trust me.'

Gaia laughed and shook her head.

'This just gets better and better! No, I won't do it Aran. It's too big a risk. There are too many holes in it. You're asking me to put everything on the line and all I can see is danger. I know things are bad in this place, but I'd rather wait and get through the becoming, then take my chances in the haven. Thanks for the offer, but count me out.'

Aran put his head down, and picked a small stone from the dirt, rolling it between his fingers.

'I'm disappointed, but I understand. If you change your mind let me know. There's still a place open for you. I want to go soon, but we've got a couple of weeks yet.'

Aran stared at her, the light from the candle giving his expression a sinister edge.

'And I can rely on you to keep quiet about this?'

Their eyes locked as Gaia returned the stare.

'Of course. However crazy this is, and however pissed off I am that you've dragged me into it, I'm no snitch. You can trust me, but the same goes for you too though. I know nothing, right?'

'No problem.'

There was a sound outside, something above them. The branches shook, but only for a moment. They both froze, their breath slowing to nothing. The slightest noise seemed to echo around them. All they heard were the incidental sounds of the woods, the gentle purring of nocturnal living. The branches shook again. This time it was more vigorous, followed by a flapping sound and a loud, rapid clicking. Gaia looked at Aran, alarm on their faces. He gestured and threw her a quizzical look. She frowned and mouthed to him:

'*Night birds.*'

Aran shook his head, but Gaia nodded. She was sure, and had heard this before. The candle was still lit, so she licked her fingertips and snuffed it out, plunging them into pitch black. Aran grabbed her arm. Gaia eased her hand forward feeling his knee, and leant towards him, her head seeking to find his. She wanted to whisper to him. Her head searched the darkness, trying to sense where his face was, to feel the warmth of his body, and the faintest indication he was near. She felt the heat of his panting breathe. His face was close. Angling her lips reaching for his ear, desperate to release her whisper, she inched towards him. Her lips glanced his skin, the faintest brush of his smooth and delicate cheek. She moved them along the line of his face towards his ear. All the while Aran was still, frozen like stone. Her lips stroked his ear, like fingertips, and Gaia whispered.

'It's the night birds. I know it is. We need to get out of here now.'

Gaia felt his head move in a nod, Aran took her arm and together they stood. She moved behind him, her finger hooked through one of his belt holes. He edged forward step by step, tiptoeing his way towards the entrance, as she shuffled behind, feeling her way in the pitch black, clinging to him. They could nothing, but he knew the layout well enough to feel their escape. Together they eased through the dirt, inching forward. Her senses had awoken and come alive, her hearing picking up every rustle, the buzz of the silent air, and the occasional flurry of the clicks and flapping from above. The violent shaking had stopped, but they knew they were still there. Her feet reached forward, stroking the darkness and the ground below. Aran stopped at the entrance, turned and took Gaia by the arm. His fingertips touched her face and moved to her chin. Gaia sensed his lips as they moved to her ear.

'What now?'

Gaia could only just make out his words. Aran did not speak, rather let them drift from his breath. She put her head to his, and traced her lips across his face again. For a moment their lips brushed, not a kiss, just the softest connection. She whispered again, only the delicate waves of her breath carrying the words.

'Open the door and we run for it. If we split up I'll meet you at the edge of the woods.'

Gaia felt Aran's hand grip her arm, as his other hand reached out and took the branches of the door. He squeezed harder, and moved the branches back, the glow from the light of the crescent moon appeared as they parted. They both stepped out, as Aran eased the branches back. In an instant they darted into the woods. Gaia was quick, but she let him lead, tucking in behind, as he weaved his way, this way and that. At first they heard nothing but the crack of the branches underfoot and their own panting. Then they heard them overhead, swooping sounds as the birds dived towards them. The noise of the clicking growing louder and softer. Soon Aran and Gaia reached the edge of the woods and stopped. Aran lent on a tree to gather his breath as Gaia peered out into the opening, looking for any signs of movement, listening for any more noises. There was nothing. They were safe for now, waiting while their breath slowed. Gaia spoke, her voice a soft whisper.

'Looks like they've gone, but we need to get back to our dorms quickly. What happened tonight stays between us.'

Aran stood up straight, and reached out and held Gaia by the arm. He looked at her, his face pleading. Her eyes locked onto his lips, with the thought of them touching only moments ago. She watched as they moved, carving out his words.

'Think about what I said Gaia. This is the best chance you'll get to escape. Trust me!'

With that Aran headed out into the opening and across the field towards his dorm on the far side of the encampment. Gaia watched as his shadowy outline moved away, lit by the moon, but drifting out of view. She steadied herself before setting off. There was a lot to think about, but now was not the time. Moving across the field to the dorm, Gaia paused outside the entrance, listening for any trace of sound or movement inside. There was nothing, so she tried the handle and pulled the door. It did not move. Gaia tried again, arching the handle further to make sure it was not caught, but still it failed to budge. She tugged again, a little harder, but fearful the noise might alert Hakan.

Gaia's thoughts drifted back to leaving earlier, retracing the steps in her mind. She was sure the door was not locked, but doubts set in. A flash of panic ran through her as she wrestled with the images in her head. Fumbling for the key in her pocket, Gaia placed it in the lock, turned it and felt the click. As the handle moved the door eased open. She crept through the narrowest of openings and closed it. Tiptoeing through the passage towards the main sleeping area there was a voice, echoing in the passage.

'Good evening thirty seven.'

Gaia jumped and turned. Hakan was there. Standing in the shadows at the far side of the passage by the bedroom door. His body was smothered in darkness, but the face was clear as he lent forward into the light, eyes dark and intense.

'Where've you been?'

Gaia's heart was like a hammer smashing at her chest. She could not breath, her mind was whirling with panic, her mouth felt dry and rancid. Survival mode kicked in. Despite the chaotic churning of her body and mind, the brain took control forcing out some words.

'Sorry leader, I felt ill and needed some air. I didn't want to disturb anyone. I didn't go far. Just for a short walk.'

There was a long pause. The knife was in. Hakan wanted to twist it.

'Mmmmmm, ill. You do seem a little anxious, let's say off colour. How did you manage to get outside given that the door was locked, of course?'

Gaia's heart was in her mouth.

'There was a key in the door. This one. I assumed it was yours.'

Gaia reached in her pocket and held out the key. Hakan stepped out of the shadows and towards her. He was wearing pyjama bottoms, but no shirt. She could see his naked torso, covered in thick black hair. He shuffled across the hall, bare-footed, silent, stopping just in front. Hakan waited, looked down at the key in her hand. He took it and lifted it close to his face twirling it in his fingers, studying it, staring at Gaia, leaning in close.

'So it is.'

Hakan winked, and eased his head back. There was a long pause and silence. Gaia could smell his stale breath. A grin crept across his face, as his pale blue eyes pierced hers. He stood silent, staring, waiting for her to speak or move.

'Now get back to your dorm and we'll keep this our little secret, shall we? But you owe me, and I'll expect something as a token of your gratitude for my silence and discretion. Just let me have a think about it. Now off you go.'

'Thank you leader.'

Gaia turned and made her way to the door of the dorm. She grabbed the handle, and was just about to open it when Hakan spoke again in a low, sinister snarl.

'Good night Gaia. Remember, this is our little secret.'

Gaia opened the door and rushed over to her bed, undressed and climbed into bed staring at the familiar patterns of the bunk above. Her head was awash with the events of the night, her veins pumping adrenalin and fear through every muscle and sinew. Fists were clenched in anger and frustration. She was vulnerable now, and knew it was only a matter of time. Hakan had something over her, the power to manipulate her for his own ends, and Gaia knew what that meant. There was the meeting with Kali in the morning and whatever that would bring. There was a lot to consider, and she needed to sleep, but it was elusive that night. Gaia drifted into a state of semi-consciousness, neither asleep nor awake. Nightmares plagued her, as all her worst fears played out.

Morning came, and the light of the sun crept through the cracks in the curtains. The sharp, piercing shafts penetrated the windows, and pinned the wooden floors. Gaia gazed at them, and tried to count them, feeling their warmth as they grew in number and intensity. She was trying to forget the night before, but there was no avoiding the truth. Gaia had mulled the thoughts, possibilities and implications over and over, tossing and turning them all night. She had wrestled and weighed them a thousand times, now knowing what had to be done.

4

Gaia sat at the end of a long table in the large hall of the refectory. The community were having a breakfast of porridge and toast with tea and/or coffee. This was the offering most mornings, though occasionally they would have eggs in various forms. Bacon was a rare treat, and marked a special occasion. Today was any other day, at least for the community.

The hall was full and bustling with activity. It was always this way with over four hundred people to get through in two sittings. Gaia was in the first sitting, the early birds without the worms. They had a brief window to arrive and finish. Anyone who was outside their slot would do without, and go hungry till lunch.

Gaia looked at her bowl, and played with her porridge. Her appetite had abandoned her. Her head was heavy with the haze of lost sleep. There was the meeting with Kali after breakfast. Her stomach spat bile and burned at the thought of their impending discussion. Aran sat a couple of tables away, his back to her. Gaia had noticed him enter, collect his food and make his way to the table. Her heart had jumped when he entered. Part of her had hoped that he would come and sit next to her, or at least near. She was hoping they might be able to share some words between casual morning chat. Yet the lucid part of her brain, the piece not swimming in the stupour of her mental hangover knew it was foolish. Instead Aran took his seat without acknowledgment, or eye contact, making a point of staring at the floor in front, a fixed gaze unbroken. He seemed determined to avoid any connection with Gaia, any recognition, wary of arousing any suspicion.

Part of Gaia felt bitter. The situation Aran had put her in, the choice he had asked her to make. This made things impossible for them. If Gaia agreed to go she would have the opportunity to escape, but the chances of success were slim. She forced the porridge down, followed by the cold, soggy toast and stewed tea. Eating was monitored, waste was not tolerated. At worst it would alert them to unusual behaviour, a change in the regular pattern. This might lead to unwanted attention and a discussion with the leaders to find the issue. This was something Gaia wanted to avoid at all costs. Kali gave her enough attention without adding further reasons, and now there was Hakan to think of. He was also in the hall, sitting at the top table with the leaders. He was laughing and joking with a couple of the others. Gaia had looked across a couple of times. On one occasion he caught her eye, grinning and looking away, returning to his breakfast banter unphased by any of the events of the night. Hakan was aware he had another victim in his snare, lined up, waiting. This victim was different. He had something on her, a bargaining chip, more power than usual. This victim was vulnerable and weak. He was not ready for her yet. He would keep her waiting, worrying over what might happen, and when. Power was Hakan's weapon. Power and its abuse. It was the basis of all human interactions. He betrayed the power entrusted him, a betrayal of his role and responsibilities, of all that he stood for, and was meant to be. Hakan had power over those he was supposed to protect, but it was never absolute. Sometimes victims were clever enough to disarm the power. Sometimes the victims were not prepared to sit back and allow it. Sometimes they would act. In this case the potential victim had other ideas. Gaia would not be taken at any cost.

Gaia moved to the table where the dishes were left. As she approached Aran moved towards the table. She tried to remain calm and act as normal. One by one, she placed each item in the designated bowls. Aran approached and stood near, not speaking, but placing a napkin by her hand on the table. He put his things away, flicked her hand, and moved towards the door. Gaia reached down and picked up the napkin, slipping it into her pocket, while looking around at the table of leaders. They were all engrossed in one of Hakan's tales, his stories of fantasy, told in such a way to make him believable. Hakan the raconteur, the entertainer, weaving webs, the cover for his evil. No-one was looking. No-one had spotted Aran's subtle act. The rest of the community were all either deep in conversation or staring at the walls, wrestling with the last traces of tiredness. They sat, ate, drifted. They were the indifferent, and the lost.

Gaia left the refectory and returned to the dorm. It was a good moment to look at the napkin. Some of her roommates were in the dorm, busy getting ready. The morning gathering was soon, and the allocation of tasks for the day. Gaia would attend, but meet Kali before embarking on her task. She needed to see what was on the napkin first. Read it, then dispose of it. The longer she had it, the more likely it would be found. At least that was the rationale to cloak her curiosity.

The rain rattled as it peppered the roof, a dreary backdrop to the chatter of the girls. After a bright, sunny start the clouds had swept in bringing a cloak of grey, wet, misery. The outdoor tasks would be all the tougher for most, but not Gaia. She did not mind the rain. It was comforting and reassuring. The rain was a screen, a bubble wrapped around her, protecting. Warm rain made her feel comforted, cold, biting rain alive, with its sharp, stinging prods of the skin. Often she would focus her mind on each of the drops as they stung her face. Her cold, tingling face, so cold that every ounce of pain would be amplified. Pain was there to be controlled, to be conquered. Gaia would soak the pain, absorb it, but she would not suffer. It was not allowed.

The sodden walk back to the dorm had done Gaia good. She had cast off the heavy haze of her restless night and was now feeling more alert. She was nervous about meeting Kali, curious too, but her spirits had lifted a little. The napkin had given her a boost. It was contact with Aran, however small. At least he had not abandoned her, and been too disheartened by her concerns. Gaia was keen to inspect the napkin further, to see what secrets it held.

Gaia sat on the bed, removed her boots and lay on the blanket, turning her back to most of the rest of the girls mingling around the dorm. She reached into her pocket and removed the napkin. In itself it would not arouse any suspicion, but she needed to be careful. She lay the napkin on the blanket by her chest, leaving her hand upon it, hoping to at least partially conceal it. There was the writing, small and faint. Gaia moved the napkin along the blanket closer to the top of her chest, seeking the right position to suit her eyes. Discretion was important. One of the spies might be watching and report any strange behaviour to one of the leaders. You could never be too careful. Trust no-one, and suspect everything. That was the key to survival in the community. It was nestled in the right position, just enough to read without the letters being too blurred. There were six words. All that was needed.

We must go soon. Be careful.

Soon. It was vague, but the implication was clear. Something had changed. Something had alarmed Aran. Giving the note to Gaia was dangerous. It was in a crowded room with the leaders present, and there was always the potential someone would see. They may have been seen. One of the spies may have noticed and could be ready to tell the leaders now. Aran said they had a couple of weeks, but not now. If Gaia was to go the decision had to be made. However, her concerns still remained. There were holes in the plan, aspects that needed a lot more thought. Then there were the others. Who were they? Gaia still had doubts about Aran, in two minds. It paid to be this way about everyone. Adding more people to the mix was worrying. The two week timescale had been a concern, but this change was alarming. For now she would have to put her concerns on hold and prepare for the gathering and her meeting. Thoughts of escape could wait till later. Gaia ripped a piece from the napkin, tore it into tiny bits and ate them. She repeated it until all the writing was gone, placing the remains in her back pocket. In rainy weather it would be easy to dispense with in the mud or drains outside.

....

The gathering was as always. They sat in the dome in their allotted places and listened to a leader speak. There was a reading and a few minutes of meditation. This was meant to focus the mind, cleanse it of all thoughts, seek a higher, purer mental state. The training required you to expel all thoughts, to let go. Gaia found it impossible that morning. There was too much jostling in her head. She went through the motions, but her mind was filled with thoughts of Aran, Kali, and Hakan, of the escape, the meeting, the threat.

They were put into teams and allocated their tasks for the day. Three teams were to go on hunting missions to seek and destroy rats. Others were to build walls and barriers at key areas of the encampment. A couple of groups were sent on beach fishing expeditions, with rods and nets rather than boats, casting from the beach beyond the castle. When the tide was right and the weather favourable this could yield plenty of fresh bounty. Other teams were given physical training tasks - running, weights, boxing, hand to hand combat, and the use of light weaponry such as spears, daggers, hammers, and axes. Some of the teams were classroom-based and would continue their training in theoretical knowledge - maths, engineering, and construction. The tasks were varied and allocated across teams on each days. The intention was to give everyone a strong grounding in essential skills to make the step to the next phase. Everyone was monitored and assessed by the leaders. Some were allocated certain types of tasks more than others and it was clear that they were being steered into particular areas. Teams were never the same though. The leaders liked to keep them guessing and mix things up. Gaia was not allocated a team or task that morning. This was on account of her meeting with Kali. Perhaps Kali would allocate this following the meeting, or maybe she had something else in mind.

When the teams had gone Gaia was instructed to make her way to one of the breakout zones where Kali would be waiting for her. The breakout zones were similar to the large dome but on a much smaller scale. There were cushions, but these were random not numbered. They were spread around a central pole with a small raised wooden platform in the centre with a single cushion for the leader, to sit over and address.

Gaia entered and saw Kali sitting on the leader's cushion. She was in a meditative position, legs crossed, arms either side, with wrists resting against her knees, and finger and thumb touching to form a loop. Her back looked stiff and straight, head pointing forward, eyes closed, with no expression on her face. The tent was silent but for the gentle rustling of wind through flaps in the roof and sides. Gaia approached, her footsteps were gentle and measured, placed with quiet precision. As she neared the central platform Kali spoke without opening her eyes or breaking position.

'Sit thirty seven.'

Gaia sat on the cushion nearest the platform, in front of Kali, waiting while Kali continued in silence. Kali was a woman of great natural beauty, something neither age nor the weight of her position had weathered. She had long, brown hair which was always tied up. Her face was long and slim, her features angular and sculptured, and her lips were narrow, almost without colour. Kali had one feature that marked her out from everyone on the island. Her right hand had a small extra finger protruding from the side by the little finger. It was of no use, but it was distinctive, odd. Gaia had never seen this in anyone else, or heard of it. Kali never spoke of it, and no-one dared ask, but made no attempt to conceal it. As with Gaia, Kali was someone of few words, choosing the words needed, no more. Kali was precise and clinical in both her commands and singular and boundless capacity for cruelty.

Gaia waited and after minutes that seemed much longer Kali opened her eyes. She remained in the same position, staring forward at nothing. Kali stood, twisted her neck, stretched her arms out wide and out front. She reached down and touched her toes a few times, placed her hands on her hips, and rotated her body from side to side. Her head switched between each side as she moved. Stopping her warm down, Kali moved forward to the edge of the platform in front of where Gaia sat, towering over her. The platform, her height, and Gaia's seated position all conspired to create a huge gulf between them.

'Thank you for coming thirty seven. I'll keep this brief. Do you know why you are here?'

'No Leader.'

Sweat trickled down Gaia's brow. Kali had a commanding presence. All felt weak before her. Kali waited and spoke, her voice booming overhead.

'We've some concerns about your behaviour. Things have been noticed by us, other activities have been brought to our attention. I needn't go into detail or spell them out. You'll be well aware of what I mean. I just wanted to let you know that you are being watched, very closely. We expect to see an improvement. I personally expect it, or there will be consequences. Do you understand?'

'Yes Leader, though I'm not sure what you refer to. Could you give some specific instances.'

Kali's blue eyes lit up, her nostrils flared, and face twisted as the muscles around her lips tensed. Scowling she spat a reply.

'You know full well. I needn't and won't give examples.'

Gaia looked back at her. Their eyes locked in a silent duel. Gaia knew she would lose, but she wanted to send a message, a momentary, futile message. Gaia understood, but would not take this lightly. She focused all her anger and disdain into her stare, hoping her feelings would transmit into the eyes of the enemy before her. Kali knew, and could sense the resistance from Gaia, the simmering resentment. It was always there with Gaia, but it was all for her own good. Someday Gaia would understand. This was not the cruelty she thought it was, it was a gateway to kindness, to understanding, to becoming. Structure was strength. Gaia needed to learn that, and one day would. Kali would make sure of it. The moment of deadlock passed. The message sent, received and cast aside. Kali moved onto the death of the girl the day before.

'Now something else, the incident with two, six, four yesterday. It was unfortunate, but you did the right thing. She was weak, you were strong. If you'd gone to help her you'd have been killed and weakened the lines for us all. You recall the stag story? Together we are stronger. Always remember that. It is more important than you know.'

Kali waited for a response, but there was none. Gaia sat and looked up at her, this time trying to conceal her anger. Gaia wanted this over with. The leaders threats were cloaked in compliments, but it did not fool Gaia. There was no point in responding, or fighting back. The revenge would come soon, in another way. Kali would feel the full extent of Gaia's fury someday, paying the highest price for the way she treated all the young. They would all pay. Kali had trained Gaia, given her precious skills, and these would be turned on her and the other leaders without mercy. Kali had created her own downfall, Gaia.

There was a noise at the back of the tent. They both turned to see Freya standing by the entrance. It was not clear how long she had been there, whether she had heard the conversation, just some, or none at all. Gaia knew that Freya was one of Kali's spies. She had always known this and these appearances confirmed it. Why was it always Freya? Gaia hated Freya, almost as much as she hated Kali. Freya was the golden girl in looks, skills and behaviour. Her hair was shoulder length and blonde, eyes the customary blue, but a doe-eyed giddy kind of blue. Her beauty was unrivalled within the community, with porcelain, translucent skin without fault or blemish. However, her smile was her greatest weapon. Her smile and her body. Both were perfect, and Freya could disarm any boy and many of the girls with either. Where she excelled in every way on the outside, she commanded a steely resolve on the inside. Like Gaia, Freya was a survivor, someone who knew how to succeed, but with no reservations about pursuing the most desirable route with a singular and ruthless focus.

There were lots of rumours about Freya, perhaps more than any other on the island. There were whispers of her liaisons with others, with boys, girls, and even leaders. Whatever was or was not true, Gaia knew Freya could not be trusted. Gaia would be extra careful around her now, would watch her, let her know of her suspicions. Gaia would not let this lie.

Kali nodded her head in permission, and Freya spoke. Her voice was calm and controlled.

'Apologies Leader, but the mission to seek the rats is about to leave. They are waiting for you before they set off.'

'Thank you seventy three. We're coming now. We've concluded here. Thirty seven follow seventy three and join her group. You'll be coming on the mission with us. Go and get kitted out and we'll see you both by the main gate in five minutes.'

This was as Gaia had feared, her worst nightmare. Not only was she allocated the most dangerous task of the day, but she was going to have to put up with Freya in her team, and be led by Kali. Gaia and Freya had been in teams together before, more often than Gaia would have liked. Today of all days Gaia could not bear the thought of seeing Freya's face. The last 24 hours had changed everything for Gaia, thrown things into turmoil. She needed to regroup, time to think. She was starting to feel the tiredness seeping back. Her morning bounce was fading, and later would be a struggle. A search and destroy mission was dangerous at the best of times, but she was not in the best mental shape. Gaia would need to perk up and be on her guard.

5

Gaia and Freya went to the main dome and collected their equipment for the mission. This time Gaia took a dagger and an axe, Freya a dagger and spear. Both were masters in their use, both had been trained to kill, a match for anyone, or anything. Neither spoke at any point. Gaia had no idea what Freya thought of her. She did not care, but she sensed that Freya had picked up some of the hatred towards her, so kept a respectful distance. Though they were very different, they both knew the other was a formidable foe. Despite the simmering hatred there was mutual respect.

They made their way to the main gate to join the teams. There were three teams of twenty, each with their own leader. They were a balance of boys and girls, mostly made of elder members, those that were close to becoming. There were a smattering of the fearless and more able younger cohorts, there because they had shown promise and were seen worthy of the experience. The teams stood apart, but near. They were gathered around their leader listening to the strategy and orders for the mission. Each team had a discrete role, frontline, rearguard, and support. The mission was clear, to scour one of the zones on the island, to find concentrations of rats, and where possible kill them. Gaia and Freya were to join Kali's team.

They joined their team, all huddled around Kali, focusing on her calm, precise words. It was then Gaia noticed Aran, on the edge of the group, obscured by a couple of taller boys. He looked up as they approached, caught her eye and looked back at Kali.

Gaia could see he was surprised and was trying to mask his discomfort. Gaia moved into the main body of the group, near the back, and away from Aran. Freya moved to the front, almost standing under Kali's nose. Gaia tried to listen, but most of the words drifted in and out in waves. She would catch the odd word, register it, the ones that seemed to have more relevance. 'Rearguard' was the one word that kept puncturing her dazed stupour.

Once the briefing was over they moved through the main gate. It was a large wooden structure, taller than the walls that held it. The walls were to be heightened and strengthened given the growing threat from the rats. This was deemed a key task for the community. One of the teams was working on a section of wall. Once through the gates the teams set off down the main road and through the derelict village. The road had long been neglected. It was functional and passable now, but few vehicles used it. Only the trucks that came and went, ferrying each wave of cohort on and off the boats that landed at the small jetty at the edge of the village. The shops and houses of the village had been left to rot and crumble, their quaint charm long since faded. Most were made of whitewashed stone with crooked roofs of slate tiles. Gardens were overgrown with weeds and wild flowers, wooden fences, rotten, gates hanging off or gone. There was an old pub, the Red Lion, the broken sign still hanging at the front. No longer expectant, no longer welcoming, the windows were broken and boarded up. There was an array of disused shops: a butchers; a general convenience store; a bakers; and a post office. All now lost and unwanted, all waiting for a purpose that would never come again, monuments to the days that came before.

They passed a red post box, and a narrow cast iron box with a rectangular chessboard of small glass windows. Gaia had read it was a phone box where people would go to speak to each other using machines. Gaia had entered it once. It was empty and stank, a damp, musty odour with a hint of stale urine. Wires spewed from one of the walls where the telephone once was before it was ripped out. A noticeboard was on the wall above with various numbers and graffiti etched on it. There was a drawing of a penis and scrotum, along with some ample breasts, and many strange shapes, symbols, and numbers Gaia did not recognise. A different language for different times.

The houses in the village all had a uniformity in their look which once gave them their charm. Gaia had always thought the village would have been a beautiful place to live. The isolation of the island had both complications and appeal. The accessibility would have made it a very insular, self-contained community. Even now that she knew there was a road to the island, the causeway, it would still have limited access dictated by the tides. It would mainly have been populated by those that were born there, and had grown atuned to this unique way of life. Or maybe those that came here to escape, to get away from the mainland and live life in a different way. How ironic she thought. Their refuge was her prison.

Gaia could never decide whether, given the choice, she would live somewhere like this. The point was she had never been given that choice. Everywhere had been chosen by others. Her whole life had been spent living with and for others. A prison made and controlled by others. Despite its rugged beauty and charm and the appeal of silence and solitude the island was the latest in a long line of prisons. She could not disassociate the island from the chains that bound her, therefore it could never win her heart. It was a place of beauty to behold, but beauty lay in the beholder's eye. The eyes through which Gaia saw it had been clouded by the darkness of the community, their power and control.

Given the choice where would Gaia live? She had often dreamed. Perhaps an island of her own, or somewhere on the mainland? A large house with acres of landscaped gardens of flowers and veg, and a family of her own. All Gaia wanted was somewhere she could be herself, determine her own life, drive her own destiny. Anywhere but here. Did such places exist? Were there people out there leading such lives free of the community? Gaia doubted it. All she had been taught, all the whispers, every indication was that way of life had disappeared. It was gone, destroyed forever. It was as Kali said. Together they were stronger.

Gaia's knowledge of the world was limited, drip fed, controlled. She knew that large parts of the world were no longer accessible. They were poisoned, destroyed, populated by deformed creatures. Other humans had survived, rebuilt again, started over as best they could, as the community had done. Living on an island, albeit a large one as the mainland was, had saved the community. They were told it was something in their genetic code that made them special, had helped them survive, made them immune to the poison. The blue eyes were the indicator. That was why all in the community were bred, and the whole reproductive process was controlled. It ensured the gene pool remained pure. All impurities or mutations were identified and destroyed.

The narrow gene pool caused problems. There were some conditions and diseases that were caught within the pool and were difficult to contain or filter out. The main one was the fading of memory. This was common amongst the elders. For some their memories would disappear and they would lose their ability to function. The condition varied in its speed and severity, but a great many of the elders suffered it. Most developed it early in the final phase. They knew of it and prepared for it, but few spoke of it. The community had a special place for them. They were taken away and cared for, but never seen again.

The community had been built by the survivors. They had begun again, started time all over again. They had moved back to a simple life, an existence based on community, on working together, on the common good. They believed they were the chosen ones, trusted to start again. Who had chosen them, no-one knew. Maybe it was just life itself, their existence and survival. They were determined to learn from the mistakes of the past and not repeat them. The fragile morality of the old beliefs and religions had failed to provide the moral guidance that was needed. Instead they had bickered and fought over their gods. The truth was they all seemed to worship the same god, but in different ways.

The panacea of science had promised redemption, a world free from disease, where food was genetically engineered and plentiful. A world where man need not fear nature. A world where man could tame and conquer it. A world of electricity, of powered vehicles that cruised the roads, and soared across the skies, of weapons that could kill men, women, children in far off countries with the push of buttons and the turn of dials. Pandora had been unleashed and could not be controlled. Frankenstein's monster was growing, but few saw it, and none took heed. The arrogance and folly of humanity marched on.

The scientists were supported by governments and companies, the former driven by domination, security and power, the latter by profit and greed. The law was meant to replace the moral vacuum left by the holy men, to provide the checks and balances. While the religions fought with all that failed to tread their path, the scientists raced against each other. The quest to be the first at anything spurred them on. They were driven by man's innate desire to push the boundaries, to break new ground. Man's great dynamism, and contradiction. Money was plentiful and the scientists fed on it. Like parasites sucking on blood they grew ever bigger, ever stronger, ever hungrier. Then the poisons came. It was an attempt to modify the food, to genetically improve it. A company involved in secret research got greedy, sloppy. Something went wrong, and the food chain became polluted, infected, poisoned. It spread everywhere. Humans died, animals too. Some of the latter survived, but they changed. In order to survive they changed, such was the order of things. Mutant strains emerged, creatures that were so different from their former species to be almost another species all together. Except they were no longer mutants. They were the survivors, they became the norm. This was the law of nature, as it had always been. Humanity lost sight of that, and almost perished.

Now the community remained. The community and the outsiders. The shadow that hung over the community was of paranoia and fear. Everything within was driven by the fear that this could, but must not happen again. All that was encouraged and allowed, all that was frowned upon and forbidden, all that was created, all that was destroyed, all that was taught, all that was learned. Everything. The impulse, the drivers all centred around the new way, and a dogged determination to not go back to the old ways. With paranoia comes control. The need to exercise and maintain it at all costs. The community had developed an internal logic based around collective need. Every phase of development was seen as a precise stage to prepare community members for their contribution. Every decision, every task were centrally determined, planned and controlled. This was the new law.

The old ways were gone, the old beliefs and religions had been discarded and burned. Science had been trimmed to its essential core, a pick and mix of the elements that would assist function and development, but only the basics. Communal life, simplicity, that was the new way forward, the only way forward given the limitations the community faced. Survival was their foundation stone and core. From that they would build a new success, a new form of happiness, one gained through commitment to the community itself. The individual was nothing, the community was everything.

As they moved further along the road, nearing the edge of the derelict village the skies opened up and unleashed a deluge of rain. It was sharp, piercing rain, liquid needles stabbing at every inch of their bodies. The team put on their flimsy waterproofs which were no match for the torrent of miniature blades. Within seconds their clothes were soaked through. Each of them clung to their cold, shivering bodies, heavy and sodden against their skin. Their boots turned a dark brown as they absorbed the water. They leaked, and began to squelch with the invading rain. Droplets of water ran down Gaia's face, dripping from her nose and into her mouth. She could taste the rainwater on her lips, feel its icy grip.

Gaia looked ahead, at nothing in particular, any focal point would do. She concentrated on her feet, putting each one forward, one after the other, feeling the squelch of the boot and sodden sock. She focused on the rhythm of her marching, beating out a strong steady beat. The harsh rattle of the driving rain added a further layer to the tune, the rustle of the others as they marched alongside the final dimension to the medley of sounds. This was nature's ensemble, the music of living, the music that is in everything. Gaia always listened, always tried to find the music, the rhythm, the tune. Sometimes it was only fragments of sound, other times a wall of symphony. She found it most of all on the beach, in the sea. It was always with her, and she always heard it and felt it most when connected to nature and away from people. The music of people was less appealing to Gaia. It was there but it lacked something. The balance of nature, its interconnectedness, its beauty, that fed into its music. The harmony of the eco-system, each plant, tree, animal, all an essential piece of a connected whole. That balance fed into the music. With people it was different, with people it was artificial, contrived. Humanity would tinker, would change, would upset the balance, and that made for chaotic music, discordant, without melody or harmony. The music of nature was what Gaia listened for and found.

The team reached a crossroads, and took a right turn heading off to the far side of the island. The side away from the mainland, and away from where Aran claimed the causeway was. The tide was low so if there were a causeway it would not be concealed. Missions were led to that part of the island, but the leaders would know when it was safe depending on the tides. Today the timing was against them so the mission was led away. There was no explanation, no questioning of this. Why would anyone? Only the leaders, and Aran knew of the causeway. Gaia had never known. It was controlled, like everything else. Even those elements of her existence she thought were tiny and random were controlled. This was the way of the community. Everything was controlled.

Despite the treacherous weather the team moved along the road at a brisk pace. The mission was headed by another group about one hundred metres in front. This team of twenty was led by Tarkan, a male leader of considerable ability and respect. He kept himself to himself, just got on with his role, no complaints and no untoward behaviour. As leaders went he was OK. He did not abuse the trust he had been given. There were no good guys here, but for Gaia Tarkan was as close as a leader could be to one.

The support team in the centre were a further fifty metres behind the front team. They were headed up by a female leader, Shia. Gaia knew little of her. Young and new to the island she seemed competent, if a touch nervous. She had not yet built up the aura of confidence that commanded respect. It would come, as it did with most of them. Some had it from the moment they arrived, with others it took time to build. Those who had been on the island a long time had it without thought. Those like Kali.

Aran was in the support team. Gaia could make him out through the spray of the beating rain which blurred her vision. He was at the back of the group, head moving from side to side, always on the lookout, always alert. They were in open ground, with no woods or foliage at either side. The rats would not be here, and if they did attack they would be seen in good time. This was not the place to feel vulnerable, but that would come soon, further down the road where the overgrown fields began, backed by thick woodland.

Gaia's team were at the rear, led by Kali. Freya was at the front just behind Kali, her shadow as always. Freya was small and slight in comparison to Kali, but mirrored her in many ways. Gaia watched the way Kali and Freya moved. Even the rhythm of their steps was identical. Left-right-left-right, marching in perfect time together. The arch of Freya's back mirrored that of Kali. Freya was almost a part of Kali. To Gaia she was an irrelevance, something temporary. Without Kali Freya was nothing.

Gaia sneered, her bones were aching now with the chill of the rain as it seeped into her pores. Her hands were stiff, finger tips wrinkled and white. The mission was risky, the weather an added danger. The distance they could see ahead was short. They were more vulnerable and exposed. Despite its melody, the sound of the rain dampened everything around them, including the sound of the rats. Ordinarily the rats could be heard from some distance, but the cacophany of the hammering rainfall limited that. Once they reached the stretch of road lined with the overgrown fields and woodland they would be a moving target. The weather also limited their movements. The effects of the rain on their skin and joints, the weight of the water in their soaking clothes. All combined to slow them. They needed to be as mobile and agile as possible, but they were not. The leaders knew this. They all knew it. Many heads were down, faces grim.

Gaia hoped the weather would narrow the scope of the mission to no more than a scouting trip. The teams needed to avoid the risk of encountering groups of rats. They knew where the rats favoured for their lairs. In this weather the rodents would tend to stick close to them. Unless the creatures were hunting. There was always a chance the teams would encounter a group of hunting rats. Usually, the hunter groups were smaller and easier to deal with. They never hunted in the large pack numbers that attacked the community. These rats only ever attacked in those numbers when they were desperate. Attacks on the community were a last resort, hence their infrequency and savagery. The creatures feared humans more than humans feared them. At least in the past that had been the case, but things were changing. The behaviour of the rats was changing. The world was evolving and so were they. The rodents numbers were growing, and they were attacking more often, and more effectively. As the rats evolved the balance of power was shifting. The balance of fear was moving.

The team at the front stopped, the others followed their lead. Tarkan signalled them to enter the field on the left. It was a long stretch of open field, thick with tall grass and wild flowers. On a sunny day it would have been idyllic, picture book, but today it looked limp and grey. Beyond the field was the start of some woodland, a small copse of well-established trees. The wood was known to them, a popular site for lairs. The missions had destroyed several, but the rats kept coming back.

The front group moved through the tall grass and paused at the edge of the wood. The other teams followed. Once they had all crossed the field the first team made their way into the trees. The woodland had become wild and untamed. Brambles, weeds and an assortment of wild plants spread across the floor between the trees. Walking was difficult as the plants were thick and strong, many with harsh spikes that either clung to their trousers or ripped through and scratched the flesh. The first team used their spears, machetes, and boots to hack a pathway through. The other teams waited and watched. The rain was less severe now. They were sheltered by the canopy overhead. The sound of the downfall had changed. The rhythm and rattle was different as the drops smashed against the leaves above. Still they listened. They were trained to listen and look for any signs, any movement or sound, any small change, however suspicious. There was nothing, just the sound of the rain.

Gaia focused on the cracks between the trees, scanning the furthest point for any movement. She noticed Aran approach, but did not respond. He waited, not wanting to speak for fear of alarming her, crouched by her side. Gaia scoured the dark woods, head moving back and forth. She could see the vapour from Aran's breath from the corner of her eye. Without stopping and breaking her focus Gaia whispered.

'What do you want?'

'I just wanted to check you were OK after last night, and if you read my note?'

'Yes, I read it.'

'And?'

'And what? You tell me. What's changed so suddenly?'

Gaia continued to look ahead, scanning the woods.

'I can't say here, but there've been some things, worrying things. I'm planning to leave in the next few days. There's a full moon and I can't wait another month. It's too risky. Are you in?'

Gaia took her time before answering. The options played out in her mind, but Kali and Hakan kept flashing through her head.

'I could be, but don't build your hopes up. I think you might be right about me being watched. I had a meeting with Kali this morning. Let's just say she's keeping close tabs on me.'

Gaia paused, thinking about Hakan and the incident the night before. Should she tell Aran? Perhaps it was best if she was honest with him.

'Something happened last night when I got back to the dorm.'

Gaia stopped looking into the woods and faced Aran. His face was wet, skin red with the cold.

'Did someone find you?'

'Hakan was waiting for me when I got back. I gave him some bullshit about needing some air, but he knew I was lying. I had to give him the key. I said it was left in the door.'

'You did what?'

Aran stabbed his spear into the sodden earth.

'Don't worry! He isn't going to say anything. The problem is now he has something on me, and you know what that means with Hakan.'

Aran was well aware of the behaviour of some of the leaders. Boys were largely left alone. It was the girls that suffered at the hands of a few. Hakan's reputation was known, and Aran knew what this meant for Gaia. She now had to make a tough choice.

'I'm sorry Gaia. You know it's only a matter of time now. He won't let this go.'

'I know, but Hakan is just one more reason to get out of this place.'

'I understand, but I need to know you're committed to this. I can't carry people.'

There was a pause. Gaia began to scan the woodland again, not looking and not caring. She focused on Aran's words, her excitement, her fear. There were doubts, but Gaia knew what she had to do.

'Count me in, but there's a condition. There are holes in your plan. You need to convince me this isn't a suicide mission. Sort them and I'll come. You've got twenty-four hours. Now go, before someone sees us talking.'

'OK. Give me a day and I'll let you know.'

Aran moved away from Gaia and crouched about ten metres to her right. She continued to scour the cracks in the trees while they both settled in and waited for their orders.

Gaia was annoyed and relieved. Aran's timing was far from ideal. Her mind was cluttered now, awash with thoughts of the escape. The questions tumbled inside her head, the many questions and doubts. There was the memory of the previous night, a sequence of events she had hoped to bury. The decision had been made for her though, and it felt as though at least one of the weights had been lifted. Now Gaia needed to focus. The mission was dangerous, the risks were high. Any weakness could mean there would be no need for escape. For now the rats were the main concern.

Gaia looked along the line to left and saw Freya who was looking in Gaia's direction. Their eyes met. The rain and cold weather had freshened Freya's beauty. Unlike the others who looked weary and fed up, Freya looked alive. Her pale skin almost translucent in the biting rain. Her red lips a more intense hue than ever. Freya locked onto Gaia's gaze and returned a stern, piercing stare, a knowing stare. Freya smiled. It was the faintest of smiles, just enough to let Gaia see it, to know she was aware. Freya had seen them talking, had been watching. The stare and smile said everything. Kali's eyes were watching.

The support team moved into the woods, following the path of those in the frontline who had moved on ahead. After a short while Kali gave the signal for their team to follow. They set off through the woods, one team after the other. The first ploughed a path through checking for imminent danger. The others provided cover from behind, extra eyes and ears to locate any threat. They pushed on for about twenty minutes then Gaia noticed the front team slow and stop. Their leader raised his arm and crouched low, moving towards the cover of the trees. Each member of the team splintered and found cover. They lay low facing the teams behind. Tarkan gave a signal to the other two leaders. Shia led her team off to the right, moving around and further into the woods, curving back in on the area the others had stopped. Kali led Gaia and her team in the same movement, but to the left. It was a pincer movement, forming a circle, a trap, so nothing could escape, at least not without a fight. Tarkan had found something. It was a lair.

Gaia was on her knees behind the trunk of a tall, sprawling tree. She could feel the water seeping through her trousers onto the skin, but was soaked beyond the point of caring. The others dotted the trees. Gaia peered from behind the tree into the centre of the area they encircled. There was a mound of earth overgrown with a blanket of foliage. Harsh, spiked plants hugged the earth. Gaia could not see anything unusual, though the mound itself was typical. The rats would burrow into them and create a maze of passages and chambers below. Somewhere concealed beneath the thick undergrowth would be the entrance holes, the doorways into the passages below.

The first task of the mission was to wait and observe, to see if there were any rats above ground. These would need to be taken out first. The teams would then need to locate the holes. It was never easy to find them all. Most were concealed, and several would be well away from the mound. A team member would each take a hole, cover it and wait. The leaders used smoke bombs to flush the rats out. They were a crude cocktail of chemicals that produced a noxious gas when mixed. The teams would roll these deep into several of the passages. The rats would then come running, desperate to escape certain death, fleeing the choking fumes which burned their eyes and skin. The teams would be waiting. The rats would flee one by one from the tunnels and into the traps. The knives, spears, machetes, axes would be ready, all poised for the slaughter.

Gaia scoured the area, but could see no sign of movement. Tarkan stepped out from behind his tree and approached the mound. This was the signal for the others to follow. The team members each crept out and eased forward. The rain continued to play out its relentless symphony overhead, the thick canopy of leaves and branches still providing a natural umbrella. Fragments of droplets worked their way through, enough to splatter the people and ground underneath, but without the brutal sting of the deluge overhead.

Gaia shuffled through the leaves and web of vines in the undergrowth at her feet. She kicked and crushed them as she inched forward. Her eyes surveyed the area, watching, ready, like a coiled spring. As Gaia neared the slow incline of the mound there was a gap in the foliage. The vines in front had been disturbed. There was a large hole in the ground. The earth entering the hole had marks, of feet with claws. They were unmistakable. Gaia took up a place just above the entrance, a vantage point over the rats as they fled the gas. They would be panicked and disorientated, but would still be quick. Gaia would have the advantage, but she would take no chances.

Gaia could see the others crouching at an array of entry points, most on the mound. Some had moved outwards, snaking in, looking for more, making sure that nothing had been missed, that all the doorways had been found. Soon everyone was in position, weapons at the ready. Aran was to Gaia's right just a few metres away, paired up by a hole with Freya. Gaia's heart jumped, a rush of anger rising from the pit of her stomach. Why had Freya paired with Aran? What was she up to?

The leaders prepared the smoke bombs, the plumes of smoke rising from their hands as they added the reactive chemical. Tarkan gave a signal and one by one the leaders rolled the bombs into the entrance holes, moving around in a circle till they had each planted a few. Everyone waited. It would not be long now.

The rain drummed overhead. Gaia stared down at the hole, still shivering in her wet clothes. Her teeth chattered, and shoulders ached. She tried to keep focused and her hands steady. A long razor sharp knife was in one hand, an axe in the other. The axe was heavier, but both were lethal in her hands. The rumble came from underground, muffled squeals from the tunnel at her feet. The sounds intensified, a deep thudding coupled with the beating snare drum of the pelting rain. The shrieks and squeals got louder. They were horrifying. The sound of blind panic and fear, of pain, of the rats sensing their imminent death. The creatures had no choice but to flee. It was escape or suffocate. The rodents were writhing in agony in a fiery excruciating death. If the rats did not run their throats would be ripped out with the flames, their eyes scorched with its acid vapour. The choice was to run or die, when running would mean certain death. In the immediate panic the rats would not think of this. They had no time to think. Instinct took over. The desire to preserve life, to survive was all that mattered. Something in the creatures' brain told them to run. It was the best chance they had, their only hope.

The first of the rats appeared. It was quick, but Gaia was ready. She thrust the knife into its back as it exited, and with a sharp twist severed its spine casting its quivering corpse to one side. Another came. This time Gaia swept the axe into it, cutting it in two. There were more. The slaughter was easy, clinical, routine. One after another they came and Gaia cut them down reaching a tally of eight dead. All were large, all adults. The rats' eyes bulged in fear and streamed with acid tears, the whites cracked with veins of deep red. Their slavering jaws gasped for fresh air as they burst from the tunnels. Each only tasted it for the briefest of moments before Gaia ripped the life from them.

The stream of rats slowed, but still Gaia waited. One more came, a final victim, a different victim. Its eyes were aflame as the others, it also coughed and spewed, its blazing lungs reaching out for clean air. However, this rat was much smaller. Its hairs were light and thin, the pink flesh could still be seen below. Its claws were not yet formed on its tiny feet. It was one of the young, a desperate, helpless baby rat. It must only have been a few days old, possibly even a day, or a few hours. The rat was new to this world, new to this cold, brutal world of survival, a world of kill or be killed. Its first experience was of pain, of the suffering of the gas. It may never have seen the light of day before, or felt the warmth of the sunshine on its skin. In the briefest of moments the young creature felt the cold drops of rain, tasted the freshness of the air. Those were the last things it felt and tasted. That and the burning pain in its eyes, lungs, stomach and on its skin. It was all over, the rat's short life ended. Slain by the swift, merciless flash of Gaia's knife.

Gaia studied the corpse of the baby rat. Its tiny feet twitched one final time as a spasm shot through its body. Then it was still. Gaia stared at the blade of her knife, still dripping in the rat's warm, dark crimson blood. The droplets of rain that seeped through the canopy overhead began to wash the blood away. The diluted beads trickled down the blade onto the handle and Gaia's hand. Her shivering red flesh took on a new shade. Her hand still gripped the handle of the blade, her fingers were white with the force of her clench. This was the first time she had seen a creature so young. The rats bred and matured in a matter of days so it was unusual to find one this way.

Gaia looked at the carnage that lay nearby, at the large carcasses of the slain rats. She knew that whatever this young creature was now, these fierce killers was what it would soon become. This was its place in the hierarchy of life, the new food chain. This was the price of evolution. This new world that had been rebooted by humanity, by those that had come before, by the politician and scientists. The world destroyed by those that looked to progress, but became sloppy and greedy, the unfettered and the arrogant. Together those people had become a beast that destroyed, a beast that swept all aside, all but those that could survive. This was the new world order. This was the way it was now. This baby rat, that had been full of life, of potential had met its destiny. In the new world order the rules were simple, survive or die. Gaia had intervened, taken control. Gaia had played God in a godless world, a world where the only gods were the survivors. The community were the chosen.

6

The mission left the slaughter and made their way back. None of them had been injured or killed. It was a straightforward mission, a success. A few rats had escaped from an exit they had not spotted, the only minor flaw in their triumph. Many creatures had been slain, the bulk wiped out. However, they knew that many other lairs remained. Unknown communities of rats, still waiting to be found and slain. There were many creatures that would be gathering again, preparing to attack. Others would return and find this broken lair. They would recolonise it, start again. The rats instinct was to survive, to breed, to drive the species forward. This was a compulsion, without question. The creatures desire was to be alive and survive.

For now the teams would savour their victory, though the celebrations were muted. The morning had been tough. Both the weather and the assault had exhausted them all, taking its toll on even the fittest and most enthusiastic. The leaders recognised this. They knew there was no point in moving on for further kills. This would do for now. The teams would return, freshen up, eat, and rest ready for some reflection time later that afternoon.

The march back was as before, cold and wet, but without incident. The journey was a blur, a monotonous parade, step after step after step. Gaia was exhausted, and the activities of the night before and the morning lay heavy. The body moved, regimented, precise, but her mind drifted from image to image, issue to issue, worry to worry. There was a lot to think about, but it was the thought of the dead baby rat that kept recurring. That one image overpowered all other thoughts in Gaia's head. However hard she tried to block it the image kept coming back. The incident had unsettled her. Gaia had never thought of the rats in this way, never seen them so young and vulnerable. She had not seen them as living, sentient creatures, only beasts, a dangerous enemy to be slaughtered at all costs. Like any other creature the rats were born and nurtured. They lived in families and communities, had mothers and fathers, fed, grew, became parents themselves. In turn, the rats would nurture others and keep the cycle moving. Gaia had never considered that before. It was not important, maybe too uncomfortable to contemplate. The truth and reality weakened her. She had been taught to see fierce, savage creatures, told to see only the threat. The rats were the enemy, strong and lethal. They needed to be destroyed.

The young one looked so weak and vulnerable. It was easy prey, no match for Gaia. Maybe to murder it was unfair, the strong destroying the weak. Perhaps that was where the community had got it wrong. Maybe they needed to destroy the young, not the old. By the time they reached maturity the rats were strong, determined, programmed with an insatiable desire to feed, survive, and destroy. The grown rats were a formidable enemy and they became stronger. The young were different. They could be slain with ease. They were not a threat. Maybe they should be the target, before they became strong, before they were lost. Kill the young and you kill the species. Gaia was confused, torn between her emotions of guilt and sorrow for the slain young rat and the logic of survival.

The community were too passive. The missions felt like training exercises. They needed more purpose. The leaders had been pacified by their own complacency and arrogance. They thought the community were superior, but while they sat and waited their enemy grew strong. This was no longer about missions, this was war. Either the community fought and won it or they would be destroyed. Gaia saw this. The community on the island were doomed, and the seeds of their doom lay in the young.

The mission reached the camp as the lashing rain began to ease. They took their weapons back to storage and made their way to the dorms where they showered and changed into dry, fresh clothes. Gaia sat on her bunk drying her hair with a towel. She took a brush from the drawer and combed it through her soft red hair. The hot shower had revived her aching bones. They still felt stiff, skin a little numb, but the warmth of the soothing water had returned some life and movement. Her feet were still cold, and sharp jabbing pains sliced through them. However, she could almost move her toes again.

Gaia arched her head and gazed out of the window by the bed. The rain had stopped and a few shafts of sunlight threatened to puncture the light grey, thinning cloud. In the background was the babble of the other girls. Gaia was not tuned into the words, each merging into an unfathomable jabber. The events of the morning had dissolved in the warmth of the shower, flushed away in a slow, swirling motion. There were other concerns now. Too many. Gaia had huge decisions to make, ones which would change her life forever. She had no-one to talk to, no-one to share this. There were no friends and family. Gaia had always been alone, but she had never felt lonely, until now. She needed someone more than ever.

Gaia continued to brush her hair. The slow, sweeping motion was comforting. Why wasn't there someone else to do this? Someone to rely on and turn to. Someone she loved. There was a strange sensation, as though she was being watched. Gaia turned and saw Hakan standing by the door. He was still, smiling, staring, paying no attention to the flurry of activity around, the bustle of the girls in the dorm. Hakan was only interested in Gaia.

Gaia placed the brush back in the drawer, stood and turned her back to the door. His piercing stare burned through the back of her skull. She tried to look busy, fussing over the bed clothes, trying to iron out the creases, opening the drawer and tidying. In the drawer there was a pencil and notebook, a brush, some pressed flowers in a small wooden box, and a leather wristband. The minutes dragged, but she squeezed every moment from them, stretching them to breaking point. Hoping he would be gone. Waiting as long as possible before turning. Hoping to shake him free. Gaia moved round, not looking at first, then she snatched a quick glimpse. Hakan had gone.

The bell for lunch rang. There was a flurry of activity as the girls in the dorm all sorted their things and left. Gaia stayed for a moment, waiting for all the others to leave. She wanted to make sure Hakan was gone. Gaia did not want to see him again, or feel the shiver of fear rush through her, or the hairs on her skin flare up. He was circling though, letting her know. It was only a matter of time.

The dorm was empty, the mindless chatter replaced with silence. The background noise had helped Gaia. It was reassuring. The silence left too much space to think, space to remember she was on her own, alone and lonely, abandoned. Gaia stood up from her bed and moved towards the door, stopping just short. It was Hakan. He had been there all along. Standing by the doorway just out of view. Waiting for the girls to leave. Waiting for the dorm to empty. Waiting for her. Hakan moved forward into the room and closed the door. Gaia stood a few feet away, face calm, expressionless, concealing the eruption of emotion within. She placed her arms by her side.

Hakan was strong, more than a match for Gaia. He was a leader, and well trained. He had more experience, and natural strength. Gaia had one thing he did not, desperation. This would give her an edge. Gaia also had a switch. She had learned to control it, but had experienced its ferocity when let go. She became another person, an animal, fuelled by a surge of energy, an unfettered anger that was powerful and destructive. All fear was lost, all sense of morality gone. There was a mist, a blanket which smothered all doubt, all hesitation. Gaia would attack with a swift, relentless force. Once the switch had gone controlled chaos would wash over her. If Hakan pushed her, he would feel it. Superior training was on his side, but he would have hesitation. They all did. All those that kept those shreds of humanity, the fragments of decency. This led to indecision and doubt. There was a tipping point where Gaia's manic aggression would expose this doubt, and magnify the fear. That is when he would begin to crumble, and lose control. That is when Gaia would have him, when the power of her momentum would sweep him aside.

Both stood in silence. Gaia was determined not to speak unless she had to. Hakan was biding time, weighing up his thoughts, measuring his words. He looked straight at her, eyes moving up and down, face awash with lurid pleasure, basking in the satisfaction of his power. Before him was his prey, the latest victim. Hakan had Gaia in his web, and now was the time to savour this. He would not strike yet. There was no need. She was paralysed. He had injected his crippling poison, or at least Gaia had administered it herself through her own arrogance and foolishness. Gaia had believed she could fool him, could break the rules on his watch, in his dorm, under his command. She had shown her disdain, her lack of respect and deserved to be punished. The girl was his and therefore he would decide her fate. There was no need to take this matter anywhere else. Hakan knew what she wanted, what they all wanted. The others had wanted it too and begged for it. This girl was the same. Gaia wanted attention and affection. They all wanted it. She had broken the rules, wanted to get caught and be punished. Hakan cleared his throat and spoke.

'I've been thinking about last night, about your blatant disregard for the rules. You've put me in a difficult position thirty seven, or shall we make it Gaia?'

Hakan sneered at Gaia, stepping forward and pacing around her.

'You're aware this is my dorm, and I'm responsible for ensuring that order is kept and the rules are followed. We have these rules for a reason. If we allow them to be broken everything disintegrates. All order is gone. Now we can't have that, can we Gaia? Your actions make me look weak, and I won't be made to look weak.'

Gaia remained still. Her eyes were fixed on a notch in the wood on the wall by the door. A bland, meaningless notch, but she was trying to find patterns within it, patterns and faces. They were reassuring faces, smiling back, whispering and comforting her. They were ghosts, faces of those that had been here before. *It'll be all right. Don't worry dear. It'll be all right. Don't listen to him.* Hakan stopped behind her. She felt him lean in, his warm breath touch the nape of her neck, the steady rhythm of his breathing. The warmth faded as he moved his head back and slid around to stand in front. Hakan's eyes pierced her, his face just a foot away. They burned with pleasure, the drunken pleasure of his power. Gaia clenched her fist. The mist was seeping into her mind. The anger was building. The switch poised. She held it together, pulled herself back from the brink. Now was not the time. It would come, but not now.

'I'm a man of my word, Gaia. I promised to keep this a secret, our little secret. I have and I will, but this can't go unpunished. You realise that all actions have consequences. *You've* let me down. *You've* put me in this position. *You* have to pay.'

Hakan stepped back and turned away, moving towards the wall by the door. He raised his arm and began to trace patterns across it, aimless swirling patterns, swaying his head from side to side as he did so. Hakan stared at the wall, lost in another world, consumed by his thoughts.

'So I've been thinking about an appropriate punishment, but you know I'm struggling. I must admit I don't much care for them. They're so. What's the word? Crude. Yes, crude. That's the one. I could come up with something, but would it serve its purpose? Would you learn? Probably not.'

Hakan continued to trace his empty shapes, still lost, still churning over in the cesspit of his mind.

'We need to find a way though. Some way of making you see you've done wrong. A way you can show your remorse. I've decided to let you come up with something. A way to say sorry. A way to repay me for your betrayal. So I want you to have a think. I'll give you two days. Come to my room on Tuesday evening. We'll discuss it then. Alone.'

Hakan stopped his doodling on the wall and turned to face her. Gaia remained fixed on the dancing faces in the wall, the now deformed faces. They were laughing now, cackling at her. *You deserve this. You brought it all on yourself. This is all your own fault.* Gaia's mouth was dry, her lips welded together. She ripped her lips apart, felt the skin tear from them. Gaia licked the wound, felt the flash of pain as her tongue hit the exposed flesh. She tasted the blood in her mouth, mixed with the sourness already there, a foul cocktail of despair.

'Can I go now? I'm going to be late for lunch.'

'In a moment. First, I need you to tell me that you understand what I've said. That you'll think about this.'

Gaia turned and looked straight at him, a scowl on her face.

'I understand.'

Gaia rushed past Hakan, through the door and out the dorm. She sprinted towards the refectory without stopping or looking behind. At the refectory door, her lungs burned as she steadied and composed herself, wiping the small beads of sweat from her brow. Catching her breath again, Gaia entered and made towards the serving area. Head bowed she collected her food and sat at one of the tables. Aran was sitting close by, the same table, but opposite sides a few places down. Gaia knew she could not speak to, or acknowledge him, but so wanted to see him and know he was near. She longed to tell Aran what was happening, to reach out and break the loneliness, to feel his warm breath like the night in the woods, his lips brush past hers again. Aran was all Gaia had right now, the closest to a friend, someone to trust. The only one. For now she must remain alone. It was the way it had to be. Finding the answer to Hakan was her problem. Gaia had to find it soon.

7

Gaia sat on the sand and looked at the rippling myriad of grey and blue sea. The light shimmered and dazzled as the waves moved towards the shore. The soft, sleepy sound of them lapping relaxed Gaia. She was drifting in and out of her thoughts, a half sleep. The sun already hung low in the sky, its bright glow offering a gentle hand of warmth. Gaia closed her eyes and looked straight at the sun, its piercing light puncturing her eyelids. Even the dampened brightness blinded and burned her, but she continued, pushing it to the limit. Gaia's brain told her to stop, warned her, but there was a fire, a desire that urged her on. She reached the point where she could take no more, the verge of too late. Her eyes moved away, her eyelids pressed shut. The bright flashes of circular light still played in her brain, sweeping through her mind, dissolving wisps of molten light.

Gaia sensed a presence. Someone was nearby. She opened her eyes, but struggled to see, they were still burning from the intense light. Gaia blinked hoping it would wipe everything away. There was a silhouette set against the sun, about ten feet away. The shape was familiar. As her eyes adjusted she realised it was Aran.

'Are you OK? I didn't startle you?'

'I'm fine. What do you want?'

'We need to talk. It can't wait till this evening.'

Aran sat beside her. Gaia felt his warmth as their arms touched. He looked down at the sand, began to play with it, letting it fall from his hand.

'I've spoken to the others and they're ready. They're all in.'

'Can you tell me who they are now?'

'No, not yet. You'll find out soon enough. They don't know I've spoken to you. It's the best way, just in case something goes wrong, and any one of us is caught and questioned.'

'Except you, of course! If you're caught we've all had it.'

Aran laughed, looked up at Gaia and smiled. She felt herself blushing.

'Well there is that risk, but someone has to pull it together. We could get caught together now.'

Gaia's face burned. She looked away. Aran continued.

'Trust me I've got plans for if I'm caught. Plans that'll protect you all.'

Aran picked up a stray stick and began to poke random holes in the sand.

'We're going to move at night. The day after tomorrow, Tuesday. The moon will be full, and we need some light. The tide is out in the early hours of the morning, just after midnight. We'll meet at the hideout in the woods. I'll have all we need there, but bring a bag. Remember we need to travel as light as possible, so only the essentials.'

Aran continued to fidget as he set out the plan. Gaia was mesmerised by his doodlings, now taking shape, becoming an intricate pattern.

'We'll make our way along the beach to the causeway. We need to get across it as quickly as possible. The tide will be back in and full by morning, and hopefully no-one will have realised that we are gone until then. Once the leaders realise and sound the alarm they'll have to wait till the tide is out again, or use the boats. Either way it gives us a good start on them. Once we're on the mainland we head for the river. We then make our way upstream to the hills as quickly as we can.'

'And if we make it, what happens when we get there?'

'We'll get there, and when we do we have to hope the message on the note is right and they'll find us.'

Aran kicked the sand with his foot wiping away his drawings. He pressed the palm of his hand onto the sand and began to smooth it in a circular motion.

'What *are* you doing, Aran?'

They both laughed, and Gaia reached across and messed the area Aran had just smoothed over.

'Hey, that was my artwork!'

'Mmmmm artwork, eh? You say you'll have all we need. So that's food, weapons?'

'Yes. I'll have food, enough for a few days. We can replenish supplies on the way. There'll be plenty in the wild as we go. I'll bring weapons too.'

'I want a knife and an axe. Make sure. That's all I need.'

Aran looked up from the sand and across at Gaia. He smiled. There was a warmth and reassurance. They both knew what they were about to embark on, both knew the risks.

'I'll get what you need, don't worry. Now are there any other orders you'd like to put in while I'm here? Biscuits, fruit, honey?'

'No. I'll trust you on the food front. As long as it's edible.'

They laughed. Despite all the worries, and troubles of the past few days. Despite the impending danger, and their world about to be thrust into chaos and uncertainty. Somehow Gaia felt happy now. Whatever happened Gaia had Aran with her, and she trusted him. There were reservations about the whole thing, but now it was beginning to feel right. Gaia looked across at the mainland, their destination in just a couple of days. She felt a rush of excitement and joy at the thought of seeing it again. Then the voice of caution intervened and hurled another pang of doubt into her mind.

'There's something else bothering me. The dorms. It's going to be tricky getting out. If any one of us gets caught we're finished.'

'I know. We each have keys for the outside doors.'

'That's the problem, I don't!! I told you, when Hakan caught me coming back in the other night I gave him the key. I said he'd left it in the door.'

'Damn. I forgot about that.'

Aran punched the sand, over and over, harder each time. Gaia looked on. He stopped and spoke.

'How are you going to get out without the key?'

'I don't suppose you have any spares?'

'No. I don't have any spares! Do you realise the trouble I went to steal those keys? We need to think this one through.'

Aran got up and kicked the sand back and forth with his foot. He started to pace in front of her. Gaia remained seated, in awkward silence. There was a solution, the only one she could think of. Gaia was waiting before offering it, working out the words in her head. Gaia knew the way out, what she had to do, the best solution, the only solution. The words blurted out.

'I'll have to kill him.'

Aran stopped pacing and looked down at Gaia. She gazed forward at the sea, not wanting to catch his eye. Gaia did not want him to see his reaction, or for him to see the cold indifference in her face.

'You're not serious?'

'Yes. It's the best way. Think about it. Hakan is scum. He's all over me already, wants me to come up with a way of saying sorry and thanking him. He wants me to go to his room to discuss it. You know what that means, don't you? There's no way he's getting his way with me. I'd already decided that I was going to kill him anyway.'

Gaia looked up at Aran. His face was wracked with worry. This was not a part of the plan he had imagined. Part of him knew that they may have to defend themselves, even kill at some point on the journey, but this was before they had even started.

'He's sick. He deserves it. This just gives me an extra reason. He wants me to go to his room on the night anyway. This fits perfectly. He'll be relaxed and thinking he's going to get what he wants.'

Gaia paused, waiting for a response.

'This gets rid of one of our biggest problems, and he won't be able to raise the alarm. It makes sense.'

Aran thought for a while. Gaia was right, but it was a big step. It did make sense, but was full of risk. Hakan was strong, and to say you were going to kill someone and doing it were very different. What if Hakan reacted and saw it coming? He was trained and even when relaxed was a threat. No doubt he was wary of Gaia. He would be a fool not to be cautious around her.

'How are you going to do it? You'll never overpower Hakan with just your hands. It doesn't matter how off guard you think he'll be you'll have a split second of surprise. It'd have to be quick, one blow or movement.'

'I know. That's why you are going to get me a knife. I'll need something small so I can conceal it. All

I need is one moment and he's mine. He won't be expecting me to be armed. I need a weapon though.'

Gaia was right. That was the only way, but getting a knife to her was an issue. It would mean Aran would have to steal one far earlier than he had planned. The longer the weapons were gone the more likely it would be noticed that they were missing.

'Getting the knife is risky, but it's possible. I wanted to leave getting the weapons till later, but we can get round that. Passing the knife onto you needs some thought.'

'Do you know the wooden shed by my dorm? They keep the gardening tools in it?'

'Yes. I know it.'

'Put the knife in the gutter at the back of the shed, the far end away from the door. It's low. You can reach it easily. Make sure it's there after the evening meal and I'll collect it. I can hide it in my room until it's time. Just leave the rest to me. Once it's over I'll meet you at the hideout. Make sure you're there and ready as planned.'

Aran played with the sand with his feet. One more thing troubled him.

'Have you ever killed anyone before Gaia?'

'No.'

'Don't underestimate it. We're not talking about an animal. This is a person you'll be killing.'

There was a sound in the dune grass behind them. It was a rustle, movement, something or someone. They turned, but saw nothing.

'Do you think we were being watched?'

'Possibly. I told you they were keeping a close eye on you. I'm not sure why.'

'I know. Kali made that pretty clear the other day.'

Gaia got to her feet, brushed herself down, surveying the dunes for any signs of movement.

'I can handle Hakan, but I know this throws up a lot more problems. You don't have to take me if you think it's going to be too risky. I might have blown it for you already, if they're watching me.'

Aran touched Gaia's shoulder. He paused awhile, the briefest of moments, but it was enough to let Gaia know he cared. She felt his hand, the warmth of the gesture, the tenderness.

'I need you. We're in this together now.'

The blood rushed to Gaia's face as she averted his gaze and stared at the sand.

'Thanks. Let's get out of here.'

'Good. That's settled. You're right. We need to get going.'

'You go on ahead. There's something I need to do here first. It won't take long.'

They both knew what they were about to embark on might be the end for them. They were stepping into the unknown together. It was fraught with risk, but despite all the dangers, the slim odds, the questions, the doubts, the high chance of failure. Despite all that Gaia knew to do nothing would be the greatest failure. Their success would not be determined by whether they made it off the island or found the camp in the hills. The success was in trying to make it happen, taking the first step to freedom.

Aran made his way over the dunes and out of sight. Gaia moved down further onto the beach, towards the hiding hole, to see her things, her secret hoard of treasure. This was the last time she might get to see them. They were small, insignificant things in themselves, but to Gaia they meant everything. Each represented a fragment of hope, and together kept her going. They were her tiny act of rebellion, part of her reason for being. She needed to see them one last time, to touch them, to say farewell.

Gaia reached the hole and took out the items one by one. The orange ball, the small pieces of frosted glass, the shells, the stones, all still glistening in the sunlight. The chunks of plastic and wood, her toy duck. She picked up the bottle, the biggest prize of all. That is what she had really wanted to see, to read the message inside, from the sea. It had been calling her, urging her to take action, to ask questions, to seek answers. Gaia took the fragile paper from the bottle, and stared down at the faded words. She read them, once, twice, over and over again.

'All is not what it seems. Seek the truth.'

8

The day of the escape came. There were no further conversations, no acknowledgements, only the occasional eye contact in the refectory and the gatherings. Their tasks had all been in different teams. Gaia had done some close combat and weapons training. She focused on her speed and reactions, knowing they would be critical facing Hakan for the last time. Kali had kept out of her way, though there were the usual threatening stares and barbed comments, but nothing unexpected or more intense. Things seemed to play out as normal, nothing to make Gaia suspicious.

Then there was Freya. Her behaviour had been different, a bit odd. She had looked awkward and uncomfortable around Gaia. At times Gaia would try to catch her eye hoping to throw her a set of daggers or an unsettling glare. Freya always avoided the look, lowering her head and moving away. This made Gaia nervous. She was sure that Freya had been the person in the dunes, the eyes and ears of Kali. How much had Freya heard? If she had heard the plans about Hakan it could be devastating. Freya would no doubt have reported this back to Kali who would have warned him. Despite Gaia's worries Hakan had seemed fine, or at least as much as could be expected. He went about his tasks as always, trying to be the showman and centre of attention at meals. It was all a game to paper over the cracks of his deceit. Hakan continued to build a wall of persona to persuade everyone that the rumours could not possibly be true. They were poisonous lies. It could never be true of Hakan.

That evening Gaia was in the refectory finishing her evening meal. Aran sat at a far table, head bowed, playing with his food. Gaia kept looking over as discreetly as she could so as not to arouse suspicion. There was nothing from him, no sign. He got up, took his tray and made towards the door. He looked across winked and raised his thumb as it held onto the tray. It was a fleeting signal, throwaway. It would mean nothing, unless you were waiting for a sign. Gaia was.

Gaia waited until Aran had left, giving him plenty time to return to his dormitory. Freya entered and weaved her way through the others towards the leader's table. On reaching the table Freya stood to attention, head forward, hands pressed to her side waiting for permission to speak. Kali nodded and Freya moved round the table to where Kali was sitting. Leaning over, Freya cupped her hand and spoke into Kali's ear. Gaia looked at Kali as Freya spoke, searching for an expression, a change in body language, a look of shock, worry, anything. There was nothing. Kali just looked down at the table and listened. Freya removed her hand and stood upright again, stiff and to attention. Freya waited for the signal to be dismissed. Kali flicked her hand and Freya moved away, marching out of the refectory, head forward, looking at no-one, without speaking or stopping.

Gaia looked back at Kali, waiting for any indication. It came. Kali looked up from her food and threw a cutting glance across at Gaia. It was only for a few seconds, but it was long enough to feel the burning from her piercing eyes, to see the look of utter contempt. It was an expression that Kali knew something. Kali was onto Gaia. In an instant Kali's gaze shifted as if nothing had happened.

Gaia began to panic. Kali knew something. Outside there was a knife waiting. Gaia had to pick it up without being seen, take it back to the dormitory and hide it. Later she had to use that knife to kill a leader, steal his key, flee to the woods to meet Aran and a group of others. Who were they? Then they all had to escape the island, using a causeway Gaia had not even seen, evade capture and survive on the mainland until they could get to the hills to find a community no-one was even sure existed. This was Gaia's life as planned for the next few hours and days. This was the moment she had been working towards, her chance for freedom, to be the person she wanted to be, to escape the manipulation and engineering of the community and its leaders. Gaia was so, so close, and now it was all going to be scuppered by Kali and her pathetic little runner, Freya. Gaia was sure they both knew, convinced that the message had been about her. Maybe Freya had found the knife? Perhaps Freya had been watching and saw Aran conceal it? Gaia's head was awash, her mind spinning.

In amongst the mental melee Gaia tried to consider the next move. Aran knew nothing of this. He was relying on her, would be expecting her. They would be waiting for Gaia. To abandon them would be a betrayal, but Kali knew Gaia was involved. If it had been Freya watching them Kali would know of the meeting with Aran on the beach. If Kali knew then whatever happened this was over. They were all doomed.

'I need you. We're in this together now.'

Gaia remembered Aran's last words to her before they parted on the beach. She could not let him down. If they were caught it would be together. At least Gaia would show him that no matter what she did not lose faith, was loyal and to be trusted. All this panic was speculation, assumption, paranoia. It was her mind playing tricks. Gaia needed to get a grip, take control, deep breaths, empty her mind. She closed her eyes and blocked out all thoughts of Kali and Freya. They were so often the trigger. The clarity returned, along with a degree of calm.

Gaia rose from the table, put her dishes away and left. She moved towards her dorm, approaching the wooden shed where the knife should be waiting, looking around for anything suspicious. There was nothing. Everything was as expected. The other young people were milling around, chatting, waiting for the second wave of the evening meal being allowed in. No-one seemed to notice Gaia, or care. She reached the shed and moved round to the back, scanning the area. No-one was watching. The rear of the shed had a degree of shade and protection from some storage buildings nearby. Gaia stood beneath the gutter at the far end away from the door, raised her arm, and felt inside. There was nothing. She moved around feeling further up the gutter. Again the knife was not there, only the soft, damp texture of moss and the small pebbles and debris that had built up over the years. Gaia lowered her arm, and lent back against the shed. The signal from Aran had given every indication that the knife would be here. Could it be Freya? Had she seen Aran place the knife here and recovered it? Gaia plunged her head into her hands, sighing and shaking her head. It was all over before it had even begun.

Something in the back of Gaia's mind prodded her. It was a small, nagging little doubt, a glimmer of hope. Gaia moved to the other side of the gutter to the door. Could Aran be that stupid? She lifted her arm again and felt inside. There it was. The distinctive texture and shape of the handle. Aran had only gone and put it in the wrong side. Could he get one simple instruction right? Gaia was supposed to escape the island with this guy, the one who had it all planned. They were all in safe hands. They were in it together. He needed her. Gaia could see now why Aran needed her. If he could not get the simplest of instructions right, what hope was there for the journey? Gaia looked at the knife and shook her head.

The knife was still in its stiff leather sheath. Gaia placed it in the back of her trousers and covered it with her jumper and jacket. She moved back around the shed and towards the dormitory. As Gaia entered the room and approached the bed a few of the girls were laughing and chatting. It was usual inane banter, the talk that is meant to bind us together. The kind of small talk Gaia would seek to avoid. Gaia spoke as she found and the other girls were dull and lifeless.

As the girls chatted away, none knew what Gaia was about to do, nor cared. They would soon though. Once it become known, the talk of the community. This would be the great scandal of Gaia, Aran, and the others. How they murdered a leader and fled the island. How Gaia struck him down in cold blood, in his room. Poor, innocent Hakan, slain by them. They would say he was a good leader slaughtered at the hands of Gaia. They all knew the truth, and it is only the truth that matters. Gaia did not care what others thought of her. She would never try to be what they wanted her to be be. As long as she was true to herself, that was all that mattered.

Gaia slipped out the knife and hid it under the mattress. The knife would be safe there. A few hours, and it would be time. If they got that far. If they were not confronted before that. If they were not challenged and exposed by Kali, thanks to Freya. One of these days Freya would get her just rewards. Not today. The moment would have to wait. There was still a chance for Gaia. Maybe they had not been found out. There was the possibility the message had been about something else. Until someone made a move Gaia had to assume things would go ahead as planned. Revenge on Freya would be foolish, much as Gaia would love to. It was all about sticking to the plans now, for the night to come. That was when everything would begin. So Gaia waited.

9

Gaia lay on her bed, dressed in her pyjamas. The others were all sleeping. There was mumbling and sniffling, the occasional snore. Gaia stared at the wires and frame of the bed above, her familiar nightly view, the tapestry of nocturnal doodling, her distraction. All those times Gaia had lain awake and could not sleep. All those hours she had absorbed this view, studied it. All the minutes weaving thread through the framework. All the seconds thinking who she was, how she got here, what the future held. Was life happy or not? What did she want? All those months, weeks, days, hours, minutes, seconds. All those questions. They had all led to this moment. The next few minutes would be the point of no return. Gaia would make the final break and set forward the unstoppable wheel of destiny. The next hour would change forever, determine who she would become. Gaia would embark on the most perilous journey of her short life. She was about to discover who her companions would be on that journey, the people who would make it happen. The next few days and weeks would define her future.

Why? Gaia asked herself over and over. Was the journey worth it? Gaia knew what she did not want, and had always known it. Gaia did not want to be moulded like putty, functional and forgotten. She would not be part of a structure, nothing but a small piece of the glue that held it together, a cog in the machine. The community had given her life, given her education, training, a purpose, but it had come at a heavy cost. The community had stolen her soul, defined all that Gaia was and would become. No more.

It had taken time to find the answers, but Gaia now knew what she wanted. Free to make her own decisions, and determine her own path. Free to make her own mistakes, and her own successes. Free to find out who she really was, not who they wanted her to be. Their chances were slim. There was a good chance of being killed or captured. They may fail in their ultimate goal to find the community, but Gaia had to do this. The journey was her chance. She had to grab it, and take the opportunity. Gaia was ready. This was her moment.

It was time. Gaia's clothes were ready, and a small rucksack packed. She reached under the mattress for the knife. The elastic in her pyjama bottoms was not strong enough to hold the sheath securely so she taped it to the base of her back. Gaia tested the position and angle to ensure she could reach it. She drew the knife from the sheath, and rolled the handle in her hands. The blade glistened even in the night. Gaia ran her finger along its razor edge, feeling the lightest of pressure would slice her skin. She held back, just enough to avoid drawing blood. Once this was done there would be no turning back. The knife on its own was nothing, it was lifeless. The knife's purpose defined by others. Gaia's actions would gave it meaning, and she was about to determine that meaning. In a moment the destiny of the dagger and Gaia would be defined forever. Together they would be intertwined in that one fateful act.

Gaia replaced the knife and steadied herself. She felt electrified, buzzing with the fear and anticipation of what lay ahead. Gaia took slow, deep breaths, holding it in and counting to three, then releasing and holding it. The air emptied from her lungs, filled and emptied them again. In, pause, out, pause, in, pause, out, pause. A steady rhythm began, all on the count of three. It was like a slow waltz. The adrenaline began to ease, the ringing in her ears subsided, her stomach settled. Gaia was ready. It was now. This was the point of no return. She was staring over the precipice.

Gaia glided across the wooden floor, opened the door to the passage. She left the room, and closed the door behind her, moving towards Hakan's door, his room. Gaia listened, but there was nothing. Raising her hand, there was a pause, just a moment for one final listen, then a tap on the door. There was no answer. Gaia listened again, but nothing. Another tap, a little harder this time. The door opened. Gaia jumped, startled. There was no sound, no warning, in an instant his face was there, smiling at her. Smiling at his assassin.

Hakan eased the door open and gestured Gaia to enter. It was a narrow opening, just enough for her to squeeze past, enough to make her brush past him, feel his presence. The calm composure from her breathing earlier had faded. The tension was building within. Gaia shuffled into the room, trying her best to not touch him, but her arm caught his chest. She tried to keep her back arched and away from him. The knife was well concealed, but all it took was the wrong twist of the body and the outline of the weapon might be revealed. Gaia could not take that chance. The leader was dressed in light trousers and a t-shirt. He was barefoot. Gaia turned to face him. Hakan closed the door and looked at Gaia. Up and down, from side to side, leaning his head left and right. There was a pause. Hakan continued to scan her face and body, the smile still etched on his lips.

'So you came thirty seven. I'm pleased. Perhaps a little surprised, but I think we both know this is for the best. Have you had a think about my proposal?'

Gaia was fighting the nerves and fury inside. Both were stirring themselves into an explosive cocktail. She could feel the switch twitching, on the verge of going. It was taking all her mental power to suppress the feelings and keep control. Gaia had to focus, and wait for the right moment. That time was not now. It would come soon, but not yet. She would know when, and then strike. Gaia took a deep breath, forcing out the words to keep up the charade, not wanting to give him any suspicion.

'You didn't give me any choice, did you? I know I've done something wrong, and I don't want any trouble. Yes, I'm thankful you haven't reported me. I've come to say thank you and discuss how I can repay you.'

Hakan grinned, a half grin, but Gaia could see he was satisfied with the response. There was a pause. Hakan screwed up his face and shook his head.

'Yes, I think a thank you of some sort is in order, but the key question is *how* you'd like to repay me.'

Gaia took a deep breath, composed herself. Her heart was racing, hands trembling.

'I don't know. How would you like me to?'

Hakan moved closer, brushed past Gaia and sat on the bed. He leaned back and crossed his legs, looked up at her, the expression of smug satisfaction returning. It was a look that said he had power over Gaia and knew it. The look made Gaia want to cut his throat now, more than ever. Gaia composed herself, wrestled with the fire bursting to get out. The finger was poised desperate to flick the switch, to unleash all her hatred and anger upon him. The moment was soon, but not now.

'I was pretty clear, come up with a way of thanking me. What *I* want is not what I'm asking, I want to know what *you* want to give me.'

Hakan uncrossed his legs.

'Take your time we've got all night.'

Now was the moment. The adrenalin was pumping through her veins, stomach and chest aching. Gaia needed to focus, and channel the aggression. She could feel the sheath pressed against her skin. Gaia had to maintain the advantage, the element of surprise. She slid forward, step by step nearing the bed. Hakan's expression changed, a look of excitement seeped into it. His guard was slipping, becoming mesmerised by the anticipation, the thought of what was to come, hypnotised by the thought of his prize. This was another young and vulnerable victim at his mercy and command. The leader felt light headed, drunk on the sense of his own power. He sat up on the bed as Gaia approached, spread his legs as she stood between them. Hakan looked up at Gaia, she down at him. Their eyes locked. His were giddy with lust, hers were clouded, a thin veil drawn to mask the anger and disgust, the hatred soon to be unleashed. Hakan raised his arms and grabbed her waist while Gaia placed her hands on his head, pressing it down into the warmth of her crotch. Hakan closed his eyes, rubbing his face against the outside of Gaia's pyjamas. His mind drifted into a stupour, lost in thoughts of desire, all that he wanted to give. Hakan trembled at the thought of what this young girl was offering, willingly, without force. This was the prize, the thank you.

Hakan flinched. It was so quick he knew nothing, still lost, drowning in his sick and delirious stupour. Hakan did not feel the knife as Gaia thrust it into his neck. He did not feel the dark, scarlet blood as it spurted across the room, the artery pumping it from the clean, precise incision. So lost he did not feel Gaia push him back onto the bed and watch as he lay there quivering, flinching, dying. Hakan's final thoughts were the sick, warped images of a sordid mind. They were the thoughts of a man entrusted to protect, who abused that trust. A leader who stripped the young of innocence, and all that separates young from old. Innocence and hope. Hakan's life did not flash before his eyes, nor did he see any light. There was no tunnel. no-one waiting with open arms. There were no angels, no loved ones. There was nothing. The dark, twisted thoughts dissolved, washed away in a pool of dark red blood.

Gaia looked down at the leader's body, the still warm, but lifeless body. Hakan was weak, pathetic without power. He could no longer harm. Gaia was strong. This was why she lived and he died. Gaia looked at the knife still clutched in her hand. Half the blade glinted, the other dripped with fresh blood. There was a pause, a moment to take in her revenge. Hakan had asked for a gift, a thank you. Gaia had given him a worthy gift for the man he was. This was the truth and all that mattered, kill or be killed.

Gaia wiped the blade on the blankets and placed it back in the sheath. There was no point in hiding or concealing the body. It was unnecessary and would waste time. She pulled the leader's trousers and underpants down to his ankles, and left him there semi-naked. It was a final insult, stripped of all dignity even in death. Gaia wanted there to be no doubt in the minds of whoever found him of the kind of man Hakan was. She wanted to expose him in every sense. This was unequivocal, it would show the other leaders the provocation, the intent, and the sick mind that had led to this. The scene would confirm everything, that the whispers were true. There would be no doubt. The truth would be exposed. They could choose to ignore it, but they would know. Gaia was curing this disease, purging it from the community, performing something for the greater good. The community should thank her, but they would hunt her down.

Gaia searched for the key, in the bedside cabinet, the desk drawer, under some papers on the desk, but it was not there. She searched his clothes pockets, his jacket, and trousers. They were all empty. Gaia needed that key. It must be somewhere. Where would he keep it? Of course, it was obvious, you keep a key in a door. From the lock hung a bunch of keys. How stupid of her. Gaia removed the keys, and looked one last time at the leader's body, swamped in blood, all life gone. Gaia felt no remorse, no guilt, only satisfaction, the smug satisfaction that once swept across Hakan's face, but had now gone. Now it lay on the face of Gaia.

Gaia left the room and locked the door. She tried the keys in the outside door, one of them worked. Returning to bed, Gaia changed out of her pyjamas, put them under the blankets with a few other clothes and the pillow. It made an unconvincing body up close, but at a distance in a dark room it would suffice. The time was pressing, the window of opportunity limited. As long as they were not discovered until morning they would be fine. The tide would buy them some time.

Gaia heard a noise. It was at the far side of the room, from one of the other bunks. It was one of the girls. Gaia lay on her bed and watched. It was Clara, a tall, dark haired girl. Gaia knew her a little. They had done some tasks together, spoken a couple of times. Clara was one of the glamour girls, the ones Gaia hated, the girls that obsessed over their looks. Clara loved the attention of the boys, and attracted a lot.

Clara tip-toed across the dorm and to the door, eased it open and left. Gaia needed to act. She grabbed her rucksack, took the knife from the sheath and moved to the door. She pulled it ajar, and peered through the thin crack. Gaia saw Clara standing outside Hakan's door tapping on it, as Gaia had done moments earlier. Clara was dim, shallow, and weak but did not deserve to die. She was another of Hakan's victims, like all the others, as Gaia could have been. However, Clara could not be trusted to remain silent. Gaia could tie her up and gag her, but that would be risky. Gaia could wait to see if Clara gave up and returned to her bed. There was no reason for Clara to be too suspicious if Hakan did not answer the door. The last thing to suspect was that the leader was dead. Clara would not want to raise any alarm without good reason as it would lead to awkward questions. Time was ticking, and Gaia decided to wait a little longer, hoping Clara would return to bed.

Gaia waited, but Clara continued tapping. Clara stopped, turned and lent her back against the door, pushing her head back and looking into the air. Clara's face was cast in despair, as tears streamed down her cheeks. She slid down the door and sat on the floor, her head in her hands. Gaia could hear the girl's gentle sobbing, whimpers of desperation. What kind of a spell had Hakan cast? This pathetic creature wanted him, cried for him. Gaia pitied Clara, as a victim and for her weakness. Clara had surrendered to the leader, allowed him to take her, own her. Now in rejection Clara was lost and broken.

Time melted away like a candle. Gaia would need to make a move soon. The delay was jeopardising everything. There was no turning back now. Gaia had crossed the line, and could wait no longer. Gaia had to act now. Control was the key, always, and there was now only one option that allowed Gaia to remain in control. She would take Clara with them. It needn't be the whole of the way, only until they escaped the island. Then Clara could do no damage, and they could let her go. The community would find her, but Gaia and the others would be gone. It was far from ideal, and Gaia knew it. The others would not be happy, but it was the best option.

The decision had been made, and Gaia needed to act now and get to the hideout. The others would be there and waiting. Gaia gripped the knife, sprung through the door, and rushed across the passage. She pounced onto Clara before there was time to react, clasping her hands against the helpless girl's mouth to prevent any screams. Clara's petrified eyes stared back at Gaia, filled with alarm, fear and a quizzical look. Gaia pressed the blade against Clara's neck, her skin was soft and smooth. Gaia's voice was a soft, precise whisper.

'Try to stay calm. Make a sound and I'll cut your throat. Do you understand me?'

Clara nodded, her bold blue eyes still flooded with fear.

'You're going to stand and turn around slowly. Face the wall and put your hands behind your back. OK?'

Clara nodded again, as Gaia guided Clara to her feet, keeping her hand pressed against the girl's mouth at all times. Gaia could feel Clara's body trembling, sense the panic, see it burning into the girl's eyes. Gaia turned Clara around and pushed her face against the wall, the knife against her throat, Gaia's hand still pressed on Clara's mouth. Gaia leant in and put her mouth to Clara's ear.

'Now I'm going to take my hand from your mouth. If I even sense a scream I'll cut it from your throat. I don't want to hurt you.'

Gaia eased her hand away from Clara's mouth, feeling the girl's saliva in her palm. Clara remained pressed against the wall, not wanting to move, still paralysed with fear.

'I'll explain everything soon, but for now all you need to know is you're coming with me. You're not in any danger, just so long as you do as I say and don't try anything stupid. Do you understand?'

Clara paused, and shook her head. Clara whispered, her voice soft, fragile, pleading.

'Yes. Please don't hurt me.'

'I won't unless I have to. Now I'm going to tie your hands.'

Gaia stood back pressing the blade of the knife against Clara's back. Gaia opened her rucksack with her one free hand and removed a bundle of string. Using both hands she unravelled a piece, cut it free and bound Clara's hands together behind her back. Gaia took out a handkerchief.

'Turn and face me.'

Clara turned. She was taller than Gaia, had long dark hair with a natural beauty that was in no doubt. Her cheeks were flushed red and draped in her tears. The self pity of rejection had been replaced with confusion and fear. Gaia forced Clara's mouth open and shoved the handkerchief in, just enough to muffle any sound, but not choke her. The look of terror had begun to subside, and was being replaced with disdain.

'Before we get going I need to make this very clear. Don't get any ideas. You're coming with me. Do exactly as you're told and you'll be fine.'

Gaia took some spare clothes from her rucksack, unbound Clara's arms and passed them to her. Gaia found some boots by the door.

'Put these on. They'll have to do for now.'

Once dressed Gaia ties Clara's hands again, in front this time, making sure they were secure. Gaia led Clara to the main door, unlocked and opened it. The fresh, cool air of the clear, crisp night swept through the door and blasted them. Tugging at Clara's bound hands, Gaia stepped outside, locked the door and led them across the field and into the woods. A bright white moon shone high overhead. It had already reached the peak of its journey across the sky and was making its slow and true descent towards the horizon. The night had not yet fully matured, with the brightness of the moon still far from waning. They needed to make the most of its light and guidance. Gaia found its glow comforting.

They entered the woods, Gaia dragging Clara behind her, clutching the strings that bound her. Clara stumbled and faltered, lacking the heart or conviction, trying to be as awkward as she could. Every now and then Gaia would flash the knife in her hand just to remind Clara. There should be no doubts that Gaia would use it, if only as a last resort.

They followed a rough path into the woods. It was not clear or laid out, but Gaia was processing the route all the time, confident her strong memory would get them to where they needed to be. Soon they reached the area, though it was difficult to tell in the dark. Gaia recognised the thicker foliage of the bush where the hideout was, and the branches of the door concealing the entrance. Gaia stopped and listened. There was no sound other than the gentle hush of the night breeze as it danced through the trees, and the rustle of the leaves and branches as they swayed overhead. There were no voices, not even whispers.

Gaia led Clara to the branches of the entrance and peeled them back. There was the passage, the arch bent overhead. Gaia could see the glow of a candle at the end of the entrance tunnel ahead, the silhouette of what appeared to be two figures sitting on the logs either side. Gaia could not make out the faces, but was sure one of them was Aran. She dragged Clara through the entrance, pulling the branches behind, then made her way along the short, narrow entrance. As they entered the domed area of the hideout the faint light of the candle revealed the right side of Aran's face, looking up at her. A smile, a mixture of worry and relief was stretched across his face. Sat on the log opposite Aran was another boy. Gaia recognised him, but did not know his name. Such was the narrow entrance that Gaia's body had concealed the surprise behind her. The boys had not yet noticed they had a visitor, an extra guest for the journey, an unwanted and unwilling guest, a prisoner.

'What kept you? Is it sorted?'

'Yes, but we've got a problem.'

'What is it?'

Gaia moved round to reveal Clara crouching in the opening to the passage. Clara's mouth was still filled with the handkerchief, hands still bound by the string. The faces of the others dropped. Aran thrust an angry look at Gaia.

'What the hell's she doing here?'

'I had no choice. I found her whimpering outside Hakan's door, as I was about to leave. She just sat there, wouldn't budge. I couldn't get out and the time was getting on. I waited, but I had no other choice. It was too risky to leave her.'

'This blows everything wide open.'

Aran looked across at Clara. She gazed back, her eyes pleading for pity and mercy. Aran was a boy and Clara knew how to play them. Perhaps he would take pity and leave her, or set her free. The boys would see the madness in this, the insanity in Gaia. There was no getting through to Gaia, but Aran was different. He would come round. Aran knew Clara, and was well aware of her style. He had seen such girls before, and had no time for them. Aran looked away at Gaia, the source of this problem. The explanation had better be good.

'What have you got planned Gaia?'

Gaia moved round and sat on the log beside the other boy who remained silent. He deferred to Aran, the leader and orchestrator. Gaia gestured to Clara to sit on the log opposite. Clara stepped over the candle and sat beside Aran, hurling a bitter, accusative glance at Gaia. Clara lifted her bound hands, winced as if in pain, and shuffled and fidgeted. Gaia ignored her.

'I know how this looks, but if I had any other choice I wouldn't have brought her. We can take her with us, and leave her once we get across the causeway. We tie her up, but in good view. They'll find her in a few hours once the tide goes out. We'll be long gone by then.'

Aran shook his head, banging his forehead with his fist. The last thing they wanted was to drag an extra body along, a reluctant one at that. There had to be another way.

'Could we not just leave the girl here? We can keep her tied up and gagged.'

'It's too risky. She'll try and escape and we haven't got anything strong enough to keep her tied securely in here. That string I've used for her hands is no good. It'd take her no time to get out of that. There's too many risks leaving her. Once she gets free, she'll just alert the leaders and we've lost our head start. No, we can't risk it.'

Aran thought for a while. Gaia was right. There were too many problems in leaving Clara here. Like Gaia, Aran would not contemplate killing an innocent. He knew that Gaia being here meant she had succeeded in killing Hakan. That was different. Hakan deserved what he got, but Clara did not. She was not a threat to their lives and killing should always be the last resort. It would be cold, heartless, brutal murder. They were better than that. They had to take her with them.

'OK. I don't like it, but we'll have to go with it, but you watch her and if she tries any funny business you deal with her. If you don't I will. Did you hear that Clara?'

Clara nodded, still trying to plead for mercy with her eyes, clutching the faintest thread of hope they would change their minds and leave her here. Unable to plead her case in words Clara replied with desperation. Her eyes were the key. They were so powerful, the weapon of choice, but missing the mark, failing to win Aran over. Both Aran and Gaia had other priorities and worries. They were smart, and ruthless, and knew Clara would try to get free. They were right. There was nothing Clara would like better than to see Gaia get caught and suffer for this humiliation.

Aran gestured to the boy by Gaia's side who shuffled round to face Gaia, and held out his hand.

'Gaia this is Yann.'

'Hi. I've seen you round, but I don't think we've spoken.'

Gaia took his hand. His grip was limp and flimsy. Yann replied.

'I know you. So you're part of this crack team Aran has put together.'

'Yep. I hope I come up to scratch.'

Yann had short, jet black hair, with skin dark and pimpled. His lips were prominent, pouting, the skin cracked and flaky. He was thick set, not muscular, and not fat, but stocky. His face was round and full, and even in the dim light Gaia noticed his eyelashes were unusually long for a boy, giving his face a feminine quality. Yann's cheeks looked flush in the cold night air, the crisp, biting weather highlighted the purple spots that littered his face in clusters. Gaia looked at Aran.

'Are we waiting for anyone else?'

'One more. She should be here by now. If she's not here soon we'll go. We can't afford to wait any longer. We need to get to the causeway before the tide turns. Once it does the water comes in quickly, especially when the moon is as full as this.'

There was a brief silence. They all gazed at the flickering candle, drawn by its mesmerising glow, the only glimmer of warmth in the cold darkness. The night song of the woods played out beyond the protective canopy of branches. There was a crack, the sound of a branch or a twig breaking. There were footsteps, light, and careful but still noticeable. They all tensed, and Gaia put her hand on the handle of her knife. Everyone held their breath and looked toward the tunnel that led to the doorway to the hideout. They could not see the end, but they listened, searching the darkness, grasping for clues. There was the sound of the branches being pulled back, the movement of someone entering, the swish of the foliage returning. There was the shuffling of footsteps, and a face came into view. It was the face of a girl. At first it did not register with Gaia, at first unsure, but the realisation hit her, the shock, the horror, the surge of emotion. It was her, the one person Gaia had never imagined, Freya.

Gaia jumped to her feet, and moved towards Freya. The knife was from its sheath as Gaia grabbed Freya by the hair, pulling her head to the floor, and dragging her body down to the ground. Gaia placed her knee on the top of Freya's back, and pinned her to the earth, her face biting the cold dirt. The knife was hanging by the side of Freya's face, a warning not to move. Aran dived at Gaia, while Yann flung himself back in shock.

The speed of Gaia's movement took everyone by surprise, especially Freya who lay there with no attempt to react.

'What the hell Gaia?'

Aran grabbed Gaia, and eased back. His hand was touching Gaia's shoulder. He was gentle, wanting to reassure, careful not to cause any further alarm. Gaia's face was seething with anger, a mist cast across her stare.

'What do you mean? What's *she* doing here. She works for Kali. It's her spy.'

Freya remained silent, her face still pressed into the ground, lips contorted by the pressure of Gaia's weight. Aran looked puzzled, still nervous and wary of Gaia, not wanting her to react. He wanted to give her time to simmer down, so he could explain.

'No Gaia. You're wrong. She's coming with us. I've been planning this with Freya for a while now. She's one of us. You can trust her. Believe me. Now let her go, and I'll explain.'

The expression on Gaia's face changed. Something had registered. The switch that had been triggered was clicking back into place. The blind intensity of her anger had been punctured by Aran's words. Gaia was processing them, trying to make sense of them. *You're wrong. She's one of us. You can trust her. Believe me.* Could it be true? Freya? The person she had hated because of Kali. Aran had to be wrong, he had to have been duped. This was all part of Freya and Kali's plan, a trap to snare them.

'No way Aran. She's tricked you. She's Kali's spy I know it!! I've seen her crawling up to her, whispering. Just today I saw it. She was probably telling her everything. I bet they're coming now. It's over. We're finished.'

'No Gaia! Listen. You're wrong. Put the knife away and let her go. Let me explain. You're hurting her. Please Gaia. We have to go.'

Gaia removed her knee from Freya's back and got to her feet.

'OK, explain.'

'I'm not explaining anything until you step back and calm down.'

Aran's words washed over Gaia's anger and emotion, smothering them. She was lost, confused. Part of her wanted to believe Aran, but as soon as she grasped at the comfort of his words, more emotion swept in. The anger and voice of caution returned telling her to be careful, of the danger. Trust no-one. The words and emotion wrestled inside. Gaia's head was a whirlwind of confusion.

The image of Kali kept flashing into Gaia's head. The cold, bitter face staring back at her. Kali's menacing eyes punctured Aran's reassuring words. The sly, knowing grin stoking the fire of hatred from the pit of Gaia's anger. Gaia looked at Aran. The faint glow of the candle was just enough to show the fear in his face. His eyes were pleading, begging her to listen. Aran was poised, ready to take action if need be. Everything now hung in the balance. The next few moments would define the journey. They stood at a crossroads, one path leading to the precipice, the other uncertain, but still offering a glimmer of hope, a fading one. These were the pivotal moments that define life, the important choices. The outcome would determine all that came after. Aran pleaded again, one last time.

'Please Gaia.'

Aran's voice was slow, measured. The tone and tempo of his words had been just right. Each one hit Gaia like the strike of a hammer, forcing home their message. Each cast out the image of Kali from her mind, destroying the anger and emotion. She placed her knife back into its sheath and stepped back.

Freya still lay with her face in the dirt, thick saliva running from her mouth, and mucus from her nose, both mixed with soil. She was shaking, face pale with shock and anger. Freya knew how close she had come, what Gaia was capable of. Freya stayed, not wanting to move and alarm Gaia. Aran would explain, calm the situation.

Gaia sat on the log. Clara and Yann both shared a look of apprehension and fear. If they had been in any doubt of Gaia's capability, the danger she posed, those doubts had gone. The speed at which Gaia moved, the clinical way she had immobilised Freya, the precision of her attack. Gaia was someone they should fear. Any thoughts Clara had toyed with of escaping, of waiting for an opportunity to act were now gone. Clara knew that to act would be to die. Yann had looked to Aran as his leader, the dominant one who had developed this plan, the one he would defer to. Yann knew that no-one led Gaia.

Aran sat opposite Gaia who was staring forward, eyes distant, almost lifeless. Aran looked at the others, saw the fear in their eyes. Time was melting away, and their opportunity with it. All was not yet lost, but the key lay with Gaia. Aran had to get through to her. Gaia was a risk. Brilliant and unpredictable, but they needed her. Both Freya and Gaia were the key to this trip. Aran knew this better than anyone.

'Gaia?'

Gaia looked up, eyes flickering into life. Something clicked and the blank expression lifted. She seemed to return again, to realise where she was, become aware of the others. Gaia nodded, her lips moved, not a smile, but an acknowledgement, a sign she was ready to listen. Aran's voice was calm.

'I know how Freya's behaviour probably looked, but that was all part of our plan. Freya's been in on this for a while. She's been close to Kali for her own reasons, but there's no love or loyalty there. Keep your friends close and your enemies closer. Wasn't that one of the messages in the readings recently? You know Kali, she's shrewd. When I knew Freya wanted to escape the island she was ideal to throw

Kali off the scent. She's close to her so that would give us any clues if Kali was onto us. Freya's also been feeding Kali misinformation, leading her down blind alleys. When you saw her whispering to Kali today that was all part of it. We don't think Kali has any idea about this. If she did, Freya would know.'

Gaia was confused. Logic told her this might be true, but it went against all she felt. She had become so used to thinking of Freya as an enemy, her hatred was so instinctive that this was difficult to accept.

'Whatever you think you know of Freya, you're wrong. We haven't got time. We need to move. You need to get your head round this Gaia. Now!'

Gaia was trying to process everything. Logic and passion were still at odds inside. This was still the moment. Whatever happened Gaia was finished on the island. She had murdered a leader, and taken another member prisoner. Whatever line was in the sand, she had overstepped it. If Freya was working for Kali they would have been found and caught by now. If Aran was right there was still the chance of freedom. Now was not the time for doubt and indecision. Aran was right. They had to move. Gaia had to take control of her emotions, make the right move and go.

'Let's go. It's too late to turn back now.'

Gaia stood and reached out a hand. Freya lifted her head from the ground and rolled over, grabbing Gaia's hand and easing to her feet. They stood face to face, eyes locked. For a moment there was the old flash of hatred, of mistrust, but it faded. There was a touch of warmth in Gaia's eyes, reaching out to Freya, their hands remained locked together. Gaia looked at Freya's face still smothered in saliva and dirt. Her cheek was imprinted with the uneven pattern of the ground below, flecks of grass clung to her skin.

'I'm sorry Freya.'

Freya was cautious, uneasy, but now was not the time to continue this. Freya wiped away some of the grime from her face with her sleeve and spat on the floor.

'Let's forget about it. We need to move or this'll all have been a waste of time.'

Aran stepped forward patting them both on the shoulders.

'That's settled, now let's get off this island!'

Freya looked across at Clara.

'What's she doing here?'

Aran frowned and thrust daggers at Gaia.

'It's a long story. I can't explain now, but Clara's coming with us. Just till we get off the island.'

10

They left the hideout, each with a rucksack, all except Clara who was gagged, bound and dragged by Gaia. They made their way through the woods, Aran leading the way. The terrain was tricky, especially in the darkness. The full moon cast little glow through the thick canopy above. Bushes and vines choked the earth and made their route hazardous and slow. They stumbled often, Clara most. Gaia was becoming annoyed, convinced it was a tactic to slow them down. They were at the back of the group, managing to keep pace despite Clara's frequent falls. The branch of a vine caught Gaia's cheek. She felt the thorns pierce and rip her cold skin. The pain was sharp, lingering, made all the worse by the biting temperatures of the clear night.

Aran pressed on at a strong pace. He knew the route and wanted to make up for lost time. Catching the timing of the tide was critical. They would cross the causeway at the latest possible moment, and if they were discovered before morning there would still be the protection of the incoming tide. The causeway was a lifeline to the island, its main artery, but it had taken many lives in the past. Foolish people who tried to cross despite the incoming tide.

They reached the edge of the woods. There was a field to cross before they reached the dunes and beach beyond. They were to follow the beach to the causeway. It was not the shortest route, but it was the safest and there was no chance of getting lost. Eventually the coastline would reach the causeway. There also the rats. They roamed at night, but seldom scavenged near the beach as there was little food.

They crossed the field. The moon shone overhead casting a bright, pure light from the clear sky. As the glow panned out, and faded into the blackness a sea of stars could be seen. On a pitch black, clear night the sky was overwhelming. Millions of flickering dots of light, all of varying intensity speckled the blanket of darkness. Gaia would often gaze out of her bedside window and soak up the spectacle. Each a huge ball of blazing gas, each in its own private solar system, with its own planets, moons, and life. All so distant from where they stood. The light from some of the stars took so long to reach the eyes that they may no longer exist. They were ghosts, real and could be seen, but only echoes of something past. What chance was there of another Gaia somewhere she wondered. On another distant planet spinning around one of these flecks of light. Maybe there was someone staring back at her, looking at the same wondrous display, thinking the same thoughts. Such was the infinite nature of the universe anything was possible, anything and everything, a sea of infinite possibilities.

They moved near the end of the field, the dew from the soft grass seeping through their boots and trousers. Gaia noticed something. A shadow flashed across the grass illuminated by the moon. It was large, but fleeting. She looked up, but saw nothing. Perhaps she was mistaken. Maybe it was nothing, her paranoia yet again.

They climbed the dunes and Aran led them onto the beach, moving onto the firm, wet sand nearer the tidal stretch. The tide was still low, the shadows of the rocks and seaweed could be seen stretching out towards the calm silvery water in the distance. The calm was a deception. It would not be long before it turned. Aran stopped a moment, scanning the beach both ways, the golden sand stretching for miles. Aran pointed.

'We're heading north, following the beach until we reach the causeway. It's safer and we can keep an eye on the tide. We've got to get a shift on. It won't be long before it turns. We need to get onto the causeway before it does. We might just make it, but it's going to be tight.'

Yann looked at Clara and Gaia. He spoke, loud enough to make the others uncomfortable.

'Can't you take the handkerchief out of her mouth now? No-one is going to hear her this far out. I'm sure she got the message about not trying anything stupid. We've all seen what you're capable of.'

Gaia pressed the knife against Clara's cheek. The cold steel blade burnt her skin. Clara's eyes bulged with fear, begging Gaia to back off.

'OK. I'll take it out, but remember don't be stupid. I won't hesitate and no-one will hear you scream. Are we clear?'

Clara nodded. Gaia took the handkerchief from her mouth and put it in her rucksack. Clara gasped as though struggling for air. She bit her tongue, desperate to hurl insults at Gaia, but knowing it would be a mistake. Yann smiled at Gaia, and mouthed a thank you. Aran spoke, an anxious tone to his voice.

'We'll stick to the tidal stretch. The sand's firmer and we can move faster.'

Aran set off jogging along the beach, as the others followed. Gaia and Clara struggled at the rear, Clara trying her best to appear to be keeping up, still dragging the pace as much as she could. Gaia kept tugging at her bound hands, warning her to get a move on. Clara remained silent, all the hatred bottled and simmering inside.

They made steady progress. Everyone was fit and the pace comfortable at first, but soon Aran began to step things up. The causeway was a few miles, the distance no problem, but he was becoming worried about the tide. They had delayed far too long and the timing was tight now.

After about a mile Gaia noticed the shadow again. Once more it was momentary, something flying across the light of the moon. There was another, a large black sheet sweeping along the sand. This time Gaia heard something, a whooshing sound. Something was in the air above them. It was large, and fast. It could only be the night birds. Gaia picked up her pace, pulling Clara along. They moved up through the group first passing Yann, then Freya and reaching Aran. Gaia ran alongside Aran with Clara close behind.

'Aran, there's something overhead. I'm sure it's the night birds.'

'I know, I've seen the shadows too. Let's keep moving. We'll be there soon. If they were going to attack us, I'm sure they would've by now.'

'I hope you're right.'

Gaia had let go of Clara, and let her slip back. Gaia turned and noticed Clara had stopped further back on the beach, crouched in the sand, face down. Gaia shouted.

'Keep going I'll get her.'

The others pushed on while Gaia made her way back to Clara.

'Come on Clara. We can't mess about. I know what you're up to.'

'Can I just rest for a couple of minutes? Please!'

Clara looked up at Gaia. For a moment the pleading dove eyes emerged, but soon disappeared knowing there was no point. Gaia was beyond her charm, if anything it would make her worse.

'You'll have plenty of time to rest once we cross the causeway. Move it.'

'Can you not just tie me up on this side of the causeway? I won't try to escape. I promise. I don't want to be on the mainland alone. I've heard stories about what's over there. I'm sure you have too.'

Gaia grabbed Clara's bound hands and yanked her to her feet.

'You're crossing the causeway. We're taking no more risks.'

Gaia tugged at Clara and they set off after the others, lifting the pace to gain ground, catching them step by step. Clara's breathless charade had ceased. The pace was well within their comfort zone and she was getting nowhere with Gaia. Clara would just have to see it through. It would all be over in a few hours. If they kept their promise. Hopefully, they would all be caught before then anyway. Clara hoped the leaders had discovered they were gone and were waiting for them at the causeway. She longed to see Gaia get what she deserved.

They followed a long arching bend and soon the causeway came into view. The beginning of the long road cast a shadow on the sheen of the glistening sea. The tide had already started to move. The causeway was long, but straight and direct, leading them to the mainland and their freedom. The light of the moon was bright, its glow enough to see the end of the causeway. Aran pushed on until they reached the start of the road. They were alone. No-one was waiting.

Their path was clear. They had made it to the first part of their journey. Now they had to make the crossing, and time was running out. Aran stopped at the beginning of the road, turned and spoke.

'We're cutting it a bit tight, but we should be OK as long as we keep up a good pace.'

Freya spoke, the first time she had uttered a word since they left the hideout.

'Are you sure we'll make it?'

'Yes. Anyway, we've no choice now. We can't go back. Stay here if you want, but I'm not going back. Anyone else want to stay?'

Aran looked around the group, the moon lighting their faces. No-one responded.

'Good. Let's go. Every minute is costing us.'

They stepped onto the causeway, and began to move along the road. It was narrow, only a few metres wide, protected by a line of large boulders. It was in a poor state of repair, crumbling and potholed. Some sections had gaping holes that were now pools of seawater filled with rocks and seaweed. They were easy to dodge, but their frequency hampered the group. About half a mile along the road they came across the remains of a wooden shed. It was on a raised platform with steps leading up to it. Gaia assumed it was some sort of stopping point, a safety area for anyone who had been caught by the waves and stranded. A rusting sign stood nearby, scarred with long forgotten words that could no longer be made out.

They kept on moving with no let up. From the corner of her eye Gaia could make out the lapping waves coming into view as they edged closer to the line of rocks. What Aran had not realised was the tide would be at its highest as they reached the centre of the causeway. They had no sense of this from the beach. After about ten minutes, they neared the halfway point and the high line of the encroaching waves. Though the road was not yet swamped, it was only minutes away, and there was still ten minutes at least before they reached the mainland. Gaia was worried, and sensed the others were too. Aran looked to his side more and more as he pushed on.

Aran lifted the pace. Soon the sea had broken through the boulders and was lapping onto the road. They kept moving, splashing through the shallow water. Clara stopped. She was exhausted. The mental strain of the night had drained her, taking much more from her physically than the others. Gaia could see Clara's face in the moonlight, the weariness, the look of despair. Clara lifted her arms and thrust her bound hands towards Gaia, pleading.

'Please cut my hands free. We might have to swim. I don't want to drown. There's no way I can make it back now. Please Gaia.'

Gaia could hear the pain and desperation in her cries. Clara was right. The threat of escape and raising the alarm was over. There was no point in putting lives at risk. Gaia placed the blade of her knife between Clara's tied hands and cut the string. Clara rubbed her wrists.

'Thanks.'

'OK. Let's get going. We've still got some distance to go.'

They ran as best they could through the rising water, each step more laboured than the last. The sea slowed their pace as it closed in on them. The water was just below Gaia's knee, making running ever more difficult. The sea was freezing, Gaia's legs numb. Aran was still out in front, pressing ahead, determined to get them to the mainland, not let them down. This was his mission, and they were all his responsibility. Freya was tucked in close behind Aran, Yann a metre back. All were pushing ahead now, as Gaia and Clara dropped further back. The mainland was not far, maybe half a mile and they would be there. They could feel it approaching, as its silhouette dominated the skyline before them. Gaia could make out the beach, a small building, a gatepost and a barrier. It was within their reach, but the water was rising fast, and was now above the knees.

Gaia heard a splash and looked behind. Clara had fallen, was on her knees, the water up to her chest. Gaia ran back. Clara was exhausted, close to finished, gasping for air, no longer wanting to carry on. The freezing water was paralysing them, and Clara was not sure if she could move any further. Gaia reached out her hand.

'Come on Clara. We've got to keep moving. We're nearly there.'

'I've done something to my leg. I think I've snagged it on something. You go on. I just need a moment. I'll catch you.'

'No! I'm not leaving you. You're only here because of me. Take my hand. We can do this together. Come on!'

Clara put her head back and inhaled a huge gasp of air. She sighed and grabbed Gaia's arm, letting her take the weight as Clara struggled to her feet. Clara winced and cried as she felt a stabbing pain run through her leg. Her leg buckled as she put some weight on it. Clara stumbled, but Gaia caught her, and dragged her back to her feet. Gaia arched her body, and bent her knees so Clara could use her as a human crutch, taking as much of the pressure from the injured leg.

'How bad is it?'

'I should be OK. You may need to take most of the weight though.'

'Does it feel broken?'

'I don't think so, but it stings like hell. I'm bleeding.'

'Let's just get to the mainland and we'll patch you up there. You're going to be OK. I'm sorry.'

Clara looked away, ignoring the apology. Gaia took Clara's weight again as they edged forward. The others had stopped further ahead. Aran's voice could be heard echoing in the distance. The others had almost reached the shore, and were now in the shallow waters of the final stretch onto the beach.

'Is everything OK? There isn't far to go. We're nearly there.'

'Keep going. We'll be fine.'

Gaia and Clara battled on through the rising waters, edging onward step by step, almost falling several times. The water was so high now they could not make out the road at all. The route ahead was gone, all they could see was water well above waist high. Clara seemed to get heavier as she tired and the water deepened. Gaia was dragging her through the icy sea that now engulfed them. Walking was laboured, and they had reached the point where they could no longer go on foot.

'Will you be able to swim? That's going to be the best way now.'

'I'll try, but I won't be able to do much with this leg.'

They began to paddle towards the shore. Clara was a strong swimmer, they all were, and though her injured leg was useless her strong upper body and other leg were effective. Clara looked more comfortable now, far more than walking. The mainland was close, and the others had made it to the beach. Gaia could hear them shouting words of guidance and encouragement from the shore. She could just make out the three dark silhouettes. Gaia dived forward into the freezing water, knowing that the biggest danger would be the temperature. No matter how fit or strong a swimmer the body could shut down with the shock, slipping into a downward spiral of paralysis and drowning. The water was not that deep, but the cold meant anything was possible. Gaia's body was numb and shivering already, but it meant submerging in the icy waters was not such a shock. It gave her some time, not much, but maybe enough.

Gaia stretched her arms forward, pulling herself closer to the shore stroke by stroke. Her legs kicked as best they could, though most of the feeling in them had gone. As she moved, her mind began to drift, still trying to stay focused on the strokes, one by one. Gaia slipped into a half dream, a cold delirium, here in the water, but somewhere else. Visions flashed through her head, random images of memories, dark, distant memories, of shadows.

Gaia was in a room, in a glass box. She was tiny, lying on her back, just a baby, aware of movement around her, but helpless. There were sounds, unfamiliar at first and difficult to fathom. The baby was reaching out, trying to get attention, crying. Gaia could hear her muffled cries as they echoed around the glass chamber. No-one came, no-one saw to her, no-one comforted her. A light glared above Gaia's head, an intense, blazing light, dazzling her eyes, blinding her. She was not alone, and could make out shadows moving beyond the glass. There were other glass boxes in the room, many of them. The other sounds became clearer. They were cries, like her own, all smothered by the glass walls of the individual cells. These were the first prison cells of each young child, each baby, each life. It was the beginning of what was to come, the beginning of their unfolding future.

Gaia felt something scrape against her legs and lower body. She put her hands down in the sea, and could feel the ground below her. It was solid ground. Her mouth was filled with water, her lungs desperate for air. Gaia's stomach felt heavy with the salty liquid, as nausea swept through her. Someone grabbed her arm and shoulders, one at each side. Gaia was being dragged from the sea, her cold, exhausted body. Her legs were limp and useless dragging behind. The others turned Gaia over onto her side, as she gasped for air, lungs burning with each icy breath, Gaia coughed and vomited, a mixture of the bitter, salty sea and acidic stomach bile. Rolling onto her back, Gaia opened her eyes and saw the outlines of dark shadows standing over. There were voices. Loud, frantic cries some near, some far. Her mind was struggling to make sense of the surroundings. There was no glass chamber, no blazing light, only the moon. The large crystal moon was a pure, brilliant white. A light hanging in the sky, smiling down at her. The memories came flooding back, the island, the beach, the causeway, the escape. Gaia was on the mainland. They had made it. This was the beach, the coarse sand touching her hands. Gaia remembered Clara, and heard the cries, the frantic cries, the distant cries, the echoes in the night. They were calling her name: '*Clara! Clara!*' Gaia gasped for air and muttered some words.

'Is Clara OK? Did she make it? Clara! Clara!'

Gaia heard a voice. It was one of the shadows above talking, comforting her, trying to calm her. It was a girl's voice, but not Clara's. It was Freya.

'Try to stay calm Gaia. You made it. You're safe now. Stay awake though. If you feel yourself going don't. Look at me and concentrate on my voice. Listen to me Gaia. Stay with us.'

Gaia felt Freya strike her face a couple of times. They were firm slaps, more than enough to shock, but not to hurt. Gaia still felt the sting on her icy cheeks. Gaia whispered to Freya.

'What about Clara? Did she make it?'

'Don't worry about Clara for now. Aran and Yann are looking for her.'

'What do you mean looking for her? Is she OK?'

Gaia tried to sit up, but her body was aching and exhausted, the muscles and bones weak. Her mind was sending the signals, but they were dead, cut off by the cold and tiredness. Freya put her hand on Gaia's shoulder.

'Don't Gaia. Rest. There's nothing you can do. Aran and Yann will find her.'

Gaia lay there listening to Freya's words. Freya was close, but the words seemed distant, echoes floating into the night air. Gaia waited, her body still stiff and aching, waiting for news of Clara. That's all Gaia wanted to hear and know, that Clara was found, safe. The minutes themselves seemed wrapped in the same blanket of freezing paralysis. They hung in limbo, the crumbling sands of the hourglass trapped inside a glass tomb. The world had stopped turning, the moon paused in its journey across the sky, no longer sliding through the night and plunging into the horizon. All was lifeless, still. Everything waited for the sign, the moment when time could move on again. They were all waiting for Clara.

Freya knelt beside Gaia. Freya was silent now, her words had dissolved into the blackness. Two shadows approached, their heads dropped, shoulders lowered in sorrow and dismay. They stood over Freya and Gaia. Both were numb, not wanting to speak, not wishing to utter the words, to confirm what they all knew. Gaia asked the question.

'Did you find her?'

There was a pause, long and silent. There was no wind, no breath, no sound, nothing. Time remained frozen. They were all locked together in this moment. Aran crouched down and took Gaia's hand.

'I'm sorry Gaia. We couldn't save her. We tried. I nearly had her but something happened.'

Aran's voice trailed off in despair, faltering and fading to a cracked whisper. Gaia spoke, her voice calm, resigned to what she had known. The full impact had not yet sunk into her exhausted mind.

'What do you mean something happened?'

'I don't know. She just disappeared. We've looked everywhere up and down the shoreline, but there was nothing.'

Gaia struggled to process the words. She unpicked them, twisted them, turned them over and over again in her head. They were clear, but there was something missing. However much she rolled them over still they meant the same thing. Clara was gone, but how? All she kept hearing was *I'm sorry. Something happened. She just disappeared. There was nothing. Something happened. Something happened. She just disappeared.* What did he mean? She spoke again, her voice more desperate.

'What happened? I don't understand. How could she just disappear?'

Aran was rubbing his face with his hands, shaking his head, not wanting to answer, not wanting to think about it, unable to make sense of it. His head was swamped, a mixture of confusion, sorrow and guilt. Aran forced the words out, his voice frail almost a whimper.

'We saw you both, you weren't that far away, nearly at the shoreline. Freya and Yann went to get you, and I went for Clara. She was struggling, but she was almost there. I put my arm out, I was sure she'd made it. I was almost there and then…'

His voice tailed off again and he paused. His eyes were distant, as though somewhere else, running through those last moments in his head, just to be sure.

'As I reached for her she was just gone in an instant, dragged under.'

Gaia sat up, pain shuddering through her body.

'What do you mean dragged under?'

'Dragged under. By something. She reached out her hand, and I almost had it, but her whole body was yanked away. She screamed and disappeared. There was nothing I could have done. I had no time to react. Something grabbed her leg and dragged her under. I saw the shadow in the water.'

The silence closed in and smothered them. Gaia's mind drifted back to the beach on the island, her beach, the beach she had spent hours staring out at the sea. During those hours spent dreaming of freedom there had always been something that troubled her. Gaia had seen things, movements in the water, dark shadows and flashes just above the surface. There was something there, something lurking beneath the waves. It was large, fast, patrolling the waters. This had always been her greatest fear. It was the main reason she had not tried to escape earlier. Crossing the sea would mean facing the creatures in the water. The causeway had given her hope. There was another way to escape, a safer way. In the relief of knowing this Gaia had forgotten all about this danger. The creatures had taken Clara. Another life lost that night, and both because of Gaia. One a predator, the other a victim, but both were at Gaia's hand.

'It's all my fault. I should never have brought her. She's dead because of me.'

Aran gripped her hand, pressed it with both of his.

'Don't think like that Gaia. There was nothing you could do. You had to bring her. You had no choice. We knew this was going to be dangerous.'

'*We* knew it and it was *our* choice. We were prepared to take the risk, but Clara didn't have any choice. I forced her to come along. I made her, and now she's dead. She begged me to leave her on the island. Begged me not to take her across the causeway, but I wouldn't listen. It should have been me, not her.'

Tears ran down Gaia's face, warm tears that trickled a path through her ice cold cheeks. Aran held her hand, squeezing it, trying to make her forgive, desperate to help her through this.

'No Gaia! It was all of us. We'll deal with this together. Somehow we'll get through this. Any one of us could have changed this, but we didn't. We all agreed to bring Clara with us. I left it too late, and we cut it too fine. I should have realised. I should have given us more time for any delays, so we still had time to get across. Don't blame yourself for this.'

Yann stood in the background, head bowed. Freya was still crouched beside Gaia, the other side of Aran who was still pressing Gaia's hand. Freya spoke.

'What happened to Clara. None of us could have known, and we can't change it. It's done. She's gone. Now we have to choose. Either we stay here and mourn, or we make a move and deal with this together as we go. We've come this far, we made it across. Let's push on, but let's make a move quickly. We're out in the open here and losing our advantage. The leaders will be coming for us soon.'

Aran let go of Gaia's hand and sat back onto the sand.

'Freya's right. We make our way inland, find a safe place and we'll deal with this then. We need to give ourselves a good head start. As soon as they find out we've gone they'll start the hunt. Once they get word to the mainland there'll be a lot of them after us. Can you walk?'

Gaia stretched her legs, grabbing Freya's hand and lifting herself forward. Gaia's clothes were soaked and clung to her skin. She was shivering, and though her lungs were clear she still felt queasy from the saltwater. Freya passed Gaia something. It was an oatmeal bar, mixed with fruit and bound with honey. Gaia nibbled, tasting the honey and chewing at the tough texture of the oats and fruit. Gaia's jaw was stiff, but she managed to swallow, feeling the rough texture scrape down the gullet and hit the pit of the stomach. Freya spoke.

'That'll give you some energy.'

'Thanks.'

Aran and Freya helped Gaia to her feet. She steadied herself against them. Her head was dizzy, spinning from the surge of blood pumping round the veins. The group stood together and looked out at the sea, at Clara's grave. They waited awhile, heads bowed, lost in silent thought. Yann whispered under his breath, Freya clasped her hands together in front. Aran put his arm around Gaia and held her close, Gaia's head resting on his shoulder. Gaia did not know Clara, their paths had been forged together through circumstance, through Hakan.

Gaia could just make out the shadow of the island in the distance. She looked up and down the beach, bathed in white moonlight. The sand was smooth, with only a few rocks and pebbles. Their footprints were the only disturbance on the golden velvet carpet. Just down from where the group stood there was a small wooden hut. In front of it was the barrier and start of the causeway, the road stretching back onto the mainland. The hut was derelict, long since abandoned, of no use in the new world. The island had few visitors, and even fewer left. The road leading away from the causeway was lined with overgrown hedgerows which protected large ragged, grassy fields. There was no sign of anyone else. The only sound was the waves crashing against the shoreline, making their presence known echoing against the moonlit sky. The dark isolation felt ominous. Aran broke the quiet.

'Are we good to go?'

Aran took Gaia's hand and pressed it against his forehead. It was a simple gesture, a connection, one of reassurance and affection. Aran knew the death of Clara would weigh heavy on them all, but more so on Gaia. The pressures of the evening had thrust a heavy burden upon the group, something they could not cast aside. Gaia had crossed a line, had murdered to get this far. Aran knew what the others did not. They were all following Aran's lead, his plan and direction.

The others followed him, but not Gaia. She carried a different burden, the weight of her actions. Gaia had blood on her hands, and Aran knew how she must feel. The group had a lot to deal with, but could not sit and dwell. They could deal with the emotion in the days ahead when they reached their destination, the freedom of the new community. Gaia knew this too. Despite the guilt and heartache of Clara's loss indecision now would make everything in vain. Gaia spoke, her voice just above a whisper, still cracked with emotion.

'I'm fine. Now let's make a move.'

11

The group moved onto the road and over a wide, wooden bar gate into a field. The grass was thick and long which made progress heavy going. Their clothes were still soaked through adding more weight to their cold, weary limbs. The field edged upwards in a steady incline away from the coastline, sometimes golden, but tonight draped in a grey, deathly glow. They walked at a steady pace, Aran still leading the way, determined, as he had been the night before. The dark shadow of some woodland was up ahead at the far edge of the field. Aran led them around the woods conscious of the thick undergrowth, the darkness, and unknown dangers that may lie within. They hugged the perimeter where the grass was shortest. Aran was heading inland at an angle, keen to reach a river as soon as they could. There were several in the area, but he was unsure how far. Once they had found one, they would trace the path upstream leading to the hills and the new community, their new future.

Gaia knew a bit about this part of the mainland. She remembered studying it in one of the earlier phases, in the old building many years ago. They were in the north, on a much larger island that stretched for miles. It had thousands of miles of coastline, dramatic cliff tops, and pebble beaches. Many were lined with beautiful golden sand, as they were here. In the days before the new world this part of the mainland had been known as Northumberland. It was an ancient land where waves of tribes and communities had arrived across the ages. Some had conquered, others lived alongside. It was whispered that many years ago warriors had come from countries across the sea. This was where the community got its pure blood from, marked by the blue eyes they all shared.

There had been much bloodshed in this area, and there were many ancient monuments to this history of warfare. Large fortified dwellings known as castles littered the landscape. There was also a long stone wall that stretched right across the north. This had been built by an invading army and named in honour of their leader. It was built to protect the invaders, to keep out the people of the north. They had a reputation for being wild, fierce and unconquerable. They were the free spirits, the ones that could not be tamed.

Now very few people lived in the north, only a few community settlements. Many of the old villages and settlements had been occupied by the outsiders, who had tried to build new communities of their own. It was rumoured most were wild, lawless places, though some offered refuge and hope. This area of the mainland was mostly abandoned fields, and ancient hills, rivers and woodland. It had been a land of farming in the past, the fields grazed by livestock such as sheep and cattle. Those animals had left the fields, died or slaughtered by man and beast.

The remoteness of the north was one of the reasons it appealed to the community. It was why it had been chosen to train and nurture the young. This was where they would Become. It was a place of isolation, where you could be unnoticed and lost. It was somewhere the community could contain and control. There were few outsiders so security was less of a worry. The main problem was the creatures. There was the added appeal of the islands, chosen for the Nurturing phase. These were uncertain and volatile years for the young, a time they were vulnerable to dangerous influences and ideas. It was deemed vital that discipline, structure and routine were instilled in their lives. They must be taught in the ways of the community without distraction or temptation. The islands were perfect. What better walls of protection than the sea?

The island was the only training community for miles. It was rumoured to be a special training centre where only the chosen were sent, the elite. Gaia was sure they all thought this, or wished it to be true. It was the nature of being young to believe you were special and chosen.

The deserted area was to the group's advantage in reaching the hills. They were unlikely to encounter many people. The main threat were the outsiders and the creatures. The outsider were those that had survived but lived alone, those that had managed to break free, or had been cast out. Gaia knew such people existed, and the young had been taught to treat them with caution and contempt. The outsiders were different, not of pure blood. They were feral, dangerous, and to be avoided. These were the people who could not fit into the structure of the community, abide by the rules, or contribute. The young were taught the outsiders were mad men and women, social deviants, crooks, and criminals. The outsiders chose to live off their wits and wickedness and were beholden to no-one but themselves. They gave nothing to anyone and received nothing in return. If the outsiders threatened they were dealt with. Those that kept away were tolerated. The community did interact and trade with some established groups of outsiders. Deals and treaties existed with some that could be trusted, but in the main they were avoided. The young all knew the outsiders had a fierce reputation. The outsiders and the creatures would be as much of a threat as the leaders who would soon hunt the group down.

Morning was upon them. The moon had almost completed its slow journey across the sky. It was about to be smothered by the light of the rising sun, the ball of flame that gave them life, the fire that warmed them. Gaia was hoping that the warmth of the sun would breath new life into the group, give them new vigour, new enthusiasm, new hope for the day ahead. On a mundane level, Gaia hoped that it would dry her clothes, and warm her aching bones. This was the first day of the group's freedom, when all they had done would be known. It was the point of no turning back. There was a long road ahead, of uncertainty, and danger, but also potential, opportunity, and hope.

The night had been clear, with no clouds in the sky, the moon a beacon and guide through the darkness of their journey. The temperatures had been close to freezing. The seawater that soaked their clothes and limbs made matters worse. They were tired and exhausted. The physical exertions of the escape could be felt already, but the emotional toll was higher and weighed heavy upon them all. There were wounds, fresh and still open, stinging from raw exposure to the elements. The wounds would heal in time, but the scars would remain.

Gaia watched as the sun crept over the horizon and the first shafts of the cold dawn light illuminated the hazy, red sky. The grass was heavy with small droplets of dew. Tiny beads of crystalline water clung to each blade, shattering with every step, plunging to the bed of earth below. Aran stopped on the brow of a hill, the others tucked in behind. He crouched low, peered over the edge, and down into the field below. At the far end of the field by a small copse of trees was a farmhouse. It was tired, old, and looked deserted, but it was shelter and somewhere they could get some rest. The group needed to eat, dry their clothes, and recharge. The farmhouse was an ideal place to take stock and plan their next steps. A place they could reflect on the night before and begin to treat their wounds. Gaia shuffled in the grass, moved closer to Aran.

'Does it look safe?'

'I don't know. It's hard to tell. It's still early. If anyone's in there they may still be sleeping. There's no smoke from the chimney and it's very cold. If someone was up you'd have thought they'd make a fire straight away. I reckon we wait a while, just keep an eye on it and look out for any movements. If we think it's clear we'll go down and check it our more closely.'

Aran swivelled round to face the others.

'Freya and Yann. Stay up here and keep an eye out for anyone approaching. If everything is clear we'll signal you.'

Yann gave a thumbs up.

'OK. Sounds like a good plan.'

Yann took off his rucksack and placed it on the grass. He lay down using it as a pillow, closed his eyes, and began to drift off. Yann was silent, nonchalant, almost indifferent. Gaia had not paid much attention to him so far. He was quiet and had stayed in the background, deferring to Aran, but it was clear Yann was more relaxed about the escape than the others. Aran rolled his eyes at Gaia, and smiled. Gaia returned the smile, and felt a rush of warmth run through her, the first time she had felt any comfort in hours. Gaia moved closer to Yann and spoke.

'You're pretty laid back about things Yann.'

Yann opened one of his eyes and smiled.

'Who me? Why worry I reckon? We all think the world is screwed, but it isn't. We are, humanity I mean. We didn't destroy the world, only ourselves. The problem is we think the world is all about us. Look at this morning. I mean look at this beauty. The world is still as beautiful as it ever was, we just can't see it.'

Yann closed his eye.

'Now if you don't mind I need some rest.'

Aran and Gaia exchanged another glance. Freya followed Yann's lead, and rested her head on her rucksack.

'If he's grabbing the chance we may as well make the most of it! Give me a nudge when you're ready to leave.'

Aran gestured to Gaia. They both looked at Freya, who was already bedded down with eyes closed, chasing Yann into the land of dreams.

'It makes sense Gaia. There's no use all of us keeping watch. We need to take as many opportunities as we can to rest. I'll be fine on my own.'

They were all exhausted, but Aran and Gaia were filled with nervous adrenalin, of their responsibility, guilt, shame and remorse. Gaia needed sleep, but could not.

'I'm fine for now. I'll watch too, if that's OK with you?'

'If you're sure.'

Gaia and Aran sat awhile in silence, both scanning the landscape below. The farmhouse was dirty white, a two storey building surrounded by an assortment of barns and outbuildings. The paddocks and pens were empty, long since redundant. A red tractor stood by one of the barns, its tyres were flat and the bodywork rusting. Gaia looked at the windows to see any sign of movement, but there was nothing. Everything was still and silent, wrapped in the golden hew of the first dawn light and slight haze of the delicate morning mist.

'It looks deserted. I can't see anything. Do you want to go check it out?'

Aran had a cautious look on his face. There was something troubling him, something not quite right. He moved closer to Gaia and pointed to the farmhouse.

'There's a couple of things I'm a bit worried about. Look by the side of the house, on the right. Can you see the small shed?'

'Yes'

'Do you notice anything strange about it?'

Gaia peered at the shed. The door was open, it looked as though it was filled with logs, but there was something there. The roof and walls were draped with small white objects hanging from strings. Gaia squinted, but could not make out what they were.

'What's those white things hanging from the strings?'

'Exactly. I think they're skulls. They don't look human. I think they're animals. They're either trophies, a collection of kills, or they're a warning.'

Aran was right. Gaia could just make them out now. From this distance they were small, but once you worked it out, you could see they were skulls. Gaia whispered.

'I reckon we check it out at least. We're armed, and there are four of us.'

Aran thought for a while, still filled with doubts, not wanting to put any more lives at risk. This was their reality now, danger and uncertainty.

'OK. Let's do it.'

Aran woke Freya. Gaia and Aran left their rucksacks and took the weapons. Gaia had a knife and axe, Aran a machete and spear. They made their way behind the brow of the hill to a treelined fence that snaked its way down towards the farmhouse. Following the line of the fence using the trees as cover both kept low. They neared the farmyard, jumped the fence and crept behind a barn. Aran slipped into the barn and Gaia followed. The building was damp and musty, with little in it other than some farm implements that had not been used for years. They tiptoed to the far wall, facing the farmhouse just metres across the courtyard. They peered through a gap in the wooden walls. The door of the farmhouse was closed, the white paint dirty and flaking, the wood rotten. The windows of the house were filthy and a couple of panes were broken. Curtains hung from the upstairs window, tattered old orange rags that were closed. Aran looked at Gaia and pointed to the far side of the barn. There was a small door which was ajar. He made his way to it, and crept through, keeping tight against the wall. Gaia followed as Aran edged his head around the corner of the barn checking the farmhouse again. The house was still wrapped in silence, nothing stirred.

Aran gave Gaia the thumbs up and pointed to the small shed by the side of the house. Gaia could see the white objects more clearly now. Aran was right, the assortment of macabre trophies were strung together on thin lengths of rope. They looked as though they had been there for some time. Gaia could make out size and shape now. They were distinctive, and even without the flesh it was clear what they were. They were the skulls of rats.

Aran darted across the courtyard and crouched behind the shed. His head was pressed against the wall, between two sets of hanging skulls. He beckoned to Gaia who ran across the open yard and leant beside him. Aran put his mouth next to Gaia's ear. It reminded her of the night in the woods, the night when their skin first touched and lips brushed. It was when they were first united, together in fear, when Gaia first felt the surge of confusion inside, the rush of warmth and passion. The same mix of emotion surged through her body, as his soft lips pressed against her. Aran whispered.

'It looks clear. We'll go round the back and see if there's another entrance. Check the windows. You go that way, I'll take this route. I'll meet you round the back.'

Gaia felt Aran's hand grip her wrist and squeeze it. She acknowledged the touch, and Aran smiled at her then darted around the back of the house. Gaia crept to the front and slid along to the window, crouching low and peering through the dusty glass. There was a huge iron stove against the far wall, covered with several large silver pots. A table stood in the centre of the room. It was large and surrounded by six wooden chairs, five of which were tucked under, one pulled out. On the table was a cup, a plate, and a clear glass jug half filled with water. The floor was grey uneven slabs of stone. Against the far wall behind the table was a tall kitchen dresser, the shelves filled with an array of cups and plates. There were photographs. In front of the dresser by one of the cupboard drawers was a pair of boots which were open with laces hanging loose. In the corner near the boots was a shotgun resting against the wall. Gaia had seen all she needed. Creeping under the window, Gaia followed the walls of the house around to the back. Aran was by the door under a small, wooden porch. Gaia moved to his side and whispered.

'There's someone in here, or there has been.'

Aran eased his head back and nodded. Leaning into her, his warm breath touched the side of Gaia's cheek.

'I know. There's someone in the chair in one of the rooms. I can't make out if he's asleep, or dead. He's old though, much older than any of the leaders. He looks frail and I can't see any weapons. I've tried the door and it's locked, but there's a window around the side of the house. It'll be easy to open with my knife. We'll get in that way. Watch my back.'

Gaia nodded, and followed Aran as he moved back around the side of the house. They approached the window. Aran eased his knife in the gap in the middle of the two sections of the frame, and slid it across tugging at the latch. It moved. He turned and winked at Gaia, lifted the bottom section and climbed through. Gaia followed him.

They entered a narrow passage, the floor was bare exposed wood and creaked as they moved. The house stank, a mixture of damp and stale urine. Pictures hung from the walls, all crooked and thick with dust. The passage was littered with rubbish, clothes, empty bottles, cans, and old paper. At the far end was a door. It was open, just enough for one of them to squeeze through without disturbing it. There was a staircase and and a door at the far end of the passage led into the kitchen.

Aran crept forward, and there was a loud groan from the floor. He paused, listening, but there was no sound. Aran took another step, and there was another creak. He looked at Gaia and grimaced, but again nothing stirred in the house. Both edged forward step by step towards the room at the far end of the passage. The floor let out an array of cries as they shuffled forward, but there was no sign that anyone had heard them. Aran paused at the door, raised his arm and squeezed through the gap. Gaia waited outside, for a sound, a signal, but there was nothing, only silence. She peered through the crack in the door, but could see only flashes of the furniture. Impatience got the better of her, and Gaia crept through.

The room was large and cluttered with rubbish everywhere. A couple of bookshelves lined two of the walls. They were packed with an assortment of volumes. An open stone fireplace dominated the front wall, a wooden mantelpiece surrounded it. The walls were covered with pictures, ignored, in disrepair, and badly hung. A battered leather sofa hugged the main wall, and an armchair sat alongside it. In the armchair was an old man, dressed in a three piece suit and tie. His thick woolen socks each had a hole exposing his gnarled big toes. He had long grey hair which was lank and curled, and his face was covered in a scruffy beard. Gaia guessed he was at least seventy. His arms were resting on his stomach. By the side of the armchair was a glass, mostly empty but for a few drops of clear liquid. By the glass was a dark green bottle. Gaia looked at the old man's chest, at the slow movements of his breathing. The man was alive, but still had not stirred. Aran stood nearby, machete in hand and at the ready. Aran was staring at him, waiting, not sure whether to wake him, hoping the old man would notice they were there. Gaia moved over to Aran, tried to catch his eye, but Aran's gaze stayed fixed on the slumbering heap in the chair. Gaia decided to make the first move and kicked the old man in the shin. Without panic or fuss the man opened his left eye and smiled, then his right. He sat up, a broad grin still stretched across his rugged face.

'Good morning. I've been expecting you.'

Aran tightened the grip on his machete and stepped back. He was poised, waiting for a move, ready to react. The old man sat forward, placed his elbows on his knees, raised his hands to his face and began playing with his beard.

'Welcome. I'd ask that you have the good grace to show a weak and elderly man a little respect in his own home. Could you do that for me?'

The elder cast a glance at both Gaia and Aran, fingers still combing his beard. He spoke through his grin, the voice calm, but with a mocking tone.

'Here's me, a creaky old fellow, unarmed and defenceless. I think you could show me a bit of courtesy and put away those knives. What do we say?'

Gaia looked at Aran, knife still in her hand, but now lowered to her side. Aran looked like a coiled spring, but his face began to ease and lose the tension, his body started to relax. Aran raised his eyebrows at Gaia and placed the machete in its holder on his belt. Gaia followed and put the knife away. Aran put his hand out to the old man, who accepted and shook it.

'I'm Aran, and this is Gaia. We're sorry to barge in like this. We mean no harm.'

The elder lifted himself to his feet. He was stiff and unsteady, as he moved around the armchair, leant and picked up a pair of slippers. They were red checked tartan, ripped and full of holes. The man sat back down on the armchair and placed the slippers on, stretched his legs forward, and leant back into the chair, folding his arms across his chest.

'It's OK son. It pays to be cautious these days. You never know what you'll come across. Now would you like a cup of tea?'

The elder looked at Aran and Gaia in turn. His face beamed a look of delight, the broad grin still painted on his face. Gaia noticed his eyes. They were hazel, not blue. She had never seen anyone that did not have blue eyes before. Her life had been immersed in the community where all eyes were the same colour, still distinctive and unique, but with that unmistakable tinge. The old man's were much darker, but still sparkled with life and warmth. Despite these strangers in his home the man seemed unperturbed. He had the look of a man beyond caring, someone content to wake each day, see the sun again, feel the rain, and celebrate that he was still alive and free to experience another day. Even in this bleakest of worlds there were those who found some kind of happiness in living. Aran spoke.

'That'd be great. Thanks. There are two others though. We have two friends, waiting up on the brow of the hill.'

'There are two more of you? Go get them. I have only one condition.'

The smile slipped from the elder's face, replaced by a stern look.

'In my home you carry no weapons. You can put them by the kitchen door till you're ready to leave.'

Aran frowned and looked at Gaia. There was a moment of awkward silence broken by the old man.

'I know you've only just met me, and you're suspicious. Why wouldn't you be? But there's one of me and look. I'm hardly likely to overpower four young people, am I? You're my guests now, the first people I've seen in a long time.'

Aran nodded.

'Of course.'

The old man led them to the kitchen which was bigger than it had looked through the window. Larger and messier. It stank of stale fat, and had the same damp, musty smell that infested the whole house. The man went to a drawer and took out a key, then moved to the front door, unlocked and opened it. He gestured to Aran.

'Signal to your friends. I'll stick a pan on and make some tea, or do you prefer coffee? I've got some grand homemade coffee. I make it from dried dandelion leaves. It takes a bit of getting used to.'

Gaia and Aran both half laughed and spoke in unison.

'Tea'll be fine thanks.'

Aran left to get the others, while Gaia waited as the old man filled a pan of water and placed it on the stove. He sat at the kitchen table, in the solitary chair not tucked under. He gestured to Gaia.

'Have a seat young lady.'

'Thanks.'

Gaia sat opposite the elder, who leant back in his chair, hands behind his head, staring up at the ceiling. He flopped forward and rested on the table and began twiddling his thumbs.

'Sorry. I should introduce myself. I'm Jack. I assume you're running from the island.'

'How'd you know?'

He winked at Gaia, continued to play with his thumbs.

'Oh I've had a few pass through here over the years. They come and the leaders follow. I expect most get caught.'

Gaia shuffled in her seat, hands nestled under her thighs.

'We've got a bit of a start on the leaders, but we won't stay long. We had a tough night, and just need a bit of time to rest. Don't worry we've got our own food. We can share some if you like.'

'Thank you, but I've all I need here, enough to last me for now anyway. You're welcome to have what you need. You'll need your supplies for your journey. Where are you heading?'

Gaia picked up a pencil on the table and began to roll it between her fingers.

'I'd rather not say. If you don't mind.'

'Don't worry, there's no need. I know where you're heading. The others were heading there too. I hope you find what you're looking for. Remember things aren't always as they seem.'

Jack stood and shuffled over to the stove. Aran knocked and entered, moving over to the table.

'I've signalled to the others. They're on their way.'

'Get four cups down from the dresser young man. Mine's over there on the table. Then have yourself a seat with your friend. The water won't be long.'

Aran took down four cups. They were thick with dust. He picked up a tea towel from the dresser, but it was damp and dirty. Returning it, Aran wiped the cups with the sleeve of his fleece, placed them on the table, and sat next to Gaia. As Aran sat he nudged Gaia's leg. As Gaia looked at Aran, he frowned and focused his stare at something across the room. She followed his eye-line and saw the shotgun leaning by the wall. Jack approached the table with a large brown teapot, and filled each cup. Just as he had finished there was a gentle knock on the door and Freya entered followed by Yann. They waited in the doorway.

'Come in. Take a seat. Your timing is perfect. Tea is just brewed. Now I'm Jack.'

Jack moved towards Freya and Yann reaching out his hands.

'Aran. Would you like to introduce me to your two friends.'

Aran spoke as Freya shook Jack's hand. Yann stepped forward holding out a solitary fist. Jack gave it a puzzled look and raised his fist to meet it. Yann nudged Jack's and gave a thumbs up, nodding his head in excited recognition of their meeting. Freya sat at the table, smiling at Jack, who nodded with a warm grin.

'This is Freya.'

'Hi'

'And this is Yann.'

'Pleased to meet you Jack.'

Yann pulled out a chair and sat beside Freya. Jack opened his arms and laughed.

'I'm pleased to meet you all. It's a pleasure to have some life in this old house. I don't get many visitors round here. Only every now and then.'

Jack caught Gaia's eye. They all sat at the table, drank their tea, and chatted. Jack was animated and told stories of his life and how he came to be here. The old man lived alone and had done so for years. He had a wife, but she had gone. Gaia sensed a tragedy in Jack, there was a deep sorrow in his voice as he spoke of his wife. The old man never told them how or when she had gone. Jack spoke of the others who had passed through. Some were runners from the island, some were outsiders on journeys further north. No-one ever came from the north heading south. The old man told them of the rats, and the skulls, how he had hunted them for years, killed many, but not for some time now. The rats feared him, and left him alone. Jack had been an expert hunter in his day, but those days were gone. As the old man serenaded the group with his tales his lively, friendly spirit was a welcome tonic after the traumas of the day before. Jack was the first outsider they had encountered and was nothing like the outsiders described by the community. Jack knew he was getting old and entering his final days, but he was content and ready for whatever the future held. Something Jack said stuck with Gaia, it was something simple, but powerful.

'I've lived the life I wanted, and the mistakes I made were my own. I've tried to find the joy in life, even in this broken world. I'm ready for whatever is next.'

Soon the arduous night caught up with the young and Aran, Freya, and Yann moved to the living room to rest. Yann and Aran lay either side of the sofa while Freya sat in the armchair. The plan was to grab a couple of hours sleep, but Gaia still did not feel like resting. She wanted to stay and talk to Jack. He had sparked her curiosity, and there were many questions. Gaia also welcomed the old man's warmth and humour. All the adults in her life had been cold and calculating with roles and functions. Gaia had never known someone who was so open, without any agenda. Gaia could tell Jack loved the company and enjoyed chatting. He missed human contact, but had grown accustomed to being alone. Jack knew these moments would be rare now, and may be the last time he ever saw others. This was the old man's opportunity to share his memories, a last chance to leave some kind of marker, however fleeting. When he died nothing would remain, no memories and no love. There would only be his decaying corpse which would crumble and scatter to dust.

Jack and Gaia stayed at the table, exchanging stories and telling jokes. Gaia had never laughed as much. The memory of the night's escape, of Hakan and Clara had been nudged to one side. Jack was her tonic, her therapy. Gaia asked the old man many questions, about the world before, about life within and outside of the community. Jack was coy when speaking of the community, wary in contrast to his relaxed openness on most other topics. The old man dodged many of the questions, shifting attention with a joke, a reference to something else, or a question of his own. After a while Jack went quiet, something forced its way into his mind, something he had buried or been avoiding.

'What's wrong Jack?'

Jack's face was stern, his mood shifted. For the first time Gaia noticed the weathered cracks in his face. Without the glow of joy and laughter the old man looked weary.

'You don't have long here young lady. You'll have to leave soon. Maybe an hour. They'll be after you now. You know that?'

'Yes, I know, but I'm trying not to think about that for now. It's nice just talking to you. I've never done this before. It seems strange saying that, but the leaders never treat us in this way.'

'I know my dear. The community have all been robbed of the wonder of being young. You aren't allowed to enjoy your youth and they make sure no-one ever gets old.'

There was a long pause. Jack stared at his hands, rubbing his fingertips against his thumb in a slow, steady circular motion. After a while the old man spoke, his voice cracked, just above a whisper.

'I wish I could be your age again. You've everything to live for when you're young, but they take it from you. At least I had the opportunity to grow old. It's made me cherish my younger days even more. Don't waste these years. Promise me, you'll make the most of them.'

Gaia reached forward across the table and cupped Jack's hands. She had so many questions, but there was so little time. A thought popped into her mind, something bizarre but important at that time.

'You've got milk. Fresh milk. How come? Do you have cows?'

'Ah, yes the milk! Come with me, there's something I want to show you.'

Jack rose and took a walking stick from near the door. He led Gaia out of the farmhouse and through the courtyard behind the house. They followed a dirt track down the hill, through a gate and over a stile into a field. At the end of the field were some woods. Jack led Gaia to the edge of the trees and paused at an opening. He beckoned Gaia to come alongside him and pointed through a gap. There was a large open area beyond the trees, and in the centre were a herd of large white cattle. They were all the cleanest and purest white. Some had long curled horns, and swishing tales with tufts of hairs on the end. Others were slightly smaller and without horns. There were the calves, suckling from bulging udders. It was a large herd, maybe forty or fifty in total. Gaia gazed in wonder, transfixed by their majesty and beauty. The beasts were like nothing she had ever seen. The horned cattle looked proud, muscular and strong. They were alert, looking all ways, keeping watch and protecting the others. Jack whispered to Gaia.

'They're a special herd called the Chillingham cattle. They've been here for centuries. No-one knows where they came from, but this is their domain. I watch over them. They know me, trust me, and the mothers let me milk them.'

Gaia looked on, mesmerised.

'They're so beautiful. They look so pure.'

'They're magnificent creatures, but you must be wary of them. They don't take to strangers. The bulls are wild, and a bit mad.'

The calves that had finished feeding were playing, butting heads with one another, chasing, and skipping as the adults watched on. Their mothers and fathers stood protecting them. Parents Gaia had never known. Gaia thought about Jack's words, the centuries they had lived here in this small part of the world, how no one owned them, how they lived wild and free to roam as they pleased. Jack took Gaia by the arm.

'Come with me.'

The old man led Gaia along the edge of the hedgerow that lined the fence, and further down the hill to the far side of the woods. There was a gap which Jack ushered Gaia through. They entered the woods and stopped after a few yards. About six feet away lay the corpse of a calf. It was rotting, flies hovering over its decaying flesh, maggots devouring it. The once bright shiny white carcass was now dull and grey. Its head was large and deformed, the mouth open in anguish.

'This is the thing you have to understand with the herd. They're pure and breed only amongst themselves, so they've got a very narrow gene pool. That creates all sorts of problems, birth defects and mutations like this calf. When a calf is born, one of the males checks it over. If it's pure it's welcomed and reared by the herd. If there is anything wrong with it, even down to a marking on its hide, it's taken away and left in the woods to die.'

'What? Murdered!'

'Yes. Murdered for the greater good. The herd can only survive if it maintains its purity, and doesn't become contaminated. They won't tolerate impurity, as it threatens their survival, and the survival of the herd is everything. That's why the males are crazy. They're inbred and that can lead to madness. Narrow gene pools, you see. It always leads to these problems. So what you see with the herd, it comes at a price. All is not what it seems.'

Jack led Gaia out of the woods, into the field and back up the hill. The sun was much higher in the sky now. It looked like a bright, warm day was ahead. The Chillingham cattle were etched on Gaia's mind. Purity at all costs, and the preservation and survival of the herd. The sacrifice of the individual for the greater good. These were all things she knew well.

'Were you ever a part of the community Jack?'

'Not really. Not as you know it. Look at my eyes. What do you see?'

Jack stopped and faced Gaia, stretching his face, his eyes open wide.

'They're brown.'

'Exactly. You know what that means to the community. I'm not pure. I'm contaminated.'

They moved on and Jack continued.

'I was one of the survivors. Me and my wife. We were both very young when the poison came and everything collapsed, but we got through it. In the early days those that were left found each other and formed groups. It was the best way to survive. Those days were scary, everything was in chaos, it was lawless. People designated themselves leaders, and tried to organise things. They claimed it was better. Then came those that wanted to cleanse the community of the unwanted. Criminals were banished at first, then any dissenters, anyone who didn't agree with how things were being run. Things got more extreme.'

Jack paused for a moment, bent forward hands on his knees, catching his breath.

'The leaders issued decrees to purify the community. At first it was all about identifying the outsiders and segregating them, but people started to be expelled, more and more of them. Rumours started to spread that people were being murdered or fed to the creatures. It was madness. They started to set out more and more definitions of who were the pure. Then it was eye colour.'

Jack's voice trembled. He was still out of breath, but Gaia knew it was more than that. Recounting those times must have been difficult.

'Only those with blue eyes were classed as pure. Me and my wife knew we weren't safe so we fled, along with many good people. The paranoia and obsession with control all led to what you were and not who you were. The community made us all criminals. We fled north, as we'd heard it was quieter here, that few had survived. We wanted to get as far away as possible from the madness. We found the farmhouse abandoned, and decided to make it our home. So that was how it happened. That was the community I knew.'

Gaia was shocked by Jack's account, horrified by the way the community had developed, the things it had done to the others. They were innocents, people who were persecuted just for being different. All her life Gaia had been shaped by the community, her thoughts, memories, and history were all implanted by the leaders. Everything Gaia thought she knew, all she had ever known was only ever the community's story. The young were given no other perspective or accounts. Now Gaia knew all she had been told by the leaders was a lie.

'I hadn't realised it was this way. That's not the story the community told us. We've always been taught to be wary of the outsiders, that they're all criminals and dangerous.'

'They would tell you that. It's all part of the control. Do I look dangerous? What do you remember of your childhood Gaia?'

Gaia could remember very little. There were flashing images, mainly of the old house and the dormitory where she was nurtured. The memory of the night before came to her again. The sense of being in the glass chamber as a baby. Were those memories or simply a dream?

'I've some memories of a house where I was brought up with other children, but before that. I don't know. I have dreams which may be memories of being a baby. I'm in some kind of glass incubator with lots of other babies.'

Jack stopped walking. He turned and took Gaia's hand. His voice was calm and quiet. Tears were in his eyes.

'I'm pretty sure they're memories Gaia. Look at you and your friends and how you've been raised. The community breeds babies, in labs, like factories. There are no families. Your parents will exist somewhere, but not as parents just as egg and sperm donors. You're bred to maintain that purity.'

Jack took a handkerchief from his pocket and wiped his eyes.

'The community is obsessed with survival and the leaders control of every aspect of life. Everything, especially childhood. They've stolen the joy of growing up, of belonging to a loving family and knowing your parents. You've all been engineered to perform a function, manufactured for the community to ensure its survival. That is all you are to them.'

Gaia could see the sorrow and pity seeping from every pore. Tears still trickled from Jack's brown eyes, and his lips shook with emotion. Gaia knew it was true, maybe she had always known the truth. That was what drove her to escape the community, the lie she was living. The outside world was dangerous, and Gaia would face tough choices, but they would be her dangers to confront, and her decisions. Gaia would rather live a life in peril and die free, than spend the rest of her life being moulded by the community. She took Jack's hand.

'You're right Jack, but not anymore. That's why I fled the island, why I had to escape There's something else out there for us. We've heard there are others, good people like you. There's another community where things are different and people are free. It's in the hills. Aran has a letter. I've seen it.'

Jack wiped his eyes again, and nodded.

'There are others out there. I've heard the same, and met many good people over the years. I hope you find them, I really do, but please be careful. Not everyone is good.'

Jack squeezed Gaia's hand and smiled. It was warm and sincere, from a pure heart. The old man's eyes began to sparkle again.

'We need to get back and wake your friends. You have to get going. You've got a long journey ahead of you.'

They set off and soon passed through the wooden gate, following the final stretch of dirt track that led to the farmhouse. They reached the door and kicked off their boots. Gaia went in the living room to wake the others, while Jack prepared some food in the kitchen for their journey. Gaia and the others gathered their things and packed. Jack insisted they take the provisions he had put together. There was some homemade bread, milk, cheese, and dried chicory leaves.

As they were about to leave and say goodbye Gaia took something from her rucksack. It was a necklace of St Cuthbert's beads. She approached Jack, hugged him, and placed the necklace around his neck.

'I want you to have this Jack. I made it myself. The beads are fossilised shells from the island. They're unique to a particular beach. It's my beach.'

Jack took out his handkerchief and dabbed his eyes. He wrapped his arms around Gaia and squeezed, as though he never wanted to let go.

'Thank you.'

The group put on their boots and prepared to leave, everyone thanking Jack and saying more farewells. Jack followed them through the courtyard to the beginning of the dirt track.

'Take care and whatever you do, avoid the woods.'

They set off down the track, while Jack remained at the top of the hill waving them goodbye. As Aran opened the gate at the bottom of the track, Gaia turned to wave at Jack one more time. The old man had gone.

12

The group walked for hours, through green fields and golden meadows speckled with red poppies and a rainbow of wild flowers. They climbed fences, leapt over brooks, ate wild berries, and the bread and cheese that Jack had given them. They drank the sweet milk from the Chillingham cattle, circled large woodland, and clambered up gentle hills. There was little conversation, each locked in thought, as they pressed on at a good pace. Aran was determined to make progress, and Freya followed his lead. Yann seemed to be in a world of his own, playful and dreamy, lost without the need for words. Gaia was preoccupied. Jack had thawed some of the ice she had used to protect her. Gaia tried to survive by disconnecting her emotions, it had always been her way. The journey would require all her strength, but the time spent walking, the time to think again, had churned up all the emotions she had tried to bury.

There was the sadness of leaving Jack. Gaia knew they would never meet again, and so did he. There was Clara, an innocent victim caught up in their plan. Gaia thought of Hakan. With little remorse for his death, Gaia was struggling to deal with what she had done and what it made her. Gaia was now a killer, not of creatures, but people, a murderer. There had been thoughts of killing people, mostly Kali, but a line had been crossed. Crossing it had been easy, the aftermath of emotion was not. Finally, Gaia thought of Aran. He had awoken something inside her, feelings she had not experienced before, and had not wanted to experience. Part of the reason Gaia agreed to escape was she wanted to be with him. Gaia could not stand the thought of staying on the island alone, wondering if he had made it, and was still alive. However, Aran was distant and only concerned with the escape. Aran said he needed her, but Gaia hoped this meant more than just her skills. She had hoped that Aran felt something, but there was little sign of that so far. Aran's only interest was the journey, finding the river, and leading them to the hills.

It was late afternoon, and the group reached the brow of a small hill that looked down into a deep valley. A line of trees snaked inland. Through them there were the calm, flowing waters of a river. Aran stopped and savoured the glorious view. This is what he had been looking for, the next stage of their journey completed, the next milestone reached. Rivers flow to the sea from the trickle of a tiny source. Their birth lies far off in the hills. In this case the Cheviots hills of north Northumberland. Find the hills and they would be found was the message. Aran inhaled the crisp, fresh air, a feeling of triumph sweeping through him. Yann approached Aran and patted him on the shoulder.

'We found it. Now what?'

'We head down towards the woods. We'll follow the edge of the treeline up the valley, and that'll lead us to the hills.'

Freya sat on the grass and removed her rucksack. She lay back and closed her eyes.

'Can we rest a bit. I'm knackered.'

'No. We'll head down to the trees and find a spot near the river. We can rest there for a few hours.'

Aran picked up Freya's rucksack and dropped it on her stomach. Freya jumped at the shock of the weight. She sighed and stood again, and started to make her way down the hill at a brisk pace. The others followed. Gaia moved up beside Aran, with Yann trailing behind. Now Freya was leading and driving the pace. Gaia spoke to Aran.

'Do you think they're far behind?

'I don't know. They probably waited for the tide to drop, unless they used the boats. They'd have been able to cross early morning anyway. Let's hope they didn't find anything until then. I knew there was a river if we headed north, but it's much farther than the one to the south. I'm hoping they'll head for the other one thinking we would aim for the nearest. Either that or they'll head straight for the hills and wait to head us off there. Who knows? What would you do, if you were them?'

'I don't know. I'd probably split into two groups. There are only four of us. They'll have dogs. If Kali is leading they'll be close now. Remember I've killed a leader. This isn't just an escape, it's much more than that now. Jack mentioned the other runners and that they'd been hunted down. I reckon they're more likely to chase us rather than head us off. I hope you're right and they've gone south, but we can't take any chances.'

Aran frowned, still pushing forward, trying to keep pace with Freya who was almost jogging up ahead.

'You're right. We can't afford to hang around. We need to keep moving, and rest when we can.'

'Will we keep going through the night?'

'Yes. They'll try to avoid traveling at night. They'll think it's too dangerous, so we need to make the most of that to keep ahead. The hills aren't that far away, and there'll be plenty of time to rest when we get there. We have to keep going. We know what the leader's are capable of.'

Aran and Gaia exchanged looks, as Gaia spoke.

'OK. I'll let you break it to the others. Freya doesn't look in the best of moods.'

At Freya's swift pace the group soon approached the woods. The sun was beginning to plunge into the line of the horizon. In a short while it would disappear and darkness would be upon them. The sky was clear and the moon would once again act as their guide and light the way. The moon would also highlight their presence to predators and their hunters. The woods would provide some protection. If the group stayed close to its edge, but still out of view they would see anyone creeping over the line of the valley above. That would be the only warning, buying them some time, but not much. Gaia hoped Aran was right and the leaders had headed south, and would not travel at night, but she had her doubts.

The group rested in the woods for a short while, ate some food and drank the remainder of the milk. Aran told the others of the plans for the night. Yann shrugged his shoulders, while Freya was less impressed, but showed no dissent. Freya was edgy and moody. Throughout the journey she had kept looking behind as if expecting to be caught at any moment. Gaia was watching her, wary and still not convinced Freya could be trusted. Freya's nervous mood and twitchy behaviour only made Gaia question her more. Something was not right. Gaia could sense it, and would continue to be careful around her. Freya would show her hand at some point, and when the moment came Gaia would be ready.

Darkness had swept across the sky, the moon puncturing it with its cold white light. The group walked along the edge of the woods, using the trees as a flimsy disguise. The trees were thin enough to ensure the moonlight broke through and the group were not lost in total darkness. The undergrowth was light enough to forge a path without too much trouble, and just the occasional stumble. The only sounds were the crunch of boots as they stepped on the fallen twigs and branches. Gaia heard the hoot of an owl, its distinctive call far off in the woods, echoing in the night, a haunting sound. There was the odd rustle of leaves in the bushes, a night creature startled by their presence, darting to safety deeper in the thick blanket of vines. Gaia heard the sound of rushing water to their right, as the edge of the wood thinned and the river cut close by. It faded and the quiet returned, with only the rhythm of their steps to accompany them.

They arched around a bend and came to an opening in the woods. Before them, lit by the moonlight was a huge silvery web. Each strand glistened in the night as beads of condensation flickered a hazy glow from the shafts of moonbeams. The web stretched across the opening blocking their route. At its centre was a gorgeous pattern of intricate lines with long, thick strands of silver rope reaching out to the trees beyond. Each strand supported the main elaborate structure. It looked like a silver obstacle on a magical assault course.

Aran stopped and moved behind a tree, raising his hand as the others crept up to his shoulder. Aran lifted his finger to his lips. Each of them surveyed the trees around, looking for any sign of movement. Aran darted out of the woods and past the web, the others followed and moved back under the shade of the trees. They could see deeper into the woods now. There were more webs, a vast complex, an array of shapes and sizes. The webs covered most of the woodland in front, preventing anyone or anything getting through. There were no signs of the creators of the structures. No sights nor sound of the creatures that had spun the menacing display of ominous beauty.

Aran stopped and spoke, his voice barely a whisper.

'Whatever made these things they're big. We need to keep moving and keep as close to the edge of the woods as we can. Jack was right about the woods. There are too many dangers in here. What was that? Did you hear it?'

Aran sat upright, all his senses searching the night for a sound, sight, smell. Aran was sure he had heard something. Everyone listened. There it was again, a faint rattle like dried rice being sprinkled on a drum. It stopped, but came again, louder. There was another pause and silence. Gaia looked deep into the woods, as far as the veil of darkness would allow. There was nothing. Something small and bright burned in the blackness of the woods, two small red lights, moving towards them getting larger. They grew alongside each of the rattles, their brightness intensifying.

'Something's coming.'

Gaia pointed to the red lights. There was a noise, a cacophany of deafening screeches from above. Gaia looked up and saw the body first, then the long black legs of a spider plunging towards her from a branch above. She reached for her knife, but it was too late. The creature was upon her, wrapping its strong, thick legs around Gaia's upper body preventing her from moving. The legs were covered in coarse, black hairs that felt like blades against the skin. Pressed in her face, the giant jaws of the creature salivated a treacle of white saliva upon her, as the spider continued to let out its terrifying shriek. Gaia was thrust back onto the ground, the creature still upon her, locked in its death grip. She felt a piercing pain in the throat, as if a hot poker had been plunged into her neck. Burning acid spread through her, and a feeling of nausea. She was dizzy and retched, almost choking on her vomit, as consciousness slipped away. Gaia gripped at images, but they faded, and it was darkness. Everything was gone. There was nothing. No thoughts, no images, no feelings. Nothing.

. . . .

Gaia's mind was ablaze with nightmare images. She was in a dark tunnel being pursued by a group of large spiders. There was a light, and a voice calling. The light grew brighter and a figure emerged, just the dark outline. It was a female voice, reaching out to Gaia, begging her to run faster, pleading, getting more and more frantic. The creatures were upon Gaia. The spiders caught her, pouncing one by one, wrapping their legs around her, and injecting their poison. In every nightmare Gaia thought she had made it to the end of the tunnel, to safety, but the creatures always won. As Gaia drifted away the voice was still calling her name.

Gaia awoke. Her head was throbbing with a piercing headache. Her throat felt like it was coated in sand. She tried to swallow, but struggled, went to move her body, but there was no response. Gaia concentrated on her fingers, but could not feel them, tried to move her toes, but again there was nothing. She sat upright, looking forward, and could just make out the trees and bushes of the woods bathed in the silvery blanket of web. It was daylight with shafts of sunlight piercing the gaps in the trees. Gaia's head was locked and facing forward. There was a sickness in the pit of her stomach. The nightmares had subsided, the memories of what had happened returned. Death was upon her, as Gaia drifted away again.

It was night, and Gaia was cold. Her body was numb with only a faint tingling sensation in her fingers and toes. The throbbing in Gaia's head had eased, but her vision was blurred and there was still the urge to vomit. Her mouth was dry, like it had been stripped of all its skin. There was a noise and vibrations through the strands of web that bound her. It was the same rattling noise from the night they were attacked. It was quiet, distant, and intermittent at first. The rattle got louder, the vibrations stronger. Gaia sensed something by her side, heard the rattle, then it stopped.

There was a long pause, no sound or movement. Gaia saw it, a huge black monstrous ball of coarse black hairs with bulbous red eyes. The creature's legs stretched out, straddling Gaia's helpless body. Its scarlet eyes blazed, the dripping jaws inches from her face. Gaia could smell the spider's rancid breath, see the thick saliva oozing from its mouth. Its teeth were large, pointed, and menacing. Gaia tried to move her arms, but she was trapped, wrapped in the binding coffin of web. Her veins still oozed with the burning poison that had paralysed her. This was the end, and Gaia was helpless. This was the moment of death, but Gaia felt no fear. Despite the imminent doom there was a strange calm, a resignation towards her fate.

The jaws of the spider moved closer, pressing close to her face. The creature surveyed her, smelling every inch of skin. It was poised, ready to make its move. The spider arched and stiffened. There was a deathly screech as the creature's body lurched backwards. Someone was upon it, and with a few sweeping movements had driven a blade through its skull and a spear into its writhing torso. The assassin was sitting on the creature, waiting until they were sure it was dead. In the dim light Gaia could not make out the face. They moved forward and into view.

Freya took her knife and cut away the thick strands of web that bound Gaia who flopped forward into her arms. Gaia was limp and could not move her legs, or arms. Freya whispered in Gaia's ear.

'Keep quiet. I'm going to get us out of this.'

Freya threw Gaia onto her back and carried her to the edge of the woods away from the maze of spider's webs. Freya set Gaia down at the base of a tree, wrapping her in a blanket, and placing a cup to Gaia's lips. The spot was sheltered, concealing Gaia.

'Here. Drink this. It tastes awful, but it'll take away the numbness and sickness.'

Gaia drank the concoction as best she could. Her lips were still numb, as the liquid dribbled down her chin. Gaia's throat raged with every gulp, but she managed to swallow, hoping it would ease the symptoms.

'I need to go and get the others. Wait here. I'll be back soon.'

A look of panic swept across Gaia's face. Freya touched Gaia's cheek. Freya's look was warm and reassuring, then she sped into the woods. Gaia lay against the tree, as her body began to shiver, frenzied and uncontrollable. Her teeth were chattering. She was not sure if it was the effects of the potion, or her body feeling cold as the numbness wore off. Despite the discomfort Gaia thought it must be a good sign. The shivering eased and sickness subsided, as Gaia gazed up at the moon. Feeling began to return, though her mind was still fuzzy.

Freya slipped through the trees, alert, looking each way, pausing and listening, seeking out any signs of the spiders. As Freya reached the clearing there was a huge web. The others were wrapped in cocoons, their silvery coffins. Aran's eyes were closed. Freya crept towards him and cut through the thick strands of webbing. He began to stir as Freya eased him from the cocoon and laid him over her shoulder, her legs buckling under his weight. A few metres away Yann hung, bound in the web. His eyes were flickering, sweat poured from his forehead. Freya carried Aran back through the trees, her movement strong and steady despite the heavy load.

Freya returned and set Aran down beside Gaia, giving him some of the bitter brew. Aran coughed and spluttered, but drank. He looked exhausted, his face an ashen white. Aran was only just conscious, and did not seem aware that Gaia was there, as his head flopped and rested against Gaia's. Freya darted into the trees again, her steps light and assured. The spiders would be near, and would sense any vibrations.

As Freya reached the clearing a spider was edging its way across the web. The creature was creeping towards Yann whose eyes were now open his face filled with terror. He was trying to scream, but there was no sound. Freya gripped her knife and waited. The spider edged towards Yann, its huge black legs reaching out towards him. It paused for a moment, to sense vibrations, or look for danger. Freya waited till the spider was just upon Yann, its attention on the prey, then Freya lurched across the clearing and thrust her knife into its head. There was a loud crunch as the knife pierced the thick shell of the creature's skull. The spider let out a shriek and began to writhe. It lurched back as though to attack, but Freya twisted her knife in a swift movement and jumped back. The spider fell on the floor, its body twitched as dark red blood and the green pulp of its brain seeped from it. The red bulbous eyes dimmed as life disappeared from them. Freya stepped over its dead carcass and cut Yann free, thrusting him on her shoulder and heading into the trees.

Gaia's head rested against the tree, her mind a mixture of haze and pain. Despite the confusion, there was the warmth of relief. Aran was alive, they had been saved. The seeds of comfort began to trickle through her body and ease the pain. She whispered, her voice frail.

'Are you OK, Aran?'

'Gaia? Is that you Gaia?'

'Yes, it's me. We're safe now. Take it easy and try to relax. The potion will kick in soon, and you'll feel better.'

'What happened? I just remember…'

Aran began to tremble, his body twisted and head shook, face taut and pained. The shivering faded and stopped, a cold feverish sweat dripped from Aran's brow. Gaia ached, the whole of her body was throbbing. Freya returned with Yann and laid him beside Aran, tending to Yann with the antidote. Freya took some biscuits from her bag, broke small pieces off and fed them to Gaia and Aran, washing them down with sugar water.

'We need to get some energy back into you. You've had a lot of poison in your system. The stuff I gave you should help. How are you feeling?'

Aran was dazed, and though Gaia was recovering she was still groggy and weak. Gaia spoke, still struggling to force out words.

'I've felt better, but I don't look as bad as Aran. How did you escape?'

'I didn't. The spiders never got me. I managed to slip away when they attacked, and I've been watching and waiting for the right moment. Those things are everywhere. The woods are crawling with them.'

'Are we safe here?'

'We should be. They don't stray out of the thicker patches of trees, it leaves them too exposed. We're all still here. Let's be thankful for that, though we've lost a day.'

Gaia remembered they were being hunted. They were lucky, but the spiders were a distraction. A day was a lot of time to lose. The hunters would not be far.

'Shouldn't they have caught up with us by now?'

'If they'd come north they'd have been onto us. I'm pretty sure of it. I didn't see anyone pass this way when you were out. Maybe Aran was right and his plan worked. They could be moving along the southern river, or headed straight for the hills. Either way they're probably ahead of us somewhere, and we need to be watching our fronts and backs.'

Yann began to shiver as the potion took hold. Freya moved to him, holding his hand as he shook. Once the shivering passed Yann tucked into the biscuits and sugar water with the gusto of someone who had not eaten for months, begging for more once they had gone. Gaia and Freya watched as Yann ate. Freya spoke.

'How you feeling Yann?'

'Hungry, thirsty, numb, bit of a sore head. Other than that I couldn't be better. Just glad to be alive.'

Yann laughed, a deep throaty laugh which turned into a coughing fit. He drank some water, as Freya spoke.

'Take it easy. You need to rest. We all do.'

'Don't worry I will. As if I need an invitation to take it easy.'

Freya wrapped the others in an extra layer of blankets and huddled them together. Freya insisted on keeping watch while her three companions got some sleep. In the morning they would need to set off again. It had been a close call, and only thanks to Freya's courage were they all still alive. Limp, weak and wounded, but alive. Their wounds were minor and the strength would return. Sleep was troubled and filled with nightmares. The visions of terror would continue to plague them for days. Gaia dreamt of Kali. They were both in a damp, musty room with no windows. Gaia sat in a chair, and Kali circled her. Kali was talking, but Gaia could not make out what was being said. Gaia was drowning and Kali's hand was reaching out to save her. That was all she dreamt, over and over throughout the night.

13

Warm strands of sunbeams stroked Gaia's cheek as she stirred. It had been a troubled night and Gaia still felt sick and weak. The feeling and movement had returned and her head was no longer throbbing. The misty haze that had clouded her thoughts had lifted. Freya sat cross legged on the ground, wrapped in a blanket, still awake, surveying around them. Freya paid close attention to the brow of the hill, and the woods. Aran and Yann were still sleeping. Both had colour in their cheeks, but Aran seemed troubled. His head would arch and twist as he let out tiny whimpers. Yann looked calm, his breathing the only indication he was still alive. Freya noticed Gaia was awake.

'How are you feeling this morning?'

'Still groggy, but much better than yesterday. I didn't get a chance to say thank you properly last night for what you did.'

'Don't worry it was nothing. You would have done the same.'

Gaia felt a twinge of guilt in amongst her gratitude. Would she have done the same? Aran and Yann, yes, but would she have saved Freya, and saved her first? After all those thoughts Gaia had about Freya, all the anger, bitterness and revenge Gaia's enemy had turned into her saviour. Maybe Gaia was wrong? Freya had proven her loyalty and courage. There could be no question of Freya's commitment to the group. After a long silence Gaia spoke.

'I always thought you were Kali's runner, her spy. I was wrong. I'm sorry.'

Freya smiled, an awkward smile, not wanting to answer, but feeling as though she should.

'You don't have to apologise. I don't blame you. We can't be sure of anything now. You just have to do what you need to survive. We need to get the others sorted, make some breakfast and make a move. Do you want to see what it feels like when you stand?'

Freya helped Gaia to her feet, walking a few steps arm in arm, Freya taking the weight. Freya stepped away and allowed Gaia to move on her own. Gaia could feel the weakness in her legs, but there was movement, and with each step the numbness from the poison eased and strength returned. The group needed to keep pressing on. The hills were a day or so away, and with luck they could avoid the hunters. Freya was exhausted, the others weakened, but everyone needed to regain strength and sharpness if they were to stand any chance against the hunters.

Freya woke Aran and Yann who ate a light breakfast. The boys struggled to their feet, moving around to shake the last of the poison from their stiff legs. Once packed the group set off, heading along the edge of the woods, following the treeline, wary of entering too far into the thick trees. They were still smarting from the encounter with the spiders, but there was little talk of it on the journey that morning. Each was trying to deal with it, all were thankful and relieved. Jack had been right. *Fear the woods.* The group had been complacent, too confident in their own strength and abilities, flushed with the arrogance of youth and inexperience. The young led a sheltered life on the island. There was the growing menace of the rats, but the protection of the community and the waters around the island meant the rodents were the only real external threat. Most of the danger on the island came from within.

The mainland was the group's first taste of freedom, but now they faced many more threats, most unknown. The mainland was vast and open in comparison, the terrain, animals and people were different. The beautiful, barren landscape meant the threats were spread more thinly, the likelihood and frequency less. Even the beauty was a threat. It lured the young into a false sense of comfort and safety. The gentle, rolling hills, and glorious meadows, the lush green quilts of grass and lines of trees had stood for decades, some centuries. The landscape had evolved, the changes subtle, seasonal, across oceans of time. The blanket of green enveloped in the arch of bright blue skies, the brilliance of the sun, and the pure, protective light of the moon.

In beauty there was darkness and terror, and in nature such sublime horror. The world gave birth to this terrible beauty, nurtured it, watched it flourish. Nature was to be admired in all its wonder, but it was also to be feared. The group could not conquer or master their surroundings. Humanity had tried that, and failed, in the days before the poison. Gaia and the others had grown in the confidence of their escape, but also grown in arrogance and folly. The group thought they knew the world, the dangers, but were wrong. Nature had reminded them.

Beneath the naked tranquility and charm of the wilderness there lay a darkness. There were the places the light had been smothered, where the beauty had not touched. There was death and destruction. The creatures waited and would kill without thought or feeling. They killed without remorse. For the creatures it was instinct, the purest instinct, the foundation on which feeling and thought were built, survival. It was all about survival, as without it there was no love or freedom. Without survival there was nothing.

As early evening approached the group reached a bend in the line of trees. The river still lay within the dark core of the woods, with the occasional sound to remind them. A falcon hovered in the sky above, staring down at its prey. The majestic bird dropped like an arrow, plunging towards its unsuspecting victim. The falcon disappeared in the long grass for a moment, and emerged prey locked and wriggling in its talons. The bird flew off into the distance, fading into a tiny dot and vanishing from view.

The trees spread out from the base of the valley and stretched up the hill. The group snaked around a bend and saw the battered ruins of a castle in a field the other side of the river. The stone walls stood astride a mound of earth that capped a hill. The mound was smooth and even, and the walls once a majestic golden stone were now stained with centuries of weather. In each corner was a turret in varying states of decay, the stonework had thin slats spread along the wall. The entrance was now a gaping hole where the gate and portcullis once stood. Gaia soaked up the view so typical of this part of the world. The rugged, untamed beauty of nature alongside relics of man's fallen past. While the group stood in awe, Yann broke the silence.

'That's some building. Are we heading up there?'

Everyone looked to Aran, still seeing him as leader, but Gaia was worried about him. Aran had struggled all day. They had all been tired, but Freya had given everyone some herbal potions, mixed with plants she was gathering on their way. Freya was demonstrating her knowledge and training with a typical absence of fuss. The homemade medicines were working on Gaia and Yann. He had floated through the day as if the spiders had never happened. For Gaia, the aches had dissolved and her body returned to some normality. Though Gaia's strength was returning, she needed frequent rest. They all did. Sleep was an imperative now, and the shelter of the castle was inviting.

Aran had wilted since the spiders. His grit and determination, the resolve he had shown in the early hours of the escape had been sucked from him. Aran's shoulders hung in silent despair. He had said nothing all day, on a couple of occasions stopping and moving out of sight to vomit. All benefit from the food and tonics were being purged from Aran's weakened body at the time he needed them most. Freya had taken his place at the front and now led the group. Everyone waited for the others to respond to Yann's question. They all wanted to go to the castle, but it was Gaia who took the initiative and responded.

'I think we should. We need to rest tonight, and the castle looks a good place to shelter.'

Yann continued to look at Aran for a response, but Aran's head remained bowed in silence. Gaia stared at Freya, and waited. Freya shook herself from her exhausted daze and spoke.

'I agree with Gaia. We need to sleep. I'm shattered. The only problem I can see is the castle is on the other side of the river. We might not be able to get across. We'll also have to go through the woods to get over. We all know that isn't a good idea.'

Gaia pointed in the direction they had come.

'I spotted an area back there. We passed it a few minutes ago. The trees thinned out. I couldn't see the river, but we're quite a way up the valley now. I don't think it'll be that wide this far up.'

Gaia had edged closer to Freya and was speaking in a low voice, dropping it to a whisper.

'I'm worried about Aran. Look at him. He needs sleep, desperately.'

Yann was with Aran behind Gaia and Freya. Yann had lain on the grass. Aran had sunk to the floor, one knee on the ground, gasping for air. Aran gave a gagging sound and threw up on the grass. Freya looked at Gaia and frowned. Freya addressed the group, her voice more commanding.

'We'll head up to the castle, eat and rest there for the night. We all need to sleep.'

Yann sat up and nodded. Aran wiped his mouth, struggling to his feet. Yann jumped up, helping Aran stand, taking his weight. Yann frowned.

'That sounds good to me. I'm starving. Have we anything better than those biscuits we've been eating all day?'

Aran and Yann shuffled towards the girls. Aran's face was ashen, and as he spoke his voice was throaty and cracked.

'We can't stop. We need to keep moving. We've lost too much time. They'll be on us soon.'

Gaia grabbed Aran by the arm and looked in his eyes. They were dull, lifeless without any sparkle. His breathing was laboured.

'Listen Aran. You're weak and need to rest. If they were following us they'd have caught us by now. You were right. They've probably gone straight to the hills or taken the southern river. They've got to be ahead of us now. They'll be waiting somewhere up ahead. If they are we're going to need all our wits to avoid them, or strength to take them on. Tonight we rest, no arguments.'

Aran frowned, a look of resignation in his face. Gaia was right. He was exhausted and desperate for food. There was a burning ache in his stomach, mixed with the spasms of sickness. If they group did not do something now Aran could spiral into something deeper and much worse, illness which might cripple him for days. Aran sensed he might be on the verge of a fever. Freya was skilled, trained in basic medical care and could help him. Freya knew what was needed, but he had to work with, not fight her. Gaia simply cared. Aran could see the concern in her face, he had no choice but to trust the others.

'You're right. We're going to need all our strength. OK, let's head for the castle.'

The group doubled back a short distance until they reached an area where the trees thinned, and there was mostly undergrowth and bushes. They moved down the hill towards the river. As they neared, the refreshing sound of the water's gentle flow could be heard. The soothing trickle gave the group a momentary lift, and they were buoyed further seeing it was shallow and easy to cross. Further up the river a long legged bird stood in the water near the bank. Standing proud and majestic with a narrow pointed bill, feathers a mix of grey and with flecks of black. The bird searched the water looking for food, waiting to pounce. Gaia was trying to recall the name of the bird, but as if Yann had read her mind he spoke.

'It's a heron.'

Yann had surprised them all with his knowledge of local wildlife. Often he would spurt out the name of a bird that flew past, or a creature that shot across their path. These were the only words Yann would utter for hours at a time as he sailed along without a care. The heron stood silent and alert, oblivious to the group's fleeting presence.

They moved up the hill on the other side and soon approached the castle. It was larger and more imposing than Gaia had first thought. The distance had fooled her. The walls were high, thick and solid in places, crumbling with neglect and decay in others. The castle was surrounded by a deep moat long since dried up, and a ridge of inclining earth led to the entrance. The sun was setting below the western horizon. From their high vantage point Gaia could see the blazing fiery ball as it plunged into the hills that lay beyond. It would be dark soon, and the group would need to move to find a place within the castle. Somewhere safe where they could huddle together and keep warm. The clear skies promised another freezing night.

As they moved Gaia could see small, darting flashes zipping past. At first she heard the swishing noise as the shadows hurtled close. Gaia noticed the tiny black creatures in the air. They looked like birds, but she realised they were bats. Gaia saw the images of the night birds in her mind. They had not appeared for days, not since the escape from the island. Perhaps they only lived on the island? Nothing would surprise Gaia. Nature had been thrown into turmoil and chaos reigned.

The group entered the open central part of the castle, a large grassy area littered with the remains of walls. The rubble was a sad reminder of the pomp and majesty that once would have graced the building. The castle was centuries old, with no purpose or use for many years. Gaia spotted a sign to the right, and moved to read it. The sign was faded and covered in a mixture of moss, muck and rust. Gaia could just make out two of the words.

'It says Norham Castle. Anyone heard of it?'

The others all shook their heads. Yann had climbed over one of the crumbling areas of wall and was on his knees peering down at something.

'Look here.'

They all moved to where Yann was kneeling. There was a circular hole covered in a criss cross of iron bars. Yann was leaning on the bars and staring into the depths below. Yann hollered into the hole, his voice echoing in the cavernous depths.

'What do you reckon this is? A well? Some underground storage?'

Aran answered.

'It's a dungeon. They put prisoners in there. The bars meant people could either feed them or throw stuff at them. Usually they'd get showered in shit.'

Yann jumped up and looked at his gloves, wiping them on the back of his trousers, his face twisted in disgust. Freya spoke.

'We need to find somewhere to bed down. Best to avoid anywhere indoors if we can. The stone walls make the rooms freezing and we can't risk a fire.'

Freya found a small area which had been dug out, and perhaps had once been a room or dwelling. It offered good shelter, and the group could huddle together under their blankets for extra warmth. They ate a supper of cheese, bread, and fruit, and each drank some of Freya's tonic. She had made a special batch for Aran and assured him the drink would kill the last remains of poison. Freya guaranteed Aran would feel more refreshed in the morning. Gaia hoped she was right. They settled down for the night under their makeshift bed, smothered in layers of blankets. The moon was still full in the sky, and had not begun to wane yet. Its light dissolved some of the splendour of the stars, though together they still provided a wonderful spectacle of millions of flickering lights. Gaia, Yann, and Freya took it in turns to take a few hours of watch. Despite Aran's protests the others all agreed that he needed a full night of sleep to recover. They did not need a passenger, but needed Aran fitter and more alert.

The night passed without note or incident. Gaia took the first watch and spent her time analysing the shapes on the moon, its mysterious face, and admiring its silent beauty. For millions of years it had orbited the earth, providing stability and balance as it spun. The moon controlled the tides, therefore they had it to thank for being here. The tides had been key to their escape, as had the moon's light. In a way the moon had colluded with them, a secret fifth member. However, in its light there was also a darkness. The speed which the tides had risen had led to the death of Clara. The moon had given the group a chance of a new life, but had also taken one.

Freya took over from Gaia who settled into a deep, uninterrupted sleep. Her exhaustion meant she soon drifted despite the cold biting at her face and ears, and feet that refused to warm. Gaia lay next to Aran, snuggled in close and placed her arm over him, feeling the steady hypnotic pulse of his breathing. It was soft and comforting. This night he did not whimper, nor was he restless and fidgety. He was more peaceful and at ease, the combination of exhaustion and Freya's potion was working.

It was good for Aran that he was no longer carrying all the burden of responsibility. The mental impact had added to his troubles. The group still faced dangers, many unknown, but the biggest were the hunters waiting somewhere up ahead. The outcome of that encounter would determine the group's fate. The night was cold, but being near to Aran, and feeling his body close warmed Gaia. She wanted to nurse Aran, let him know she was there and would look out for him. They were all in this together, but Gaia was only there because of Aran. Whatever freedom meant, whatever awaited, Gaia wanted Aran to be a part of her future.

14

Gaia woke early with Aran still sound asleep beside her. Freya was eating breakfast with a blanket wrapped around her. The clear night had brought a crisp frosty morning with a sprinkling of white dust across the grass. The sun was already beginning its slow rise, but was still low and not yet sharing its gentle warmth. There was a golden red hue in the sky, and just a smattering of wispy cloud. The castle walls cast an array of shadows, and all was quiet, even the birdsong was absent. Gaia sat opposite Freya who was picking at her food.

'Good morning.'

'Hi. You feeling better?'

'Much better thanks. I don't know what you put in those concoctions, but they work.'

Freya laughed. Never the most jovial, even Freya had been more preoccupied since the spiders. As the others recovered Freya had taken on the role of leader. She was comfortable with that, but it presented a challenge. Freya did not show emotion unless it was necessary. The distractions of motivating the others, nursing them back to health, finding the plants and herbs to make her tonics had crowded her mind. Gaia was pleased Freya was showing signs of thawing. Freya whispered, conscious of Aran still sleeping.

'There's nothing to them really. It's just knowing what to look for and how to put them together. It's surprising how much is out there.'

'It's obviously a specialist role they've been preparing you for.'

'Yes. I was singled out with a few others for the training. It's mostly natural remedies, but also general healthcare, and dealing with breaks and injuries. I'd have been sent to work for medical support in the haven once I'd become.'

They were both struck by the same realisation that their becoming would no longer happen. Unless they were caught, then it was likely they would be expelled or worse. Gaia had not known any that had escaped return. No-one spoke of them or what became of them. They had crossed a line. They were free now and Gaia shook the thought of capture and its consequences from her mind. Gaia noticed Yann was missing.

'Where's Yann?'

'He's exploring the castle. He was on last watch, but was still pretty chirpy when I woke and went off soon after he ate.'

'Here he comes now!'

Yann was running across the open area, sprinting, a look of alarm on his face. He stopped, struggled to speak and catch his breath.

'You need to come with me. I've something to show you.'

Freya jumped up, and Gaia followed. Freya spoke.

'What is it?'

'Just come with me.'

Gaia looked at Aran.

'Wait, what about Aran?'

Freya and Yann were already gone, leaping over the ruins of the internal walls. Gaia was hesitant, wrestling with the urge to follow and the guilt at leaving Aran alone. Gaia scanned the area. There was nothing, not even a sound. The other two were out of view. Something snapped, the training took over and

Gaia set off in pursuit. Yann and Freya were at the far end of the outer walls, they had stopped running. Yann was crouched in front, finger placed on his lips. Freya waited, Yann disappeared into the ground and Freya followed. As Gaia neared there were stone steps descending into the darkness. She tiptoed down the steps into a freezing cold cellar. The only light came from three holes in the ceiling spread around the room. Gaia could see Freya and Yann in the shadows, standing over something, both looking at the ground. Gaia approached. At their feet was a giant rat. It was dead, a hole through its skull and another in its back. The wounds were fresh, and blood seeped from them. Freya and Yann were staring at it, looking for any final signs of movement, making sure the creature was dead. Yann whispered

'I found it just before. It was sleeping down here. I managed to kill it before it woke. I've checked, but can't find any others.'

Freya stepped away, whispering as she combed the darkness.

'They're social. There'll be others, so we need to make a move and get out of here as soon as we can. Let's get back and leave.'

They made their way back up the staircase, the freshness of the morning air hitting them as they left the underground chamber. They jogged back towards where Aran was sleeping, and Gaia woke him. Freya was agitated, keen to move, struggling to contain her concern.

'Come on Aran. We need to get going.'

'Can't I get something to eat?'

'We haven't got time. You can eat on the road. Come on, we'll explain later.'

'Is there a problem?'

Gaia tried to allay any panic.

'No, it's fine Aran. Have something quick while we pack.'

Gaia cast a glance at Freya who began to pick up the blankets. Aran seemed better, physically and mentally. The tonics and full night of rest had given him some colour. He was more alert, and eager to get on with things. Gaia passed Aran some fruit while the other two packed. Gaia kept watch, peering out just above the wall that surrounded the small, sheltered pit. Just as they had packed away, Gaia noticed something in the far corner of the grounds. There was a movement, something large and black.

At first Gaia could see only one, but more rats appeared. It looked as though the creatures were rising up from the depths of the earth, from an underground cellar where they had been sleeping and were now awakening. The rats would be hungry and desperate. The group were concealed in the pit, safe from view, but trapped. Any attempt to leave would be noticed. There was no way the group would make it to the gateway without being seen. The rats were much nearer to the entrance, and the creatures would be upon Gaia and the others in no time, heading the group off before they got near to escaping. Gaia turned, caught the attention of the others and beckoned them over.

'Look. Over there.'

Freya surveyed the area, clicking into survival mode, instincts taking control, calm and measured and searching for a solution. The group would need to act, and Freya had spotted the best option and without hesitation had a plan.

'The turret over there. We'll make a run for that. There's a door, hopefully it's open.'

Yann nodded.

'It is. I was in there this morning. There's a bolt on the inside.'

'What's in there?'

'A staircase leading to a platform.'

Freya kept probing Yann, the plan unfolding for the others. It soon became clear what Freya had in mind.

'How high's the drop from the other side?'

'It's high. You're not thinking of jumping?'

'What's down there, rocks, grass?'

Yann was starting to panic being sprayed with the volley of questions. His mind did not function this way. He liked time to think, to breath, but the group had little.

'I don't recall exactly. I think it's just grass, heather, maybe a few rocks. It's risky. I wouldn't want to jump it from that height.'

Gaia and Aran kept watching the rats. The larger ones were lying in the sun, the younger ones were fighting. There were about ten, five adults. Even the younger ones were large, and would prove formidable in a fight. There were too many to take on without risk. The group were still weak, and escape was the best option, any confrontation a last resort. Aran studied the turret Freya had spotted for the escape. He spoke.

'What about the ramparts? They're a few levels lower. The jump won't be so high.'

Freya stared at the ramparts, thought about Aran's suggestion. There was a problem.

'The rats can get onto them. We'd be exposed.'

'Yes, but the only access is through the turret or those steps over there. We'll draw them to the turret and lock the door. Once we're sure they're all there we can move onto the ramparts and jump. We'll have some time to get up there and jump. Even if they spot the steps we can be over before they get up there. That's our best chance.'

Freya looked at each of the group in turn. Aran's plan was sound, but Freya wanted the approval of the others. Yann shrugged, Gaia and Aran looked at each other and nodded. Gaia spoke.

'I say we go for it. It's the best option we have. None of us are up for a fight. There's too many of them.'

Freya nodded.

'OK. Let's make a move. Stay low and they might not spot us.'

Freya climbed up onto the edge of the pit and crept across the grass. The others followed. They each looked across at the rats who continued to bask and play, oblivious of the groups movements. Gaia noticed one of the younger rodents stop playing. Its head twitched, and pointed straight at Gaia. It was only a second, but somehow seemed longer as the rat waited, then began to run towards the group. The other young rats followed, the adults stirred and were soon in pursuit. The creatures had spotted Gaia and the others far sooner than they would have liked. Gaia shouted and began to sprint towards the turret.

'They're coming. Move!'

Freya was close behind Gaia, then Yann and Aran. The door to the turret was within reach, perhaps twenty metres, but the rats were fast. The creatures were hungry and hunting. Once the rats had spotted prey they became rabid and frenzied, desperation fueling a demonic adrenalin. The adults had now overtaken the young, their long, rapid strides eating up the earth, narrowing the gap between hunter and hunted. Gaia reached the door first and kicked it open. Freya followed. Yann and Aran still had a few metres to go, with the first of the adult rats just behind. Gaia could see their huge teeth, mouths open, salivating, ready to wrap themselves around their prey, preparing to lock tight and rip them to shreds.

Yann and Aran plunged through the door, just as the first adult rat dived towards them. Gaia and Freya slammed the door shut and felt a thud against it. The two girls pressed all their weight against the door as Yann scrambled to bolt it shut. Everyone stepped back and looked at the door, listening to the banging and scratching. There was frantic hammering and screeching from the rats, a sound the group were all familiar with, but had not heard for days. It was a noise the young people had hoped they would never hear again. The door was bulging, the hinges strained. Freya looked at Gaia, grave concern scratched into her face. Freya shouted above the din of the attack.

'Let's hope it holds out.'

Freya ran up the stairs while Yann and Aran pressed against the door trying to ease the pressure as it was battered from the other side. The deafening screeches continued, more frequent and frenzied than ever. Freya soon returned and took command.

'They're all at the door, so we need to move quickly. The drop's better from the right of the ramparts. As soon as we're over head for the woods at the bottom. At the far side I can see a church. We'll run for that. Let's go.'

Freya continued to lead, able to switch into a measured efficiency, the result of years of training. Yann seemed unfazed, almost enjoying the excitement. While Aran looked strained, the demands of this and the last few days were taking a toll. Gaia managed to smother the emotion, knowing control and precise thinking were the key to survival.

Freya led them up the stone stairs. They were narrow, steep and slippy, the morning frost on their shoes making the stone like ice. Gaia lost her footing several times as she clambered up behind Freya and Aran. Gaia could feel Yann at her back, bumping into her as she stumbled. The group came to the doorway that led onto the ramparts. Freya was already standing by one of the gaps in the walls. Looking over the edge, Freya threw her rucksack down and without hesitation jumped. Gaia peered over and saw Freya land on the grassy surface below, rolling forward and tumbling down the hill in a series of short, swift rolls. The jump was higher than Gaia had anticipated, but it was too late to back out. The alternative was far worse, the choice determined by a lack of real options.

Gaia dropped her rucksack over the edge and lowered herself down the wall. Her fingertips gripped the edge of the rough, cold stonework, body stretched, toes pointing to the earth below. Gaia let go and recalling her training, relaxed. The body had a natural tendency to tense which was more likely to lead to injury. It was better to concentrate on easing the muscles. In the split seconds of the fall Gaia tried to focus her mind.

Gaia hit the ground feet first, let her legs collapse and dived onto her side. She tumbled, head reeling, the sound of the air and crashing body loud in her ears. Something struck Gaia in the side. It was solid, probably a rock, a jabbing pain shot through her. Winded and struggling to breath Gaia was still hurtling down the hill. She tried to slow the rolls, careful not to extend her arms in case they became trapped. The seconds seemed much longer as Gaia plunged forward. After what seemed an age the tumbling slowed and stopped. Gaia lay still, dizzy, disorientated, and trying to catch her breath. A switch clicked in Gaia's mind, the survival instinct triggered. Jumping to her feet Gaia looked around. She saw Freya just a few yards away, crouched, rucksack on her back, looking shaken, but still alert and poised, waiting for the others. She looked like a coiled spring, ready to confront the rats, waiting to be unleashed. Freya approached Gaia.

'Are you OK?'

'I think so. I hit a rock coming down, but I don't think anything is broken. It just winded me. I'll be fine once I get my breath back.'

They looked up the hill, back at the ramparts. Aran had already jumped and was cascading down the hill like a boulder, plunging head first. He bounced, hit the side of the hill and flew high into the air landing with a thud a few metres from Gaia and Freya. Gaia leapt to him as he lay in a heap on the grass, dazed and groaning, but still conscious. Aran's hair was soaked, filled with flecks of grass and heather.

'You OK?'

'I should be fine. Help me up, will you?'

Gaia helped Aran to his feet, and he hobbled across to gather his rucksack, shaking his head in an attempt to cast off the dizzy haze. Gaia looked across at Freya who was staring up at the ramparts, a worried look on her face. Gaia followed Freya's eyeline and saw Yann still up there, looking down, ready to jump. Something was wrong. Yann's body was frozen, his face locked in panic. Freya cupped her hands and hollered, her voice quivering with desperation.

'Jump Yann. Don't look, just jump. Come on.'

Gaia could see the rats. Their large, black, hairy bodies were zipping by, a series of flashes as they passed each gap in the ramparts. The creatures were bearing down on Yann, and would be upon him in seconds. He still seemed paralysed with fear, unaware that the rodents were almost upon him. Gaia screamed at Yann.

'Yann. They're coming, jump, JUMP!'

For a fraction of a second Yann looked frozen, staring below in a vacant haze. Something stirred and he seemed to hear Gaia's words. Yann came to, snapped free, and realised the creatures were almost there. He grabbed the sides of the ramparts, and was just about to jump when the first of the rats dived. Gaia saw the rodent's body thrust through the air like a missile, its jaws open wide, ready to lock onto their target. The creature caught him, its teeth plunged into Yann's throat. The force of the assault hurled them both over the edge. Man and beast hurtled to the ground, locked together, Yann grabbing at his throat, trying to pull the rat from him as the creature writhed and flailed, its jaws locked in a deadly grip.

Time seemed to slow as Yann and the creature fell. Gaia could see every movement of their macabre dance, every expression of agony on Yann's face, every frenzied jerk of the rat's neck and jaws. Blood was gushing from Yann's wound, and he screamed as they hit the earth and began to roll. The rat was still locked on Yann's throat ripping and sucking the life from him. Aran and Freya began to run towards him, but stopped. Gaia was frozen in horror. The other rats were staring over the edge of the castle walls, ready to jump, but still tentative, waiting. Gaia knew the creatures would jump. The hesitation was instinctive, but the hunger was stronger, the desire to feed overwhelming. The rats would see and smell the blood, inviting them, urging them on. Time was edging forward, second by second, in a blurred slow motion. The rats would jump and, in an instant be upon the group. The rodents were gathering, the opportunity of escape was slipping away.

Gaia, Freya and Aran looked on in desperation and horror, as Yann was torn apart. Gaia watched as the life was ripped from his face and body. The remaining three knew it was too late. Once the jaws had locked onto Yann's throat it was when and not if. The moment Yann and the creature hit the earth it was over, the injuries fatal. Yann stopped fighting, every ounce of energy had gone, every last piece of life dissolved. Gaia and the others had to run, preserve themselves. The rats were coming and it was all about survival. It always had been, and always would be. Gaia barked at the others.

'Leave him. He's gone. Come on. Run!'

Freya had paused, tempted to attack the rats, exact revenge for the killing. Her killer instinct wrestled with the urge to survive at all costs. Yann and his killer were only metres away, but the rat paid her no attention, still tearing at Yann's throat. Yann was limp, soaked in a blanket of his own blood. Freya knew it was over. To attack was futile. She could kill the rat, but that would cost time, and time was their only hope now. Freya snapped out of the lust for revenge and grabbed Aran. He too had thoughts of settling scores, had the urge to attack. Freya tugged at Aran's arm, pleading.

'It's no use Aran, we have to save ourselves. Let's go.'

Aran's head dropped into his hands. He began to shake and quiver. He was losing his grip, his mind was crumbling, losing all sense of hope. Freya yanked at Aran's arm again, and began to drag him away. Something in the back of his brain told him there was still a chance. The panic began to dissolve, Aran's mind regained control. Now was not the time for risks, it was the time to run, to preserve life, to survive. Emotion was weakness. Action was strength.

The rats on the rampart were beginning to make their move. A creature's long claws and head were over the side, scratching and feeling its way down the stone walls. It fell, flying through the air towards the hillside. This was the trigger for the others, the tumble of the first domino. Another rat followed, then another, and another. The adults dived first, then the young. Even in the throws of their murderous frenzy they had a deference to order and hierarchy. It was programming, instinct, the natural way. Without order there was chaos, and in chaos there was weakness. The rats were the same as Gaia, Freya, Aran, and Yann They were all programmed to survive, hunter or hunted, kill or be killed.

Freya and Aran ran towards Gaia, passing her, as all three sprinted towards the woods. Gaia caught a glimpse over her shoulder. The last of the rats had hurled themselves from the ramparts. The creatures that had landed were huddled around the body of Yann, feasting on flesh, the blood still warm and fresh. Gaia felt sick, the image of Yann's face flashing through her mind, his smile laid back and carefree. Yann was not made for this world. Chaos was his beauty; innocence the weakness that destroyed him. Yann was for the old world, not here, not this moment.

The group charged on towards the woods, the only urge to survive. They were building a gap, putting as much distance as they could between them and the rats. The creatures were still devouring Yann, locked in a feeding frenzy. At the moment the rats wallowed in the rampant delirium of a fresh kill, but soon that would be gone and the rodents would know more human flesh was waiting, escaping.

15

Now there were three, sprinting towards the woods and the church beyond. Legs pumped hard, the grass and heather heavy with morning dew made the going tough. They were tired, but the hunger to live matched the hunger of the rats for blood. The group had a good head start, and the church was near. If they could reach it and lock themselves inside they could sit it out, and wait till the rats grew hungry and moved on. Gaia looked back over her shoulder. The rats had begun their pursuit, but had left it late. They were too overcome by their feasting, the sweet warm flesh and blood. That was gone and the creatures sensed more prey. The rats were faster and better suited for this terrain. The three still had time, precious time, now more precious than ever. Gaia kept pushing forward, Freya and Aran still just ahead. They reached the woods and zig-zagged through the few, sparse trees making it easier to navigate and plot a path. The three were almost there, the stone wall of the churchyard metres away.

Freya and Aran leapt the wall into the graveyard, followed by Gaia. The headstones were broken and neglected, the graves overgrown. The long forgotten relics of the past lay tattered in a garden of buried memories, and love that no longer survived. The group darted in, out and over the graves towards the door of the church. Freya reached it first, hurling herself against it and trying the handle. It was locked. Aran and Gaia reached her, as all three gasped for air. The rats had not yet entered the churchyard, and still could not be seen for the wall. Soon the creatures would be here and once they leapt the wall Gaia and the others had only seconds.

Freya stepped out from the stone arch of the doorway. She surveyed the roof, and set off around the church, Gaia and Aran close behind. At the head of the church was a tower, at its base a wooden door. Freya tried the handle, but again it was locked. She moved to the side of the tower and clambered up a drainpipe onto the roof.

'Come on, climb up here.'

Freya reached down and helped Gaia. Aran followed with Gaia's help. All three crept up the steep, slate tiled roof which was damp and covered in green moss. They hugged the slates, dragging themselves to the pitch of the roof, where they sat and straddled legs either side. Gaia spoke.

'What now?'

Freya was looking along the line of the roof to the bell tower. Just up from the highest point of the roof was a window. It was not within easy reach, but with some help from the others one of them would be able to get to it. Gaia looked down into the graveyard, could see nothing, but heard scratching and intermittent shrieks. The rats had reached the church and were down below. The creatures would not be able to climb onto the roof, their size made them too heavy and cumbersome to climb these walls. The three were safe for now, but knew they could not stay on the roof too long. They had to get inside.

Freya led the others, shimmying along the roofline to the window. Aran put his back against the wall, remaining seated. He cupped his hands into a cradle and Freya stepped into them and onto his shoulders. The extra height was just enough to allow her to reach the window. Freya used her knife to lift the latch and pulled herself through. Peering out over the ledge she beckoned to Gaia who stepped into the cradle, onto the shoulders, and pulled herself head first through the window. Gaia lunged forward and fell in a heap on the hard stone floor. Freya lowered a blanket. Aran clutched it and walked up the wall, as she pulled him through to safety. Aran and Gaia lay on the floor, exhausted and relieved they had made it. Freya closed the window and sat down beside the others.

The stone chamber echoed with their breathing. Each lay against the wall, perched upright, overcome with emotion. The realisation of what had happened began to seep in and the initial sense of relief was soon replaced by sorrow. Aran put his head in his hands and wept. Gaia wrapped her arms around him, feeling his sobbing against her breast. She gripped Aran's head, pressed it hard into her chest, longing to take away the pain. She felt the same burning pain, heartache, and desperation. Aran would feel this more than the others. It was his mission and idea, his leadership and responsibility. Aran had approached Yann, handpicked him to join the group. Yann's loss was Aran's burden.

'Just let it out Aran. It's hard to take in. I can't believe he's gone.'

'It's my fault. Yann was only here because of me. I should never've let him come.'

Gaia rubbed her fingers through Aran's soft hair, feeling his gentle sobbing between muffled words. Freya sat with her eyes closed, silent. Gaia continued her attempts to comfort Aran.

'Don't blame yourself. Yann knew the risks. We all did. We all chose to be here. There's nothing any of us could have done. Just remember him as he was.'

Gaia stopped. Maybe her words were futile. The truth is she did not really know who Yann was. She had only known him a few days. The group had been thrust together through circumstances, the connection simply a necessity, an unspoken contract. Yet, the intensity of their situation and the time they had spent together had given colour to Yann's character. The time had been short, but they had already lived a lifetime together. Gaia knew these moments were life-defining, the experiences special. These were the times that memories were formed.

The past few days Gaia had developed a genuine warmth for her companions. Her interactions with people had always been defined by others. There was a wall, but this went beyond that. Gaia's feelings for Aran were strong and growing, something different again. Even Freya, who Gaia hated at first had shown strength and loyalty. Freya had moved from an enemy to someone Gaia would trust with her life. Gaia had been wrong. Yann had been the quietest of them all, and in many ways the most difficult to understand. His peace and tranquility were humbling to Gaia. Yann saw the joy in life whatever chaos threw at him. His bubble was a protection, but there was a charm and appeal to such free spirit. The world was full of pain and danger, suffering and despair. Yann looked beyond and saw the beauty. Yann and the others had helped to thaw Gaia's icy heart.

Gaia continued to play with Aran's hair, the softness comforted her. Her voice was a whisper, cracked and trembling with emotion.

'Yann saw beauty in everything. He floated through life. Maybe that was his problem, but at least he was happy.'

Freya opened her eyes.

'He was one of the good guys, a pure soul but he wasn't meant to be here.'

Aran sat up and wiped his tears.

'What do you mean?'

Freya shuffled, and looked away, realising she had said the wrong thing.

'Sorry, that came out badly. I just meant that some of us are different. We've been programmed differently. We're killers. The world is destroying people like Yann, the ones with the good hearts. It's natural selection. The good won't survive.'

Freya's voice faltered, as Gaia reflected on her words. Freya was right. The three of them could run as far as they wanted, but there was no escaping the truth, no escaping themselves. The young all knew what they were, what the community had made of them. Freedom was the chance to be something different, to become who they chose.

Gaia looked at Freya, tears had filled Freya's eyes and she was biting her lip. Gaia leant forward, and Aran followed. All three wrapped their arms around one another and hugged. They were long reassuring hugs, that told them everything would be alright. Gaia and the others knew the gravity of the situation and felt the pain of Yann's loss. If they were to get through this the group could not allow the pain to break them. Freya was right. The young were different, killers, but that made them strong and survivors. Yann had been a gift, showing them all something else. He had reminded all three of their humanity, that there was still beauty and good in the world if you cared to look. Where there was no beauty you could create it. The young lived in a world of fear and brutality, but each could make it better. The new world could begin with them.

All three sat for a while, wallowing in the silence, bathing in its calm. A thought swept through Gaia's mind. She laughed and spoke.

'He knew his birds and animals, didn't he?'

Freya grinned, nodding in agreement.

'I know. Where'd he pick that up? Were you ever taught anything like that?'

'Nope. Not that I recall.'

Aran shook his head and chuckled.

'Do you think they were training him to run a farm?'

They all laughed, filled with warmth and affection. The three sat and exchanged memories of Yann. Tender and touching stories filled with the same spirit and humour as Yann. Despite the brief time together, and difficult circumstances there were fleeting moments of laughter and joy. Aran told of when he first met Yann, how Aran had approached him, how it had become apparent that Yann also wanted to escape. Aran seemed uncomfortable in recalling it, as though the memory was too private and it was not right to share. This was the part of Yann's backstory that had always puzzled Gaia, but had never thought to ask. Why did Aran pick Yann and why did he want to come? Despite his reticence Aran told them.

'I don't know, there was always something different about Yann. I thought it was a rebellious streak, but maybe with hindsight I was wrong. We'd spoken occasionally, and I'd sounded him out a bit. Nothing too obvious, ambiguous stuff. One day he whispered to me, *'Do you want out?'* That was the start. It was a risk on his part, but I guess I'd given him enough signals. Plus he didn't seem to care. I arranged to meet him one evening and told him that I had plans and if he wanted in. The look on his face when I told him.

I'll never forget it. He was like a child, could barely contain his excitement. Every time we met you could tell he was itching to go. He wasn't interested in the detail, it was just a case of wanting to go.'

Gaia butted in, there was still one question Aran had not answered and puzzled her.

'Did he ever say why he wanted to leave the island so much? I thought if anyone could cope with the island it would be Yann. He struck me as the type that would just let it all float by.'

'I did ask him and it was an odd answer. He said he was bored and wanted some adventure. He said the place drove him nuts.'

They all laughed again, but thought about Yann's words as they sank in. There was a bit of truth in that for Gaia too, maybe for all of them. There were many reasons Gaia wanted to escape. She had always been convinced it was about finding freedom and her own future. But the escape was showing Gaia that it was about other things too. The journey was about adventure and discovery. All three were young and had their lifetime's ahead. There was something deep inside Gaia, an urge to fight against being put in a box and made to perform. Gaia did not want to be just a cog in a machine, something engineered by the community to fit its needs. Gaia wanted to see what was left of the world, however messed up it might be. After a long silence Gaia spoke.

'I think Yann nailed it. That's why I'm here. Aren't we all? I want to experience life, live it. I don't mind if I die taking a few risks. I'd rather die doing something I love, something I chose to do than live a dull life shaped by the community. I want something better. I deserve it. We all do.'

Freya nodded.

'Yes, that's it for me, definitely. The hope there's something better. I don't know, it's hard to say exactly but I feel this urge to find some answers. I'm sick of being told who I'm meant to be and what my life is all about. The community say they know what's best. They talk of the greater good, but it's always their greater good and their best not mine. I'd like a say. That's all I want, a say in what I become.'

Gaia smiled. Freya and Gaia both looked at Aran who was quiet, staring into space. Gaia thought he looked lost. He remained silent.

'How about you Aran? What made you decide to escape?'

Aran continued to look away, the same vacant expression on his face, his mind elsewhere. Gaia thought maybe he had not heard, or was not listening, but he had. Every word had stung him. Aran was thinking of a response, knew what he wanted to say, but could not.

'I escaped because I had to. I had no choice.'

Aran jumped to his feet, and clasped his hands together. The sudden energy and animation took the others by surprise.

'Let's check this place out. We need to know we'll be safe here, or it'll all be over before we get to the hills.'

Freya and Gaia got up, and gathered the rucksacks. The chamber was small, almost a landing. It was empty, just a stone floor and two doorways, one leading up to the bell tower, the other down to the main part of the church. Aran led the others down the steep narrow staircase. It was dark. At the base of the staircase was a room, with no light. All three entered, as Freya felt her way around the walls until she reached a door. Freya pressed her ear against it and listened. The other two waited, as Freya reached down and eased the handle. A gap appeared, the door creaked open and light flooded in.

Freya stepped through the door and into the main area of the church, Gaia and Aran followed. The room was large and cold, and coloured light streamed in through the bright stained glass windows. On the right was a large stone basin filled with water. Most of the room was filled with two columns lined with rows of wooden benches. Between was a narrow aisle leading to an open area at the back of the church. The floor was raised and covered in dusty old rugs. There was a platform to one side on which stood a lectern. A long table stood in front of the benches and beyond were more tables littered with an assortment of objects. A large silver cross stood in the centre of the table. The windows at the back of the church were vast, magnificent displays, bursting with a kaleidoscope of rainbow colours woven into a picture of a man on a cross and some people kneeling at his feet. The windows were tall and narrow with a pointed arch at the top. Four stone pillars stretched out to the high wooden ceiling above, and around the higher reaches there were strange stone demons, and a weird menagerie of creatures. The chamber was silent and cavernous. There was a peaceful atmosphere, but there was something not quite right. Gaia had a strange feeling.

The three split and explored the room. Though there were no people something told Gaia the room had been lived in. This was not abandoned, life had warmed it. Gaia moved along the aisle, stroking the benches as she passed. In front of each was a square mat or cushion, each scarlet red and embroidered with a black cross. The colours and material were worn and faded. Books were placed on the shelves that backed each bench in front. There was a red book and a green book. Gaia picked up the green one, *The Book of Hymns*, and opened it. Each page contained a numbered set of words. Gaia wondered what they were, and read the words of one. The hymns had a strange and steady rhythm.

He who would valiant be

*He who would valiant be
'gainst all disaster,
let him in constancy
follow the Master.
There's no discouragement
shall make him once relent
his first avowed intent
to be a pilgrim.*

*Who so beset him round
with dismal stories
do but themselves confound
his strength the more is.
No foes shall stay his might;
though he with giants fight,
he will make good his right
to be a pilgrim.*

*Since, Lord, thou dost defend
us with thy Spirit,
We know we at the end,
shall life inherit.
Then fancies flee away!
I'll fear not what men say,*

I'll labor night and day
to be a pilgrim.

'To be a pilgrim.' Gaia reflected on the meaning of the words. They seemed antiquated, an arcane language she had never heard. These were the words of the days before, and of the old ways. Churches were places that housed the old religion, like the ruins of the abbey on the island. They were the buildings where communities gathered to worship a god. He had no name, it was just God. He was the old god, the forbidden god. Gaia read the words again. The rhythm and lyricism fascinated her. They were almost musical, though music was banned now in the community, it had been a part of her early years, the nurturing.

Gaia replaced the book and picked up the red one. The front read - *'New Revised Standard Version Holy Bible,'* the final two words in large bold golden letters. Gaia opened it, and the pages fell open on a section named *'Peter.'* By the side of the words were the numbers '2:18.' The paragraph read -

'Slaves, submit yourselves to your masters with all respect, not only to those who are good and considerate, but also to those who are harsh.'

Gaia opened another page, the passage numbered '28:53'

'Then because of the dire straits to which you will be reduced when your enemy besieges you, you will eat you own children, the flesh of your sons and daughters whom the Lord has given you.'

Gaia closed the book. Slaves, masters, eating the flesh of your own children. What was this? Was this what the people of the old ways thought? Gaia moved to the table at the front and examined the large silver cross. It was intricate and ornate, and as with the large window that dominated the room there was a figure of a long-haired bearded man. He was semi-naked, wearing only flowing underwear, his arms stretched out. The man's hands were nailed to the horizontal beams of the cross, and his head bowed, on it he was wearing what looked like a circular head garment made from twigs. The feet were pressed together and nailed to the vertical beam. The man's eyes were closed, and above his head was a sign with letters. Gaia gazed at the image, mesmerised by the peace and tranquility of the man. He was hanging from a cross, nailed to the beams and yet there was no pain or anguish on his face. On the contrary, he looked serene, not dead, but resigned to his fate, almost welcoming it.

Gaia heard a noise to her right. There was a door which had opened and a small crack appeared. She could see eyes peering through. They were low down, small, the eyes of a child. The door opened further and there was a little girl with long, messy blonde hair. She was dressed in a rag of a white dress, torn and filthy. The girl clutched a small blanket in her arms, her hand at her face, sucking her thumb. The child was only a few years old, her face filled with a mixture of fear and confusion. Gaia reached out her arm and beckoned the child forward.

'It's OK. I won't hurt you.'

Freya and Aran stopped wandering, and turned to look at the girl, as she inched forward across the carpet, not towards Gaia, but parallel. The child stopped.

'I'm Gaia. What's your name?'

There was no response, only bleak, sad eyes peering back at Gaia. The child continued to suck her thumb, clutching the tattered blanket. Gaia could see she was an outsider, and there was something disturbing in the girl's dark green eyes. They were empty, lifeless, not the playful, joyous eyes of a child.

'Are you alone?'

Still there was silence. The girl began to sway from side to side, her feet planted on the ground, but swinging her arms. She looked down at her blanket, placing small delicate fingers through the holes of the woolen mesh pattern. Each finger had tiny, grubby nails.

'Can you tell me your name? I promise we won't hurt you. There's nothing to be afraid of.'

'Her name is Ruth.'

Gaia turned with a start. In the doorway stood a man, at least seventy years old. He was short and stout in build, his hair white, combed across, a vain attempt to look smart. The man was unshaven, perhaps a few days of growth, dressed in a black suit and grey pullover. There was a thin, white collar around his neck. A huge gold cross on a chain hung from his neck and rested in the centre of a bulging chest. The suit was covered in stains, the edges of the sleeves threadbare and worn. Gaia looked at the man's eyes. It was instinctive, the badge, the first sign of who you were, and who you were not. The old man was one of them, an outsider. His eyes were brown, the whites cracked and speckled with a deep bloodshot red.

'What brings you to my church?'

The man's voice was deep and menacing with a throaty rattle.

'Sorry, we mean no harm. We need shelter. We were being attacked by rats. They're still outside. We lost a friend in the attack. My name is Gaia, and these are my friends Aran and Freya.'

Gaia gestured to the others in turn. Freya was alert, hand by her side over the knife, poised for any sudden movement. Freya stood by the main door to the right, listening for the rats. She could still hear the creatures scratching and shrieking. Aran was in the main aisle, holding one of the red books, looking more relaxed, his face softer and more welcoming. This was an old man and a small, young child. Neither posed a threat to the group, unless there were others. Freya was taking no chances, her instinct to mis-trust and be cautious. Freya did not like him, and there was something troubling about the girl. Gaia addressed the man again.

'Would it be OK if we stayed here a while, maybe only a few hours, just until we're sure the rats have gone and it's safe to move on. We won't impose on you.'

The man's look was stern, staring at Gaia, then the others. He was wary, but not afraid. Many people had passed through over the years, some far worse than these young people. The man felt protected, the church was a sanctuary. He looked down at Gaia's belt and saw the axe and knife. The old man frowned.

'All are welcome in this house. It is the house of our Lord. You may take sanctuary here. Come let us rest and talk. You must be hungered after your travels. I will prepare us some food.'

Gaia looked at the others and back at the man who gestured to Gaia's belt.

'You won't be needing those. You'll find no danger here. There are no threats, are there Ruth? We're a small family, just myself and a few of my children. All of us are God's children. So come, come, please. Let me introduce you to Ruth's sisters. I'm Father Ridley by the way. It's a pleasure to meet you.'

The priest stepped forward from the doorway, approaching Gaia with his hand outstretched. Gaia offered hers which the old man gripped and shook. The grip was strong, almost painful. The priest let go and moved towards Ruth, standing beside her and stroking the child's hair. Gaia noticed the girl flinch as Ridley touched her. The blank eyes fired with life, with fear. The child stood still beside him, while he played with her tousled locks, grinning. Ridley's teeth were stained yellow and chipped, a small ball of white spit clung to the corner of his lip.

Gaia was hesitant. The priest was old and gracious, but gave her the creeps. Gaia looked back at Aran who raised his eyebrows and cast a gesture of 'What do you think?' Freya was frowning and shaking her head. Gaia could see her caution and reluctance. Gaia spoke.

'Could I have a moment to speak with my friends, please?'

'Of course. Take your time. We'll just be through here. I'll make us some tea. Come through when you're ready.'

The priest led Ruth back through the door. Aran and Freya joined Gaia who spoke in a whisper.

'What do you reckon? We aren't going anywhere soon, so we've not got much choice but to stay.'

Freya looked uneasy, her face cast in stone. Aran spoke.

'I'm with you Gaia. He's an old bloke with some kids. What's he going to do? We stay here a few hours, no longer than we have to. We keep checking on the rats outside, but they'll get hungry and move on. As soon as we're sure it's safe we leave. We needn't stay here any longer than we have to.'

Freya took out her knife and began to twirl it in her hand. They were fast, sweeping and elaborate movements, tricks she had practiced many times. It was the adept skill of someone who knew her own capability, all programmed. Freya stopped and balanced the knife on the palm of her hand, point facing upwards, then spoke.

'There's something not right here. I sense it, but if you feel comfortable, fine. Like you say we get out of here as soon as we can. But this place and that man give me the creeps. I mean what was this place?'

Aran still held the red book in his hand. He passed it to Freya.

'This is where they'd sing, worship, pray. It's a house of the old ways, like the ruins of the abbey on the island. They believed in Christianity. I was told it was born on the island and spread across the mainland. For many years it was everything in the old ways, it shaped the lives and thinking. But it became part of the problem. That's why it was outlawed by the community. It looks like Father Ridley is still a believer. This is the Christian book. I think everything they believe is in here.'

Freya looked at the bible in Aran's hands, grimacing as though the book was dirt. Freya shook her head.

'Have you seen some of the stuff in there? I've just seen something about stoning your kids to death. Is that what they did back then?'

Aran grinned.

'No. At least not for many years. I'm not sure everything in the book is meant to be taken literally. The book's thousands of years old, things change, but

I guess if it's what you believe. I'm sure the old man will explain. Come on. Oh and Freya.'

'What?'

Aran's face turned much harsher, staring into Freya's eyes as spoke. His voice had lost all of the playfulness and was now full of warning.

'Keep it shut, will you? These believers are passionate. It's a huge part of their lives. Remember they're just words and beliefs. They can't hurt us, but they'll mean a lot to Father Ridley and we're his guests.'

'Words and beliefs can't hurt us. You reckon? Our whole life's been built on empty words and beliefs. Not these ones, but the leader's. Of course, they're older and wiser than us, aren't they, so we're just meant to trust them. Well, if their words were so clever how did we end up in this mess? They made it, not us. We just have to live with it.'

Aran and Gaia looked at the floor. Neither responded. There was no point. Freya was right. Freya was saying what they had all thought. That was why they were here. They were young and had inherited the mistakes of the past. The future was meant to belong to the young. They would make things right, but everywhere there were thoughts, ideas, rules that held young people back. The leaders told the young what to think and do, trained them, programmed them. Freya knew there was no point in taking her frustrations out on the others. None of this was their fault. Gaia and Aran hoped to build a better future just like Freya, but it had been a long day, and nothing would change through angry words.

Gaia and Aran laid their weapons on the table and moved towards the door. Freya hesitated, but after a warning look from Aran placed her weapons next to theirs. The group entered a narrow passage which led to a large room. The walls were plastered, though the paintwork was old and faded. A couple more crosses hung on the wall, each with the same figure. The centre of the room was dominated by a narrow, wooden table, around which were six chairs with high ornate backs. The table was set with plates, bowls, cups, glasses and cutlery. It was cluttered, but looked unused and neglected. A grimy white tablecloth with a floral pattern covered it, and two bold six pointed silver candlesticks sat on the table. The room was lined with bookcases which were full to bursting. Books of all colours and sizes, mostly hardbacks, littered the shelves. Each one looked tired and worn. The floor was dark wooden boards which echoed the footsteps. In each corner was an armchair, all different shapes and sizes, with white cloths draped across the back of the headrest. A long narrow window stretched high across one of the walls, letting in some light, but the room was dim and dreary. At the far end there was another doorway leading into the kitchen.

Ruth stood by the far side of the table, still clutching the blanket and sucking her thumb. Ridley was not there, but there was a clatter and bustle of activity through the other door. A voice shouted from the room.

'Please. Take a seat. I'll be with you in a minute.'

All three laid their rucksacks in a corner and each took a chair. Gaia's creaked as she sat. Aran and Gaia sat on the near side by the door they had entered. Freya sat alone opposite, so she could see both doorways. They waited in silence, studying the room. Gaia stared at Ruth who was still passive and unresponsive. The child's eyes had drifted back to the lifeless look of when Gaia first saw her. The fear and panic in the presence of the priest had subsided.

Ridley entered the room with a silver tray. On it was a teapot, a bowl of sugar, some milk and a plate of biscuits. He placed it down on the edge of the table, struggling to find a space.

'There we are now. Seeing as we have guests and it's a special occasion I've got the biscuits out. We don't often have biscuits, do we Ruth? Now how does everyone take it?'

The tea was poured, the biscuits shared. Gaia ate a couple. They were soft and tasted stale. Gaia noticed that Freya ate nothing and left her tea. The priest took the seat at the head of the table, Ruth standing by his side. As the old man took his seat the child's body stiffened and her eyes flared.

'Go get your sisters, will you Ruth my dear? Bring them through to meet our guests.'

Ruth left the room by the far door, as the others exchanged small talk. The child soon returned with two more girls. Both were dressed similar to Ruth in white, tattered dresses. Both were barefoot. One was older, tall and thin, but still a few years younger than Gaia. The older girl had long, black hair and piercing green eyes that shone like emeralds. She was pretty, but her face looked bitter and troubled. The second girl was between the size and ages of Ruth and the elder girl, with stunning green eyes and dazzling long red hair, identical in colour to Gaia's. This was the first time Gaia had ever seen someone else with red hair. While Gaia's hair was shiny and vibrant, this girl's looked dull and lank. The red-haired girl looked more relaxed than the elder, with a warmth, as though she was pleased to see the visitors. Both girl's eyes, gorgeous to look at, shared the same cold, lifeless stare as Ruth. All three girls lined up alongside the priest, each in order of height. Ruth nearest to the old man who smiled and addressed the guests.

'Here we are my pretty things. Now you know Ruth. This is Mary, and the older one is Rebecca. My how they grow up quickly, don't they? Mary and Rebecca these are our guests, Gaia and, sorry could you remind me of your names again. I'm getting old. The memory is going.'

Ridley leaned forward, a questioning look on his face, staring at Freya and Aran in turn.

'Freya.'

'Aran.'

'Yes, of course. Forgive me. Freya and Aran. Unusual names, but interesting. I like them.'

The old man paused, put his cup to his lips and took a long drink. Some tea ran from his mouth and down the side of his chin. The priest took a napkin from the table, dabbed it and sniffed, his nostrils flaring, a snarl sweeping across his face.

'I notice you have their eyes, of the community. I assume you're running from the island. Forgive me if you're not.'

Gaia cast a glance at Freya, an indication to remain quiet. Freya's eyes were ablaze, but she bit her lip and let Gaia answer the priest.

'Yes, we're from the island. We're looking for a group that live in the hills. Things weren't working out for us there so we're looking for something else, a different way of life. They say things are better there. It's a chance for a fresh start for us all.'

The priest placed his hands on his chin, his face pensive. He looked around at the three visitors, weighing them up. They were similar, but different. Ridley could see Freya's guarded body language, and stern expression. She was the one to watch. The suspicious one who lacked trust. The old man knew Freya disliked him.

'I thought as much. I've heard of such groups in the hills. I've had a good few people pass through here over the years and you hear these things. Maybe it's true, perhaps you'll find what you're looking for. Be on your guard though. This whole area is wild. It's filled with those that banished and fled. The community doesn't take kindly to anyone that is different. Especially those that don't think like them.'

Ridley took another drink of tea, finishing the cup, and pouring himself more. He added two sugars, stirred and dipped in a biscuit.

'How rude of me. Would anyone else like some more tea? Young lady. Freya. I notice you haven't drank yours. Aren't you thirsty, my dear?'

Freya stared at the priest, stone faced, silent. A grin threatened to creep from Ridley's lips. It was there, waiting, but the old man did not want to provoke Freya.

'You say you lost a friend. I'm sorry to hear that. Lord rest their soul. It's always heartbreaking when we lose loved ones, but hopefully your friend is at peace now. May I ask what happened?'

Gaia spoke.

'His name was Yann. We were attacked by rats in the castle at the top of the hill. He didn't get away in time.'

The priest stood from his chair and leant forward, reaching over and touching Gaia's hand resting on the table. The old man gripped it and stared at Gaia. His glare was heavy and unsettled her.

'Grieve my child. It's good to weep. Be reassured your friend is now in the arms of the Lord. If he'd opened his heart to Jesus and accepted him there's a place for him with the righteous in eternity in God's kingdom.'

Freya had been simmering, biting her tongue, trying not to let her anger boil over. Freya loathed Ridley and everything he stood for. She was playing along with the charade for the others, but could see the priest for what he was. The sanctimonious piety and sickening insincerity was choking Freya. She felt sick listening to the priest's formality and pompous words. Ridley had wrapped himself in a blanket of authority, with a uniform of credibility, but he was a fraud. The collar meant nothing, a symbol of all that had plunged the world into chaos. Where was God in this world? Where was he when Yann needed him? God had stood by while the chosen ones ruined the world, abandoned them all to live like animals. If Ridley's God existed he was cruel and indifferent, and let people suffer. God had abandoned the world to desolation and despair, and the community had banished God. This was the new world order. Freya's anger and disdain erupted.

'Yann didn't open his heart to your god, or Jesus. He didn't accept them. We didn't have time to ask him seeing as your god sat back as our friend had his throat ripped out. You see old man, we kill to survive and sometimes we die as a result. That is the way we live now. It's the world people like you have given us. We don't need your god.'

Aran stepped in, eager to snuff Freya's anger, and undo any damage caused. Aran and Gaia were both thrusting spear like looks at Freya.

'Sorry, can I apologise for my friend's outburst. It's been a traumatic day for us all. We're all feeling the loss of our friend. Freya apologise to Father Ridley.'

Aran continued to press Freya with piercing looks, waiting as she released her teeth from her lips. Freya put her head down and spat out a sorry. There was a silence, as everyone looked at her. She eased her head upwards, scowled and peered at Aran through the edge of her eyebrows. Aran was furious. Freya had gone too far, but could not care less. Freya knew what she had to do and spoke again. This time in a softer voice.

'I'm sorry.'

Aran lifted his stare, still frowning, and turned to the old man.

'I hope you accept all our apologies Father Ridley. We aren't well versed in your beliefs. They're not taught in the community. We've been taught to mistrust your ideas, programmed to attack them and sometimes the instinct takes over. I know Freya didn't mean to offend you.'

Ridley smiled, reached forward and offered his hand to Aran who took it and shook. The priest turned to Freya.

'My dear, there's no harm done. Believe me, I understand what you've been through. I know the community. I know exactly.'

There was a long pause as the priest pondered his next words, wanting to choose with care.

'I've got first hand experience of the community and their ways. Now let's forget this and say no more about it. We don't want it to spoil our time together now, do we?'

Ridley held out his hand to Freya, hanging for a moment, waiting for her to accept his token of peace. Freya sat unfazed and defiant. Despite the apology the body language spoke otherwise. Freya still bubbled with anger and was trying to dampen the urge to explode again. Aran and Gaia continued to stare at their friend, but Freya ignored them, looking down at the priest's outstretched hand. Freya waited, as the old man's hand began to tremble, not through fear, but the ache in his arm as he waited for a response. Freya reached out and took it, gripping the hand as hard as she could. Freya looked at Ridley, her face blank, all emotion buried deep inside. Her voice was a bland, lifeless whisper.

'I am truly sorry. No hard feelings.'

Freya and Ridley each let go. The priest smiled and stepped back, clasping his hands together and addressing them all, as though giving a sermon.

'Why don't you all get some rest. Those armchairs are comfy, if a little old like me. Me and the girls will prepare you all some dinner. You're more than welcome to join us. In fact you're welcome to spend the night. Please stay and rest and see how you feel in the morning. Then you can continue with your journey. Like you said, you've had a tough day and I can see that you all need some good food, wine and a decent sleep. You'll be safe.'

The group were all too tired to question. Freya was on her guard, but this was wrapped in humility after the outburst. Gaia and Aran could see no danger from an old man and a few girls, however strange they may seem. Gaia sensed something. It was a place filled with secrets, but compared to the chaos outside it was a sanctuary. The church was secure and offered a roof to sleep under. That was something they all needed.

Gaia, Aran, and Freya settled down in the armchairs in the corners of the room. Gaia soon drifted off into a restless and troubled sleep, dreaming of Kali, the same dream as before. Gaia was in the windowless room with the sick odour of damp. She was in a chair talking to Kali. The conversation was intense, and Gaia had a strong feeling of fear. There was someone in the corner, hiding in the shadows. Gaia could sense they were there, could feel their presence. Gaia noticed as the light caught the faintest glimpse of their boots. They were the standard issue boots, but there was something familiar about them. It was the distinctive pattern, the battered shape, the wear and tear. Gaia recognised the boots, but could not think who they belonged to. Gaia fought to find where she had seen them, but could not. There was Kali's face again, large, distorted and pressed into Gaia's. There was water and Gaia was drowning, gasping for air, as the liquid flooded her lungs. There was a strong arm holding Gaia down as the water was poured into her mouth. Something covered her mouth. There was Kali's face, and hand, reaching out. There was a feeling of panic, the fear of drowning, a desperate struggle for air. All Gaia could see were the boots, the familiar boots, but still she could not picture the owner, the person in the shadows.

16

Aran and Freya were at the table, the same seats as before. The room had darkened, the little natural light the narrow window provided had gone. The candles on the table were lit casting a faint glow around the room. Gaia stood up, stretched and yawned, and took a seat at the table with the others. Aran gave a warm smile, the pale light of the candles giving his face a much more colourful hue. Aran seemed to be recovering, his spirits lifting with his growing strength. The rest had done him good. Freya played with a fork, looking agitated and unsettled. The sleep had not calmed her troubles or temper. Aran spoke.

'Did you sleep well?'

'I did thanks, you?'

'Great.'

Gaia looked at Freya.

'And you Freya?'

Freya kept twirling the fork in her fingers, stabbing the table. Without looking up she forced a response.

'I didn't sleep much. I'll feel much better when we get out of here.'

Ridley entered the room with a serving bowl. It was heaped with mashed potatoes, steam still gushing from them. He placed the tray in the centre of the table.

'Good morning all. Of course I should say good evening. I trust you all slept well?'

Aran and Gaia nodded and thanked the priest. Freya grunted and continued her preoccupations with the cutlery. The three girls followed Ridley into the room, each carrying a serving dish of assorted vegetables. They laid them down on the table.

Rebecca stood nearest to Gaia. As the elder girl reached over to lay down the dish Gaia noticed her wrists were scuffed with deep, dark purple and yellow bruises. Rebecca stepped back and pulled her sleeves down, with a nervous glance at Gaia, and look of alarm in her eyes. Gaia looked across at Freya who was staring back, a knowing expression on her face.

Ridley took his seat and the young girls left the room, returning with more food and a jug of wine. Rebecca placed a plate in the centre of the table with a roasted bird on it. Ruth laid a large gravy bowl to the left side of the priest, and Mary the decanter of red wine to his right. All three girls left the room, and Freya spoke.

'Are the girls not joining us?'

'No, they ate earlier. They'll go to their rooms and do some study. They read the Lord's book each night.'

Freya continued to question the priest.

'They don't talk much, do they?'

The priest stood up, took a large knife and fork from the table. He began to carve the bird, responding to Freya as he eased the knife back and forth.

'They're quiet girls. They all had troubled lives before they came here. They're not my own children, though I look after them as if they were.'

Ridley continued to slice layers of flesh from the bird, placing each fresh slice onto a side plate. His face was intent, total concentration, never looking up from his task as he spoke.

'When they came to me they were lost and alone, deeply damaged. The poor things. Their parents had lived perilous lives. They were desperate for support, for love. That's what was missing from their lives, love. I offered to take them in and save them. Give them all the love they needed. God's love.'

The priest paused, the long carving knife still pressed against the remainder of the flesh.

'It's been a challenge. Each day we seek forgiveness for their sins through prayer. Each day we study the word of God, and the teachings of his son Jesus. Each day their hearts grow strong again. But each of them has a long road ahead before they find peace and salvation. We all do, it's the journey we have to make. It's through that journey that we learn the truth.'

Ridley sat back in his seat, and gazed at the feast before them. He opened his arms and looked up at his guests.

'I know you think you don't have God in your hearts, but may I ask that we put our hands together in prayer and thank the good Lord for the food he's given us.'

Ridley waited. Aran and Gaia looked at each other, both hesitant and unsure. Sensing their confusion, the priest pressed the palm of his hands together. Aran and Gaia copied him. Aran glared at Freya who did the same. All four paused for a moment, the warm, red glow of the candlelight flickering in their eyes. The priest closed his eyes, Aran and Gaia likewise. Freya did not. She stared across at Ridley as he bowed his head, her face burning with simmering rage. There was a look of peace and tranquility spread across the old man's face, the same look as the man on the cross. It was a knowing calm, as if nothing could hurt him, despite all the pain. The priest spoke in a hushed voice, not quite a whisper.

'Dear Lord, we thank you for the gifts of your bounty which we enjoy at this table. Gifts you have provided for us in the past and our times of need. We thank you for our guests and wish them a safe passage as they continue their journey. While we enjoy your great gifts we spare a thought for their friend who sadly is not here to savour your grace. But we know you will take care of him in your great kingdom. Thank you Lord. Amen.'

Ridley opened his eyes and lowered his hands. Freya was still glaring at him. She too placed her hands on the table. Aran and Gaia remained still, their eyes closed, hands clasped in front of them in prayer. Freya kicked Aran under the table as the priest spoke.

'We've finished. You can open your eyes again now. Thank you.'

Gaia looked at the food spread before them, a banquet she had not seen the likes of before. Aran kept the conversation ticking over, keen to placate their host and make up for Freya's rudeness.

'Thank you for this. It looks delicious. You clearly enjoy your food.'

'What pleasures are there left in this world? It is the simplest of things to enjoy God's gifts. We seem to have forgotten all that is still to enjoy.'

They helped themselves to the food, as Ridley poured each a generous glass of red wine. The priest passed around the gravy insisting they poured ample. The old man raised his glass.

'Please join me. The wine has been blessed. Now let us drink.'

The priest took a long drink, watching the others as they followed. They ate, the food was good, grown by the old man and girls in a plot of land at the rear of the church. The bird was a chicken, procured from the village nearby. Many local people would meet there. It was a trading point where you could pick up basic items, and trade for food. The priest was resourceful, the cupboards seldom bare and the table always blessed with the finer things that remained.

The initial conversation was warm and jovial, with Ridley pleased to have guests. It was a rare event and he wanted to make the most of it. Aran and Gaia enjoyed the company, and the chance to eat in comfort. Freya was polite, but Gaia could sense her tension. Gaia was troubled by the bruises on Rebecca's wrists, but for now put it to the back of her mind, determined to enjoy the meal.

Soon the conversation turned to their past, of the island and the escape. The priest sat and listened as Gaia and Aran filled in the details, Freya offering the occasional nod and grunt. Everyone but Freya was chatty, but even Aran and Gaia were still guarded. They only gave the old man enough information. Freya continued to eye Ridley, and Gaia could see she was weighing him up. Freya's mistrust was plain to see, and after a few more grunts Freya spoke.

'What about you Father Ridley? You said you've had experience of the community. Tell us more.'

Ridley laid down his knife and fork, and took a sip of wine. He leant on his elbows and played with his lips. The others waited, unsure of whether he would respond. Freya had hit a nerve, poked at something uncomfortable, as had been her intention. After another longer drink of wine the priest spoke.

'The community is a godless world. They fear everything, even each other. Myself and others like me tried to make them see that only through God's word and love could the world move forward. We had an opportunity to make amends. The old world lost its way, became blinded by science and money. They lusted after greed and progress. They walked in the wilderness and took the hand of Satan, and look where it led us. They abandoned God and he punished us. But some of us survived. This was God giving us another chance, as he had done before. It was a chance for us all to be born again. The community could've taken that chance and embraced God and Jesus, but they feared and condemned them. The community feared the truth. So they banished us, persecuted us. I got out, escaped, just like you. Before they could punish me. Some of the others were not so fortunate.'

The priest paused and filled his glass, taking another long drink. His hand was shaking, as he placed the glass down on the table and stared at Freya.

'There are those in this world who cannot find love within their hearts. But without love the world is full of hate. The community is filled with that hatred, it breeds it. There are many I see who carry that hatred within them. Cast it out. Whatever you're looking for find God's love. If you don't you'll also walk in the wilderness. But you must look for it. If you try to find God he will find you.'

Freya stared back at the priest, playing with her food. Their eyes were locked, neither wanting to break free or look away, not even a blink. Freya picked up a knife and began to spin it in her hand. She spoke, her voice calm, but with an ominous almost threatening tone.

'We've been through a lot. More than you will know. My head is spinning with those older and wiser than me telling me what's right and wrong, and what I should and shouldn't do. Maybe you're right. Maybe this god you have found has the answers, but I'd like the chance to find those answers for myself. We all do. That's why we left.'

Freya kept spinning the knife on the palm of her hand, twisting and twirling it between her fingers. She continued.

'All my life I've been told what to think, what to feel, and what to do. I guess what I'm saying is those days have gone. Now I make my own decisions. I'll make some bad ones, but they'll be my mistakes, no one else's. I'm no longer living my life for others.'

Freya stabbed the knife into a piece of chicken. There was an uncomfortable silence. Aran and Gaia looked on, each wanting to step in, but neither sure how to respond. They agreed with Freya and the Father needed to know that. The young had been let down by those that went before. The future was meant to be for them, yet still the leaders controlled them. The elders did not want to let go. The priest shuffled in the chair, his stare had softened, eyes drifting around the room. Freya knew she had rattled the old man, and decided to move onto another topic that intrigued her.

'This Jesus you talk about. He was the son of this God you say. I'm curious about this.'

Ridley sat up, surprised, a look of pleasure lit up his face. There was a moment of joy that Freya had taken an interest, and the priest was keen to enlighten his guests. The old man stood and moved to the wall, leaning beside one of the numerous crucifixes. He surveyed them all and pointed to the figure of the man hanging from the cross. The priest puffed up his chest, brimming with a sense of pride and adopted his sermon persona.

'This is Jesus Christ, the son of God. He was sent to us by his father to show us all a new way, because

God saw the world had become lost and was full of sin. Jesus was crucified by the Romans, and betrayed by the sons of Israel, his own people. Jesus died for all our sins, but was resurrected and ascended to his father. He died and was resurrected to save us. God did this to save us, to show us the measure of his love and remind us of his word. My faith in the resurrection is what makes me who I am. God has shown himself to me and I know this faith to be true.'

Freya frowned and continued to press.

'When did all this happen?'

'It was over 2,000 years ago, in Palestine, a place many miles from here. It's all written down and documented in the Bible. That is the word of God.'

The priest moved to a bookcase, took three copies of the red book and passed them around.

'Open the book. Look at the sections written by Matthew, Mark, Luke, and John. They all capture the life and words of Jesus. They're words of love and compassion.'

Freya and Aran opened up the red books and began to thumb through the pages. Gaia continued to eat her food. She had seen the words of the book earlier, and had no desire to read more. Freya stopped at a page, a smile on her face.

'Here's an interesting one. It's Matthew ten, twenty one. It says, *'And the brother shall deliver the brother up to death, and the father the child: and the children shall rise up against the parents, and cause them to be put to death.'* I must admit I like that.'

Ridley looked uncomfortable, trying to respond but Freya continued before the priest could answer.

'Oh and look at this other passage further down the page, ten, thirty four *'Think not that I come to send peace on earth: I came not to send peace, but a sword.'* Now that's what I like to hear. Maybe he's not so bad after all this Jesus.'

The priest interrupted, hearing enough.

'Those words are out of context. Jesus was love, and spoke of the importance of love. Look in John chapter thirteen, verse thirty four. Jesus says, '*A new commandment I give to you, that you love one another: just as I have loved you, you are also to love one another.*'

Freya twisted her face, a mocking look of confusion. Her voice was filled with sarcasm.

'I'm confused. Which of those do I believe? They seem a bit contradictory to me.'

The priest continued his defence.

'The testaments are complex, and contain contradictions. They have to be seen in their historical context. They must be studied. Some of the words and sentiments must be seen as of their time. But read the words, study them, and you will see they are words filled with love.'

Freya laughed and shook her head.

'What about the historical context we're in now. This godless world you describe, maybe we need sentiments that are right for now. How is your God's love going to save us?'

'Leave it Freya! Father Ridley has welcomed us, cooked for us, provided us with shelter. The least we can do is treat him with respect. I think you owe him an apology.'

Aran had heard enough. He knew Freya. There was no real interest in this other than attacking the priest. Freya believed in nothing. Aran's voice was stern and abrupt, reflecting his anger. Freya looked shocked, but tried to defend herself.

'Look I was just…'

'Apologise!'

Freya and Aran's eyes locked, as Freya fumed at her humiliation. The priest said nothing, wallowing in satisfaction, waiting for the apology to come. Ridley looked at Freya with a smug, expectant expression, while Freya took her time. She continued to glare at Aran, unwilling to look away, knowing there was no choice. Whatever Freya thought of the priest, whatever his views, Aran was right, at least for now. The priest would be found out soon.

Freya heard the words of the priest and his God, but only heard the words of man. Ridley's faith in these words had been given credence and value through centuries of blind indoctrination. Freya and the others had been spared this, but had been fed a different kind, one Freya and the other young people may never overcome. They were all controlled by a different tyranny, but Freya would walk alone. She would find her own path, her own truth. No-one would tell Freya what to do ever again, especially not an old man in a strange suit and white tie worshipping stories thousands of years old. Freya took a deep breath and uttered the words the others had been waiting for.

'I'm sorry. Forgive me.'

The priest nodded his head, a smug look still spread over his face. The old man basked in his glory, the hollow victory. It would be short-lived.

'Of course I forgive you my child. Let's say no more about it.'

They continued to eat, and after a period of silence the conversation turned to other topics - their plans, and what they hoped to find. Ridley was quiet and coy on the subject of the community in the hills. Gaia felt sure he would know of it, heard rumours in discussions with others at the nearby village. Gaia sensed the priest knew more, but would not share it. Gaia finished her food and asked to be excused.

'Is there a toilet I could use?'

'Of course. It's just through the kitchen. There's a passage at the back. It's the room at the very end.'

Gaia rose and made her way through the kitchen which had already been cleaned, the cooking pots washed and draining by the sink. The inviting smell of the meal still dominated the room. Gaia's hunger was satisfied and she was as full as she had ever been. She made her way through a door and along a narrow passage. The floor was covered in tattered carpet with a garish floral pattern. The walls had candlesticks mounted along them, an assortment of different sized candles lit her way.

As Gaia neared the doorway at the end of the passage, she heard a noise from the room to the left. The door was ajar. Gaia stopped and leaned towards the crack of the open door. She could hear something. It was faint, but Gaia focused on the sound. It was the soft whisper of a girl's voice in repetitive chanting. The words were monotonous and lifeless. Gaia leant against the door, edging it open, pushing her head through the gap.

The room was bare with only an iron framed bed against the wall, the floor exposed wooden boards. On the wall was a mounted candleholder with a solitary candle casting a dingy light around the room. On the other wall above the bed was the man on the cross again, Jesus light and saviour. On the bed sat Rebecca, reading the red book and chanting. Her voice was faint, almost inaudible. Then Gaia noticed the full horror.

At the top of the bed attached to the iron frame were a set of handcuffs. The bed sheets, filthy and torn were also stained in dark red. Rebecca did not look up. She just sat at the bottom of the bed, chanting the bland, hypnotic words. Gaia stepped back, and pulled the door to a little, pausing to contemplate what she had seen. She felt strange, a touch dizzy and queasy. Images began to flash in Gaia's mind, distorted visions invading.

Gaia made it to the toilet and struggled back to the main room, her mind a flurry of dark images, some clear and lucid. Gaia was aware of everything that was happening, but some of her mind was fighting her. This part was full of the crazed, dancing visions darting and dashing. Gaia's lucid mind was trying to suppress these wild thoughts, cast them out, control them, but she could not. Gaia sat, her mind bombarded with the building chaos. There were voices, words. They were heated and animated, but familiar. It was Ridley and Freya fighting again. This time more aggressive. Gaia looked across at Aran, his face was clear, but his head was tossing and turning, lit up with a delirious smile. Aran's face became distorted with large, bulbous eyes. He was giggling like a giant, hideous child bearing down on her.

Gaia looked at the priest, his face twisted and filled with rage. He was standing and pointing at Freya. The old man's finger morphed into a long metal sword and his face melted. Gaia saw a demon with sharp, pointed teeth and salivating jaws, the teeth of the rats. Ridley's eyes burned blood red and his head grew two pointed and twisted horns. The priest began to laugh, a loud and uncontrollable cackle. It was chilling, the sound ripping though Gaia's body like a cold knife.

Gaia could feel herself trembling. The clear part of her mind was speaking to her, reassuring her, telling her this was all a dark nightmare. The voice stopped, paused amid all the chaos that reigned inside, the demon face, the blood curdling laughter. Gaia began to panic. What if it would always be this way? What if she never woke up? What if the rest of her life was this endless struggle between clarity and chaos? What if this was all she would know? Gaia was staring at madness, what it meant to be insane, clarity and control versus chaos. A surge of panic rushed through Gaia's body, her mind now in overdrive, drowning in the frenzy of images. One by one the visions flashed through her head, dark, disturbing, delirious and delightful. Layer upon layer of twisted thoughts, simultaneously, merging into one, a collage of chaos. Then there was darkness.

17

Gaia opened her eyes. Freya was standing over her. Gaia was in one of the armchairs, head hazy, still with faint echoes of the madness from the night before. Images drifted in and out of Gaia's mind, but less intense, like clouds rumbling in the distance after a huge lightning storm. The skies were clear and blue now. There was control again, confused control. Freya reached out and touched Gaia, whispered.

'How are you feeling?'

'I still feel a bit strange. What happened?'

'Ridley drugged us. It was probably in the wine, a hallucinogen, probably from wild mushrooms. They grow all over this place and there's loads this time of year on damp mornings. I bet you had some crazy dreams.'

Gaia thought back to the night before, the cacophony of images flashed through her mind. At first the memories were patchy, just flickers, but became more vivid, almost real. The demonic face appeared, the horns and snarling teeth. There was the same surge of panic as the fear returned. Gaia was staring into the abyss again, standing on a precipice, about to plunge into a dark, spiralling black hole of madness. She was in the crazed world, her lucid mind locked in battle with wild, anarchic thoughts. Gaia shook her head, tried to rid herself of the haze.

'I thought I'd gone mad.'

Freya put her hand on Gaia's shoulder.

'I'm sure you did. The drugs unlock something in your mind, open your thoughts. They take over and you feel as though you've lost control. In the right environment they can be amazing, but in the wrong place and the situation we were in last night. I can understand why you panicked.'

Freya sat on a dining chair and faced Gaia who was looking around the room in search of the others. Aran was sleeping in the armchair in the opposite corner. The table was a mess, broken crockery and food scattered on the floor. Ridley and the girls were not there. Gaia spoke.

'How is Aran?'

'Aran'll sleep it off, like you. I'll wake him soon.'

'And you?'

Freya grinned, one of her sly, knowing grins.

'I was fine. I didn't drink any of the wine. I made it look like I did, but you know me by now I trust no-one. I never liked that slimy bastard from the start. I never trust the righteous, they usually have something to hide.'

An image flashed into Gaia's head. It was a dim, dreary, candle-lit room, an iron-frame bed, handcuffs, blood stained sheets, a girl chanting, Rebecca. Gaia struggled for a moment, thinking it was a dream, another mad thought. She realised it had been real. An overwhelming sense of pain and sorrow swept through her as Gaia felt the depth of Rebecca's suffering. An image of Clara flashed into Gaia's head. Rebecca, Clara, then Rebecca again, the two images jostling until they blurred into one. This was real, all of it.

'Freya, I saw something last night. Rebecca was in her room.'

'I know.'

Freya interrupted her, got up from the chair. Leaning forward Freya gripped Gaia's shoulders. It was a firm grip. Freya let go, knelt beside Gaia and began to stroke her shiny red hair. Gaia was crying, tears trickled from her eyes. Freya wiped her friend's cheeks, caught them with her fingers, and spoke.

'Everything is sorted now. We'll wake Aran, and decide on our next move.'

Freya got to her feet and extended her hand to help her friend up. Gaia took her arm and struggled to her feet, putting her arm over Freya's shoulder as her feet buckled.

'I'm still a bit frazzled. Where are Ridley and the girls?'

'I'll show you.'

They woke Aran who was still dazed, drifting into other thoughts, wincing at the dark images. Freya explained everything, that it would fade, they would be fine, with the occasional flashback. Freya led Gaia and Aran into the main church area.

Ridley was in front of the table by the large stained window. He was on his knees, hands stretched out straight, tied with a rope across the table. The priest resembled the cross that stood on the table just behind. Ridley's head was also bowed and he too was bleeding from his face and forehead. At first Gaia thought the old man was dead, but noticed the slow, steady movement of his chest, and heard the rattle of breathing. It was weak and laboured, he looked exhausted, near dead. Freya approached the table.

'We need to decide what we do with him. I didn't want to do anything until you woke. You might think I took matters into my own hands.'

Freya looked at Aran, who was still too dazed to catch any hidden meanings. Gaia spoke.

'Where are the girls?'

'Ruth and Mary are in a room in the back. Rebecca ran away just before you woke. She slipped out of a door at the back. We need to move quickly. She might have gone to get others.'

Aran's eyes were still glazed. The decision sat with Gaia and Freya. Gaia spoke.

'What do you think?'

Freya leant over the old man and grabbed him by the hair, pulling his head back. Gaia could now see his battered face, caked in dried blood. His cheeks and eyes were swollen, his mouth quivered as he snarled at Freya. The priest opened his dry lips, ripping them apart.

'Have mercy, please. In the name of God have mercy. Leave me here. I can do you no harm.'

Freya sneered at him, pulling his hair tighter. The priest winced with the pain, as Freya pressed her face close to his ear and spat the words at him.

'Mercy. Is that what you showed Rebecca, Mary, and Ruth? Is that what you call mercy? I've been round the back and seen the fresh graves. Did you drug their parents and kill them? What were you planning to do with us? You're a sick old man hiding behind your words. I'm going to show you our mercy.'

Gaia stepped forward and tugged at Freya's free arm.

'Let him go Freya. We need to talk about this, think it through. We're better than him.'

Freya let go of Ridley's hair and stepped back. Her eyes were still locked on the priest, her face gripped with fury and disdain. Freya wiped the spit from her mouth and spoke. Her voice was cool and calm, still in control.

'We've got two choices. We leave him and go, or I finish him off.'

Gaia was hesitant, trying to come up with alternatives, but her mind was still a blur.

'Do you not think there's been enough killing?'

Freya's eyes remained focused on the priest, locked in a cold stare.

'I think there's been too much death, and too many innocents have died, but this is different. Some people deserve to die.'

Ridley laughed collapsing into a fit of coughing. The old man looked up at Freya, swollen lips trying to force out words, bloodied eyes searching for her face. He mustered the energy, his voice frail.

'Do what you will. You can't hurt me. I've got God on my side. Whatever happens I'm prepared to face him. It's only his judgement I recognise. Only he can grant my forgiveness.'

Gaia looked at the priest's pitiful face. There was a glimmer of pleasure behind the blood and bruising as the old man still clutched his blind passion, even in the last throws of death. Gaia knelt down in front of him, much closer, so he could make out her face.

'Why'd you do it? Why them? They trusted you. They're just kids. Why?'

The old man lifted his weary head. Blood filled saliva ran from his cracked lips, head scanning the room, searching with his bruised and swollen eyes. Ridley was trying to find the girls, but they were safe. The priest's voice was just a broken whisper now.

'God gave them to me to love as though they were my own.'

The old man lowered his head and began to mumble, his voice and body draining of all energy and life, managing to splutter a few final words.

'I will answer to the Lord for my sins, not you.'

Freya stepped forward. She stood over the old man, lifted his head and stared down at his face. Without expression Freya thrust her knife into the centre of the priest's chest, lifting him from the floor as the knife twisted in her clenched fist. Ridley winced, his mouth open wide, gasping for air. Freya kept thrusting and twisting, as the priest struggled, the life seeping from him. Freya pressed her face close to his, and whispered, her face a sneer.

'Consider this an act of mercy. Go meet your saviour, face the truth and be judged.'

Ridley's body relaxed as the life slipped from him. He lurched forward against Freya as she eased the knife from his chest, a circle of dark red blood forming in his pullover. Freya shuffled back, rose to her feet, and stood over the old man. All three looked down at the lifeless body as it hung from the table, arms still outstretched, head leant forward. Gaia looked at the cross on the table, and back down at the priest. Gaia reached out and took Freya and Aran's hands.

Freya took a white sheet from one of the tables and threw it over the body. Gaia collected the girls from the room at the back of the church. They were cowering in the corner, the room they had shared for many years. This had been the scene of their torture and abuse at the hands of someone who was meant to protect. The room was sparse and filthy, both clutched the red book in their hands. They were chanting passages, dazed and in a trance.

Gaia found the girls some socks, shoes, and warm clothes. She took the red books and placed them on bloodied beds, then led each girl to the door. Neither said a word. Gaia looked back at the room, their life. It was a pitiful scene, just two beds, covered in filthy mattresses, some wall mounted candles and a crucifix. Ruth still clutched her blanket and sucked her thumb, both stared with blank expressions. The girls were gone. They had been destroyed. The priest claimed he was saving their souls, but he had taken them instead. Ridley had raped their innocence, and stolen their youth.

Gaia led them back into the kitchen. Aran and Freya were rummaging through the cupboards, taking anything useful they could find. Freya was agitated.

'We need to move quickly guys. Rebecca could have found people, raised the alarm. Let's get going.'

Freya checked outside in case any rats remained. Reassured it was clear Freya led them out the rear door and through the graveyard. They soon reached the woods that surrounded the church. The girls were slow, but followed without speaking. The group zig-zagged through the sparse trees and thin undergrowth with ease.   After a short while Gaia spotted something up ahead, something odd moving in the trees. The view was obstructed. She stopped and signalled to the others to wait. Aran stood by her shoulder and spoke.

'What's wrong?'

'Can you see that over there? There's something in the trees.'

Gaia pointed in the direction of the object. It was white. They caught brief flashes as it moved and twirled through the gap in the leaves and branches. They edged forward, and neared a gap. Gaia realised what it was. In a tree, hanging from a long overhanging branch was a body. It was limp and lifeless, twisting and twirling from a thick rope. A pair of soft, delicate feet pointed to the earth, and a grubby white dress covered a slender frame. The broken neck was draped in long, flowing black hair. It was Rebecca.

Gaia turned to shelter the two younger girls, protect them, but it was too late. The girls stood there impassive, staring at the swinging corpse. There was no reaction, no expression. Gaia turned Ruth and Mary the other way while Aran and Freya cut down the body and laid it on the ground. Freya placed Rebecca's hands on her chest and sprinkled some of the golden, fresh fallen leaves across her body until she was covered and out of view. Gaia knelt before the girls.

'Look girls. What we've just seen, your sister. I'm sorry. Maybe she's in a better place now, away from all this.'

Gaia hugged the girls, held them tight for a few moments, let them go.

'Don't worry. I'm going to take care of you now. You're safe now. I'll protect you. Do you understand?'

The girls looked at Gaia, the same blank expressions, Ruth still sucking her thumb, Mary's face cold and vacant. There was no comment or reaction. Gaia spoke again.

'We're going to the hills. There's a community there who can help us. We'll be safe there.'

Gaia hugged the girls again, feeling their bodies both stiffen as she held them. They were trembling. Gaia let go and got to her feet. Aran had approached. Gaia took his hand and whispered.

'We'll take care of them, won't we?'

Aran squeezed Gaia's hand and nodded, she put her head on his shoulder. Aran lifted Gaia's hand and kissed it. They looked at each other, his face was soft with a warm, gentle smile. Gaia felt a rush through her body again, the burning in her stomach. For the briefest moment Gaia felt safe and happy, as though nothing else mattered. All pain and fear had gone. It was as though the past few days had been just dreams. In a world of fear and chaos they still had a chance of a better future, something to live for. It was something Rebecca never had, something she never found, something they were all searching for, even those who did not know it.

Everyone gathered around the mound of golden leaves with heads bowed. Gaia and Aran held the hands of Mary and Ruth. This was their opportunity to say goodbye. The girls were silent, without emotion, but Gaia was sure they would be hurting. The sisters had spent a long time together in those dark cells, in the clutches of the priest. They were united in the bond of their pain and suffering. They had been a family of sorts, a dark, dysfunctional family. Perhaps this was the only type of family left in the world. Gaia had never known family. Her only family had been the community. Gaia had no mother or father, no sisters or brothers. Maybe that was what she was searching for? The love, security and stability of family. Maybe that was the truth she was meant to find?

Gaia gazed into the treetops. The morning breeze was crisp and biting, playing with the branches. A few russet leaves drifted to the ground lilting like boats on the waves. Autumn was in its prime, the harvest month, the time of endings, and new beginnings. The time before winter comes and the long darkness falls. Like all the seasons it heralds change. Gaia heard the squawk of a bird, a harsh and bitter call. She looked into the branches and saw two black crows with grey hooded caps. One had a small bird in its mouth, struggling, flapping its wings, desperate to escape the murderous grip. The crow played with it, squeezed the last droplets of life from its victim. The other bird stood by letting out a callous cackle, a triumphant cry of victory. They both flew down to the earth beneath the tree and began to peck at their victim, rip its small, lifeless body apart with their black pointed beaks. Gaia looked on, fascinated and horrified by the cruel sight. Ruth and Mary gazed ahead in silence letting the world and chaos drift by, the controlled chaos of nature.

The group made their way through the woods until they reached the edge of the trees. A field beyond snaked down and around the foot of a hill. The other side was where the river began again. Freya and Aran led the others across the field towards the water. The river was much narrower now, just a few isolated trees dotted its banks. The land was rising, the going tougher as they neared the hills. They would reach the lower stretches by nightfall, and by tomorrow would begin the steeper climb into the higher ground. They would continue to follow the river, to its source, to the place where its journey began and theirs would end.

Later that morning, as the sun reached its highest point in the sky they saw a small village in the distance, about a mile beyond. They could see no people, only a trail of smoke billowing from one of the chimneys. Freya led them as they crept towards a small barn, a safe distance from the village. Aran and Freya ran ahead to search the building while Gaia hid with Ruth and Mary behind one of the few remaining trees. Despite the clear sky and sunshine it was cold, and Gaia huddled close to the girls to keep them warm. The sisters were silent, still locked in vacant expressions.

Aran and Freya returned. The barn was empty apart from some rusting farmyard equipment and a few bales of hay. Keeping low they shuffled towards the building and took refuge inside, throwing down their packs and lying back against the bales. Everyone lay in silence. Gaia could still feel the effects of the drug, but the sickness had gone, replaced with a hunger. Gaia sat up and spoke.

'Is anyone hungry?'

Aran and Freya nodded. Gaia took some food from one of the backpacks and handed it to the girls. They took it, ate without speaking. It was clear both were hungry. Aran and Freya devoured the cheese and fruit, then Aran lay down and closed his eyes. Freya got to her feet and paced around the barn, disappearing for a while. Soon she returned and approached Gaia.

'Stay here and watch these. I'm going to have a look in the village and see what I can find.'

Gaia frowned.

'Are you sure that's a good idea?'

'There's people there, I've just seen some. I just want to check out if they're friendly or not. We're not far from the hills. They may know something about this community we're looking for.'

Gaia was still nervous, but knew Freya and there was little point in trying to change her mind.

'OK, but be careful.'

'I will.'

Freya winked at Gaia and scurried off. The girls were sleeping. Gaia shuffled closer to Aran and laid her head back alongside his, staring at the ceiling. It was a pitched roof of wooden beams, stained with bird droppings and peppered with old nests. The frame of the barn was metal, lined with wooden planks, many of which were rotting. The floor was scattered with hay and dirt. The opposite side of the barn had a pen for animals, with metal fenceposts and intermittent troughs. The barn smelt dank, a mixture of rotten hay and animal dung. The putrid smell made Gaia feel nauseous. Her eyes felt heavy, struggling to stay open and soon Gaia drifted and began to daydream. Her mind was filled with the picture of a moment earlier, when Aran had smiled at her. Gaia could feel all her emotions again, how the care and worry had washed from her body. She longed to know that warmth and pleasure, never let him go.

Gaia felt Aran take her hand, and play with her fingers. Her eyes stayed closed, focusing on his gentle touch. Joy flowed through Gaia's body, a warm sensation in the pit of her stomach, rising to her heart. She sensed Aran move and felt the heat of his breath against her cheek. Their lips touched. They both opened their mouths, locked together in a tender embrace. Gaia's heart was racing, her whole body felt alive. Her eyes were still shut, and a kaleidoscope of colours swirled inside. Their lips parted and Gaia could still feel Aran's breath on her face. As her eyes opened Gaia saw Aran's piercing blue eyes staring into hers. There was a life in them, something she had not seen for days. There was a joy and longing, as Aran whispered.

'I'm sorry, I couldn't help myself. I've been wanting to do that for some time now.'

'There's no need to say sorry. I've been hoping you would.'

Aran kissed her again, a shorter kiss but still filling Gaia with the flurry of emotion.

'I guess we haven't had much of an opportunity with all that's been happening.'

'I guess not.'

Aran lay back and held Gaia's hand. They lay in silence as he played with her fingers once more. After a while Aran spoke.

'You like that don't you?'

'What?'

'Me playing with your fingers!'

'Oh that, yes.'

Gaia tickled the palm of his hand, and Aran laughed.

'You don't mind, do you?'

'No, keep doing it. It's nice. I like it.'

As they sat together Gaia was overwhelmed with happiness and joy. She had never felt this way. All her life she had felt alone, something Gaia had accepted, blocking out others and forging a solitary path of her own. She had built a wall and not wanted to let anyone in for fear of what she might find. The leaders were at best functional and passive, at worst they were manipulative and abusive. Gaia had always been running, but had now found something she had longed for. Aran had offered Gaia a way of escaping the island. He had given her the chance to leave the old life behind, and find a new freedom. Now Aran had given Gaia more, something to live for. Whatever happened, whatever freedom they all found, Gaia wanted to share it with Aran. As they sat, and Gaia savoured her thoughts of happiness, Aran's breath warmed her neck. He whispered.

'I'm sorry I've put you through all this.'

'Stop apologising. I'm here because I want to be. You didn't force me to come. There's no need to say sorry.'

Aran let go of her hand and sat up. There was a long pause. Aran was sitting forward now, staring at the floor. Gaia could not see his face as he spoke.

'No. This hasn't turned out as I planned it and there's something I need to tell you.'

Gaia put her arm around him.

'What is it? Is there something wrong?'

Gaia could feel Aran's body tense, his eyes remained fixed on the ground in front. There was a long silence before Aran answered.

'I've put you all in danger, and I've not been much of a leader. I mean without Freya and you we wouldn't have gotten this far.'

Gaia turned Aran's face to hers and placed her hands on both his cheeks. Gaia glared into his eyes, her expression still tender, but with a flash of warning. Gaia studied his eyes and face for a response. Aran was looking at her, but there was something else, something troubling him. There was a sterner tone to her voice.

'We all knew the risks. We're in this together. What's happened, well we're still here, aren't we? That's the important thing. This whole place is screwed, the community, the outside world, everywhere. There's got to be something better than all of this. We're so close now I can feel it. Another day or so and we'll be there and they'll find us. I know they will.'

Aran forced a smile, a half smile betraying his doubt. He reached up and stroked Gaia's cheek.

'You're right. We're close now. They're out there somewhere. They'll find us.'

Aran's voice tailed off, as he looked at the floor. Gaia lifted his chin, her words softened, voice slowed.

'Whatever happens we have each other, and we've got Freya and the girls now. We all stick together no matter what. We protect each other and we'll get through this. And if we don't like what we find we'll start again. We'll make our own community, live by our own rules. We can do what we want now. We're free now thanks to you. Don't forget that.'

They kissed again, another long passionate kiss. This time it was different, a pledge to one another, a seal of their commitment. The future was uncertain, some of what lay ahead was beyond their control. Their lives had been determined by others, but they could build their own future, determine their own destiny. They had come this far, and were building the courage and strength to see their own potential. The journey was showing them they could find their own way.

Gaia rolled over and lay her head on Aran's legs. She gazed at the ceiling, at the shafts of light piercing the gaps. Gaia thought of the young girls still resting beside them, of their dark past. She vowed to make things right, to give them a brighter future, to help them forget and heal. Gaia thought of Freya, all she had done to protect them, of the courage and determination, steel and ruthless edge. Freya had a blinding desire to survive at all costs. Her instinct was to protect. Gaia recalled how she felt about her only a few days before. Freya was an enemy, Kali's servant, but she had shown her loyalty to Gaia and the others, had saved their lives. Gaia spoke.

'Freya's been amazing. We owe her a lot. We wouldn't have got this far without her.'

'I know you never liked or trusted her, but she's definitely proven you wrong.'

'Yes. I admit it. I got it very wrong.'

Gaia rolled her eyes and shrugged. Aran continued.

'Maybe you need to trust people more. We all do.'

'We can't help how we've been programmed. The community has made us this way. They've made us see everyone as an enemy, even each other. It's how they control. They divide and breed suspicion. We need to undo all that, teach ourselves to be something else.'

The shafts of sun continued to flicker and dance their way through the cracks in the wood above. Aran and Gaia lay together. They chatted, joked, and laughed. These were rare moments for them, of tenderness and connection without fear of being watched or facing reprisals. What had happened before hung like a dark shadow. Uncertainty stood in front. For now they ignored both, and tried to enjoy the time together. They had known each other a short while, and knew so little. Now was the time to laugh and bicker, tease and share their hopes and dreams. Gaia and Aran were nearing the end of this journey, but at the start of their own. A journey of discovery and excitement, love and wonder, heartache and pain, their time together.

Aran rested his head on the bales of hay. Gaia still had hers on his outstretched legs. Mary and Ruth lay together side by side, still sleeping. Ruth held her tattered blanket, Mary huddled in close. They all lay and waited for Freya to return, for news of what was to come. The next twenty four hours would determine where their futures lay. Either they would find the new community they were seeking, and the hope the whispers, letters, and notes had promised. They could face disappointment and uncertainty, or worse. This was the eve of their judgement and fate, all the potential and hope. Their dreams still held the promise that something better awaited.

18

Gaia had dozed, and was woken with a fright. Someone was shaking her. She opened her eyes, still dazed and sleepy. It was Freya, a look of alarm on her face.

'We have to leave. They're here.'

Gaia and Aran jumped to their feet and gathered the things. They woke Mary and Ruth and followed Freya to the back of the barn. There was a rickety old door on the side of the building facing away from the village. Freya was about to open it, as Aran took her hand.

'What do you mean they're here? Who?'

'I went into the village. I was careful. Made sure no-one saw me. I hid in a garden and waited to see who was around. A group arrived. They were armed. They were fit and well trained. You could see they meant business. They had a pack of dogs. They were hunters, no question.'

Aran scowled and cursed under his breath. He pressed Freya further.

'Did you recognise any of them?'

'No, they're not from the island but they were wearing the uniforms. I reckon they're leaders from somewhere on the mainland, or a search team. They looked mean. They were quizzing someone, one of the locals. I managed to get a bit nearer and overheard bits of the conversation. They were definitely asking about us. They described us. They mentioned Clara and Yann too, so they must think they're still with us. They mustn't have found the bodies.'

Gaia spoke.

'Are they still there?'

'No. They headed out of the village. We need to get out of here, and get to the hills as soon as we can. If the dogs pick up our scent it's over.'

Aran and Gaia exchanged concerned looks. Gaia knew this could happen, and had prepared for it in her mind. Part of her hoped it might not, and they might manage to evade the hunters. She always knew that was unlikely. They had been lucky to get this far without being caught, but the incidents and delays had meant any advantage over the hunters had been lost. The group needed to make a final push for the hills, hope the new community were watching and found them as promised in the note.

On their own the group could step up the pace with few problems. If they pushed on and walked all night they would be in the upper reaches of the hills by dawn tomorrow. However, Gaia, Aran and Freya now had the sisters. So far the girls had followed without question or complaint but the group had slowed the pace to compensate. This was a worry, but Gaia said nothing.

Gaia had heard whispers about the hunting dogs. They were bred to kill and trained to be clinical and ruthless. Their hunger for blood was insatiable. Once the hounds had a scent they would be locked onto the kill. If they were unleashed the group would have no chance. Gaia took the girls by the hand. It was hard to tell what the sisters made of all the talk, or how much they understood. Fear and tension were a universal language, and Gaia could only guess what was happening behind their dead eyes. Gaia set out a plan.

'I say we head back to the river and follow it for a while. We can wade in it for a bit where it's shallow enough. It'll slow us down but it'll cover our scent.

We need to be very wary of those dogs. We all know what they're capable of.'

Aran nodded. They both looked at Freya who gave a knowing look. Freya looked down at Ruth and Mary, a mixture of regret the girls had to face this, and concern as to how to protect them. Aran was keen to press ahead. They could not afford to wait any longer, and he agreed with Gaia.

'We can't push on as fast as we'd like, but that's our best option. We'll have to make it to the hills as soon as we can. We'll travel as best we can through the night and should be well into the hills by morning. Hopefully, the others will find us like they said.'

Freya looked less confident, but she knew they had come this far and needed to see this through. Freya had seen the hunters and the dogs, and only told the others as much as they needed to know. The danger was far greater than they imagined.

'I hope you're right Aran. They'd better find us soon. We're running out of time. This is it. Either they find us or it's plan B.'

Aran frowned.

'What's plan B?'

Freya opened the door and grinned.

'We don't have one.'

Freya crept outside and scanned the area for signs of movement. All was clear so she ushered the others through. They made their way away from the village and down to the river. The water was shallow and calm, more of a trickle, a stream. They waded a path upstream for about a mile, and took the banks on the opposite side. The trees that lined the river were patchy now, offering no cover. They kept moving, the girls followed, their pace laboured, but they did not stop. Gaia and Aran held their hands, reassured them, guided them through the tricky places. Freya led the group, keeping a watchful eye, always alert. Ever the hunter, but this time the hunted.

The group stopped for a brief lunch. Afterwards, the girls tried to sleep. It was as though they had been programmed to snooze after food. Gaia tried to keep them awake. Freya remained edgy and was reluctant to pause for long. She ate standing, and made frequent sweeps of the area to check for threats. They pushed on through the afternoon, and saw nobody. Even the wildlife was scarce with only the occasional bird and some rabbits. The one notable sight was a large bird of prey circling above. It was slow and majestic. It circled, hovered a while, and flew off into the distance. The bird reminded Gaia of Yann.

The sun disappeared and thick, dark clouds moved in. By early evening the light had faded and specks of rain began to fall, a patter at first, but soon becoming heavy. The drops grew in size and ferocity and became piercing, like splinters being hurled from the sky. The temperature dropped and the combination of cold, the biting wind, and the relentless torrential rain all conspired to slow progress and sap their spirits.

Gaia's clothes became soaked, her skin wet and cold, her bones aching with the damp chill. Gaia comforted and encouraged Ruth and Mary, but they looked shattered. Ruth's face was lost in sadness and despair, her lip quivering with the cold. Ruth's blanket was now just a sodden rag. As the rain fell down Gaia's cheeks she could not tell whether they were tears or not. Gaia moved ahead alongside Freya who was pushing on, direct and relentless as ever.

'Freya, we have to stop soon. We need to find somewhere to shelter and rest. The girls can't keep this up. I'm not sure any of us can. Look at them.'

Freya did not look or let up her pace. Her gaze stayed firm and fixed on the path ahead. She answered Gaia.

'We'll push on through the night if we can. That's what we agreed.'

'I know, but things are different now. Look at the weather. We can't keep going in this. We're hardly moving as it is. And how we going to make it through the night. The light is fading badly now as it is. I can hardly make out my feet. We'll never see in the dark. It's too dangerous. We need to stop soon.'

Freya stopped and glared at Gaia who could see she was burning with rage. Gaia had forgotten this side of Freya, the dark, bitter, angry side. Despite all they had been through Freya had been the one who had remained level-headed and calm. Freya was cold and clinical, but invariably measured and calm. She knew what needed to be done and did it without feeling or emotion. This was anger and rage.

'We agreed to keep going so we keep moving. Got it?'

Gaia sneered back at Freya, eyes flaring with rage. This was the old Freya, the one Gaia had known and hated on the island, Kali's Freya. The image of Kali flashed into Gaia's mind, the face merging with Freya's as it had so often in the past. The two became one. It was a fleeting image, but enough to unleash all the hatred again. Gaia took a deep breath, regained control and calmed herself. This was not the time. She answered Freya, smothering the anger, not a hint of it in her voice.

'You go on ahead, but you go alone. The rest of us will find somewhere to shelter. We're stopping for the night.'

Freya looked at the girls and Aran. All three had fallen in behind Gaia, as the rain pelted down. Everyone was soaked and shivering. The sisters' hair was dripping, lips seeping floods of rainwater. Everyone was exhausted, including Freya. Mixed with the desperation on Aran's face was a plea, begging Freya to listen, urging her to back down. Freya was formidable, but Gaia was a match if need be. Gaia was adamant, Aran and the girls were with her. Freya knew she was on her own. The stalemate was broken and Freya conceded defeat.

'I'm sorry. I hear. We'll find somewhere to shelter, and hopefully, the rain'll let up. The dogs might struggle to track our scent in this so we should be safe to move from the river for now. We're going to have to if we want to find shelter.'

Gaia was relieved. This was for the best, but she did not want this to escalate, or Freya to go off alone. Aran shared Gaia's relief, and reassured the group.

'I can't see the hunters following us in this. They'll have holed up somewhere too. Let's find shelter, anywhere will do and see what it's like in the morning.'

Freya was content now, but had appointed herself a new mission.

'I think I know the sort of place we might find somewhere to shelter.'

Freya set off again. The others followed. Neither the stand-off nor the rain had dampened her desire to lead. They were now well into the lower reaches of the hills. All around them were small valleys and ravines meandering off through the undulating folds and waves of the land. Stones, small rocks and boulders littered the landscape, grey stone speckled with green and yellow from the smattering of moss and lichen. The trees had thinned to nothing, leaving the group exposed to the biting elements. They could not risk finding any man-made shelters, as these would be a beacon to the hunters, an obvious place to look. This area had always been sparsely populated, therefore constructed relics of the old days were rare. Gaia had seen the occasional crumbling stone cottage, or what may have been a winter sheep pen. All were derelict, all sheep and humans now gone.

The sky had turned much darker now. There was no moon to light the way. The only potential light in the sky was the faint flickering of a million stars, but the thick blanket of dark cloud had smothered them from view. The group were at the mercy of nature, the ravages of the open moorland, and the unpredictable temperament of the bleak hills. There were added dangers underfoot with peat bogs. These were like quicksand and could swallow a man whole sucking him into sticky, airless depths and certain death. Freya knew the risks and was tracking their route with care. She led them away from the path of the river and along a ravine that veered to the left. It was lined with steep walls of rock, the path sprayed with an assortment of awkward stones and boulders. The rain and the obstacles underfoot made the going tough. Gaia's body was sapped of most of her energy from the long, arduous day. Freya was pushing on ahead, the usual singular steel and grit. She worked at her own pace and expected others to match it.

Freya stopped, found what she was looking for. Moving to the right of the narrow gorge, Freya crawled under the arch of a rock and disappeared from view. The others followed and found themselves in a low, narrow cave. It was dry and offered good natural shelter from the wind and rain. Though it was small and shallow there was enough room to sit upright. It was also wide enough to lie down. The floor was solid rock, hard and cold, an uncomfortable bed. Despite its shortcomings the cave offered what the group needed, and was far better than facing the brutality of the night. The group needed to rest, and they had found their beds for the night. They would stay, eat, and dry out as best they could. They would take stock and prepare for the morning. It was close now. Tomorrow was the day when the journey ended.

19

Gaia kept guard while the others were sleeping. The cave was pitch black. Blinded, the other senses had come alive. There were far more than five senses, but people had become lazy and reliant on only a few. This had led to arrogance, a false sense of comfort which made the species weak and vulnerable. Gaia and the young on the island had been trained to use these lost senses, to know and be aware of them - hunger and thirst, pressure and pain, the sense of time and direction. In the dark, damp cave sound and smell were alive. The moist air mingled with condensation from their breath, forming a thin cloud of vapour, layered with the smell of moss.

The sounds assaulted Gaia most of all. The patter of the relentless downpour outside. The whistling of the brisk wind as it darted through the entrance to the cave. The sound of dripping, steady and rhythmic, a living organic beat, always changing, evolving like a heartbeat. Gaia could feel her own heart beating with the dripping of the rain. It was a soft and gentle beat, deep within the wall of her chest. There was the sound of the others breathing, and their fidgeting as they slept. Gaia tried to guess the person from the sounds. Some of the movements were louder and suggested someone heavier. These had to be Aran or Freya. The direction suggested Aran who seemed restless, always twisting and turning. There was a soft, slow, steady breathing. It was the same rhythm, but barely audible, almost as one. This must be the girls. There was the occasional sound of movement outside, a stone sliding under the weight of water, or a small animal braving the weather in search of food.

The sense of danger was the most important of all. Gaia had been trained to trust her instincts, to know when something did not feel right, to sense when something was there, or about to occur. It was the toughest of all the senses to master. It was elusive, ephemeral, often subjective and pure judgement. Gaia's antenna was very different to Freya's, but both were taught to heighten their awareness, adjust, leave nothing to chance. Trust nothing and suspect everything. This was the default position, how the young were programmed.

Gaia heard movement in the cave. One of the others was stirring. There was shuffling towards her, the presence of someone at her shoulder. The darkness whispered. It was Freya.

'Do you want me to take over now?'

'If you like. There's nothing out there, just the wind and rain. It's blowing a hooley. I hope it stops by morning. To be honest I'm not that tired. I don't mind sitting here a bit longer. You can go back to sleep if you like.'

Gaia could feel Freya move beside her. Freya sat hunched up, knees tucked into her chest. Their jackets rubbed together making a scratching sound, amplified by the acoustics of the cave.

'I'm sorry about earlier. Things might be catching up with me a bit. I didn't mean to have a go at you.'

'It's fine. I think we're all on edge. The past few days have been pretty intense.'

'You could say that.'

They continued to whisper, but despite their efforts everything echoed in the small cave. Even the softest words sounded like chatter. Freya leant her head against Gaia's.

'We'll get through this. I know we will.'

There was a long pause, the silence filled with the music of the night. Freya continued.

'There's no way I'm going back. I'll die before they take me back to the island.'

Gaia listened to Freya's words, unable to see her face, expressions or body language. Gaia concentrated on the tone of her friend's voice, heard the meaning of the words, found the spaces in between. The words echoed in the cave and Gaia's mind, hearing not just what was being said, but also what was not. Gaia whispered.

'I don't think that'll happen. Even if they caught us there's stuff I've done which I'll have to pay for.'

'Me too, and there are things I can't face again.'

There was silence again. The sounds of whispers were replaced by the background sounds of the cave and outside. Gaia could hear Freya's breathing, could feel the warmth of her breath, the gentle movement of her body. Gaia could sense something. Freya's body had tensed, her breathing quickened. Gaia broke the silence.

'What things?'

Gaia could feel Freya's mounting tension, the rhythm of her breathing. Freya spoke, her voice rising above a whisper.

'You'll have heard rumours about some of the leaders, about stuff that happens, the kind of things they do.'

Freya's voice broke off. Gaia's fingers crept around the stone floor, feeling for Freya's. She found them and crawled across her cold hands, taking a firm grip.

'I understand. You don't have to tell me anything.'

There was something Gaia wanted to tell Freya, something that changed everything for the group, turning them from fugitives to outlaws. Freya was more involved than she knew. Gaia had killed a leader and Freya had to know.

'Freya, there's something I have to tell you. I haven't spoken about it to any of you. Aran knows about it though.'

Gaia gathered her words. There was a moment of doubt, worrying how Freya might react. Gaia continued, her voice broken, the words coming out in fragments.

'The night we escaped. I did something. I had to do it. I had no real choice. He deserved it.'

Gaia composed herself again, trying to slow her breathing. She imagined the words in her head, but the more she thought of them the more terrible they sounded. It almost seemed as though she was speaking of another person. Gaia could not associate the words with her actions. Three words and a name, his name. Over and over, she kept saying the words in her head. Freya was growing impatient.

'What did you do? Tell me.'

'I killed Hakan.'

Gaia spat out the words which hurtled into the cold, damp air of the cave. Gaia saw them in her mind, hanging in the darkness, waiting for Freya to grab them, process and understand them. There was a long wait, seconds seemed like minutes. Time slowed to a heavy, monotonous beat. Gaia waited for Freya to speak, desperate to hear a voice, some words, a response. Freya's voice was calm.

'I don't know what to say. I never imagined this.'

There was silence again. Gaia's heart was racing, anxious for Freya's judgement, desperate to know either way how she felt. Freya kept her hanging, not out of cruelty, but shock, and a struggle to find the right words.

'You did what you had to Gaia. Hakan was evil. They're all evil in some way, but he was one of the worst. He got what he deserved.'

Gaia tightened her grip on Freya's hand. It was a thank you. Gaia was relieved, not only by her friend's response, but sharing this with someone else. Aran and Gaia had not spoken of Hakan's murder. He would have known Hakan was dead because Gaia was there. Clara's presence would have confirmed this. Saying the words, confirming it to someone else did not lessen the act, but lightened the load. Gaia knew she would always have to live with the burden. Killing Hakan was necessary and justified, but it was still a life taken. The consequences were unknown. If Gaia succeeded in the escape and built a new life she would have to live with this. The group had all done what they needed to survive. Without survival they were nothing. They had to kill to live. That was what the community had taught the young. If Gaia was caught, she would have to face the penalty. This was her confession, some assurance and forgiveness. If anyone would understand it would be Freya. Gaia whispered.

'I was lucky. Hakan never got the chance to take advantage of me. Things were heading that way before I put a stop to them.'

Gaia felt Freya squeeze her hand, as she continued.

'There were others. Lots. I'd hear them at night sneaking off to his dorm in the night. The girls would wait till they thought we were all asleep, but I'd hear them. Clara was one of them. That's why I brought her. She was waiting outside his room on the night, after I killed him.'

Freya lifted her head from Gaia's shoulder and answered.

'It makes more sense now. I wondered why you'd brought her.'

'I didn't want to leave her and I couldn't just kill her. Clara was an airhead. She couldn't help it, but she didn't deserve to die.'

Gaia's voice tailed off to a cracked fragile whisper, inaudible even in the silence of the cave.

'Though I ended up killing her anyway.'

Freya caught the delicate fragments of Gaia's words.

'You mustn't think like that Gaia. Clara's death was an accident. There's nothing you could have done. It could have been you.'

'Maybe it should have been instead.'

Freya interrupted, her voice firm and agitated, lifting above a whisper and echoing around the stone walls.

'Stop it. Less of the 'what ifs?' This whole escape is about 'what ifs?' What's the point of thinking about them? We've got to move on, in our heads too. We can worry about all that when we're finished. You're strong Gaia, and we need you to stay strong. Don't let the doubts get to you. They'll only weaken you.'

The silence and blackness enveloped them again. Gaia wrestled with images of death in her mind, a fleeting jigsaw of visions, pieces scattered everywhere. There was the sea, blood, the moon, waves, and there was drowning. A face appeared. It was Clara's. It was blue, her eyes bloodshot and lifeless. Clara's body was washed up on a beach at night, alone, the waves lapping around her cold, stiff corpse. Gaia saw the eyes again, and thought of Hakan, his face still alive, a grin of lust and desire. He was sitting on a bed, stroking someone's hair, a girl. Gaia could not see the girl's face, but she turned and Gaia saw her. It was

Freya. Gaia sat upright and blurted out her words, louder than intended.

'Was it Hakan?'

'No.'

Their voices boomed around the cavernous chamber. They stopped, listened to the silence that had returned. Gaia feared they would wake someone, especially Aran in his fitful sleep. There was no sound, no movement, only the sound of breathing, gentle, rhythmic breathing. Freya whispered this time, much calmer, a subtle apology in her voice, tip-toeing through her words.

'It wasn't Hakan. It was someone else.'

Gaia ran through all the male leaders in her mind. They were all capable of abuse, none would surprise her. Gaia knew little of some leaders though. The acts happened in the dead of night, under cover of darkness. More often it was the dorm leader with someone under their watch. Freya was not in the dorm of a male leader. Freya whispered again.

'I know what you're thinking Gaia. Which one? You're probably going through them all and weighing up the most likely. Don't go there, please.'

Gaia continued to process each of the leaders in her mind, making a mental list, considering who was the most likely. Freya continued.

'They're all the same Gaia. Liars and frauds. Every single one. Male and female.'

They are all the same. Liars and frauds. Every single one. Male and female. It was then Gaia realised. Everything pointed to one person, the one Gaia would never have imagined. Gaia had heard rumours about Freya and her links with leaders. Gaia had always thought Freya capable of anything and stopping at nothing to win favour. Freya could never be a victim to Gaia.

Freya was always in control, would never let anyone take advantage of her. Gaia now saw her friend was vulnerable, just like all the rest. Freya had been abused by those she trusted. Freya was a victim, and it was clear to Gaia who the abuser was. Gaia spoke the name that Freya had not, that she could not. Gaia spoke for her friend.

'It was Kali.'

Freya did not speak. She did not need to. Gaia knew she was right, and the absence of words confirmed it. Gaia felt Freya squeeze her hand. They sat together for many minutes, listening to the sounds of the room, the shuffling and breathing. They listened to the outside, the wind and rain. Neither spoke for a long while. There was no need for words. There was simple comfort in each other's presence, in being together.

Gaia understood her friend now. The layers of judgement and prejudice had been peeled away. Freya's actions and words had shown Gaia another person. Was it the real Freya? Maybe not, but sometimes the veil is lifted. We get to realise who a person is and what made them. The other person becomes a mirror in which we see a reflection of who we really are. Freya had become a mirror, and Gaia had come to know more of herself through the reflection. Gaia did not always like what she saw. She did not like knowing she was wrong or enjoy overcoming her prejudices. Yet, Gaia was humble enough to accept and learn from this. Freya had shown Gaia how to be stronger and survive, revealed their shared humanity, and made Gaia want to become better. Freya had grown from enemy to friend, someone Gaia trusted with her life.

As the two friends sat in silence, listening to the myriad of sounds around them, something new could be heard. Gaia could just make it out. It was very faint at first, so much so Gaia thought she may be imagining it. Freya's body stiffened, Gaia sensed the tension mount in the cave. The others slept on, oblivious, but both Gaia and Freya were focused on the new sound. It was in the distance, but getting nearer. It was muffled, dampened by the rainfall, drifting in and out of earshot in the swirling wind. There was no doubt it was there, getting louder, still faint, revealing itself more and more. The sound grew until it was unmistakable, familiar and distinctive. It was the sound of dogs barking.

20

The dogs were near, but the wind and rain made it difficult to tell how far. The sound was nearer than either Gaia or Freya wanted to admit. Perhaps the creatures were at the start of the ravine, crossing it, but moving away, following another path through the hills. The route the group had taken was a detour, the terrain tricky. It was not a route you would choose to take, only for a purpose. The group had sought shelter, now the dogs sought them. If the dogs had picked up a scent, if tracks had been found Gaia and the others were in trouble. It would be the end. There would be no escaping the dogs. Gaia, Aran and Freya could put up a strong fight, but it would be futile. The dogs were fierce and could tear someone apart in seconds. The best hope for the group was that they had not been found and this was a coincidence. Gaia and Freya listened, hoping the rain had washed away all traces of scent, all footprints, all indication the group were here. The two of them waited and hoped, cold sweat dripping from their brows.

Neither of them seemed to be breathing, all senses focused on the sound. The danger was smothering them, pressing down like a heavy weight, a poisonous cloud suffocating them. For a moment the barking stopped, and there was nothing but the wind and rain. It started again, louder than ever. Gaia's heart was pumping, and her mouth was dry. The adrenalin surged through Gaia's body, a cocktail of fear and anticipation. Freya was still locked in cold sweat, hoping the others would not make a sound. Gaia put her hand on her axe, knowing it was futile, but seeking reassurance through its presence.

The barking faded, still there but more distant. It flared up once again, as the howling wind picked up the waves of sound and tossed them through the night like an ocean storm. It was difficult to judge where the dogs were. Neither Gaia or Freya could be sure how near or far. Gaia was sure they were getting close, could feel it. The young had been programmed to trust their fear and judgement, take no chances, expect the worst and prepare. Gaia's programming ran through her head. It was instinct now, who she had become. Both girls were ready, like arrows in a bow, pulled back and poised to be unleashed.

The barking ceased, but the two girls did not trust the silence, sure it was a trick of the swirling wind. The sound returned for a moment, but it was fainter, drifting away to the point of silence. The two of them held their breath, strained their ears, but it was gone. Gaia's heart slowed and the adrenalin eased. They were safe for now, the dogs had moved on. The girls waited awhile before speaking, until they were sure it was safe. Freya touched Gaia's hand and whispered.

'That was close. It was the hunters. Must've been. They must be crazy looking for us in this weather. Or desperate. Maybe they're worried. We could be nearer to the others than we think.'

The group were well into the hills, but the area was vast. The note said find the hills and we will find you, but the other community did not know Gaia and the others were coming. There'd been no signal, no advance warning, which made the group so much harder to find. Perhaps the search had alerted the community, perhaps the hunters had been a signal the group were on their way. Gaia and Freya could not be sure. The leaders and the dogs knew where the group were heading and were searching. That gave the hunters a huge advantage. Gaia and Freya now knew the hunters were near, and would close in soon. It was only a question of when. There would be other teams of leaders and dogs searching and time was against the group. The garrote was tightening around the groups' throats, the screws on their thumbs. Gaia and the others were not caught or dead yet, but they could feel the leather strap gripping their necks and choking. If the community in the hills did not find the group soon, the life would be squeezed from them. Gaia spoke.

'What now?'

'We sit it out for the rest of the night, and set off again in the morning. I'd hoped the rain would ease or stop, but it mightn't be a bad thing if it doesn't. This weather's better for us than it is them. It covers our trail and makes us harder to track. Get some rest. You'll need it. It's going to be a tough day tomorrow. I can feel it. I'll keep guard.'

'Are you sure?'

'Yes, I'm positive.'

'Thanks.'

Gaia touched Freya's hand again. This was their new communication in darkness. Gaia edged her way through the pitch black to her makeshift bed. She wrapped the blankets around her, and lay against the rucksack. It was hard, lumpy, a lousy pillow, but it was better than the cold, hard surface. Gaia listened to the shuffling of the others. Aran was still restless.

Gaia dreamt that night, the same dream with Kali in the room. The other person was there, Gaia could see their boots. The person was in the corner, their lower half kept coming into view. Gaia still could not place the boots, but the thought of who they belonged to was haunting her. She was poised on the edge of knowing. Somewhere in Gaia's head she knew, but could not find the answer. Gaia kept willing herself to get up, lunge towards the corner, drag the person from the shadows. Gaia could not move, she was trapped and bound to a chair. Kali was shouting at her, hurling abuse. Kali was unleashing a venom, a tirade of verbal attacks, spitting in Gaia's face as she bellowed. Gaia focused on the boots, desperate to know who they belonged to, hoping they would step out and reveal themselves. Gaia heard herself calling in her mind, *Who are you? Show yourself. I know you. Tell me who you are!'* The person did not step out. They did not speak. They remained in the shadows.

The dream ended, as it always ended. It faded away, dissolved into the pit of Gaia's sleep. It was always before the person revealed themselves, before Gaia could see their face. When she woke the dream always remained, its presence hanging heavy like a dark cloud for most of the morning. It wrestled with Gaia's other thoughts, played on her mind. It toyed and teased - the image of Kali, the room, and the boots. There was a feeling of fear, drowning, and hatred, the most intense hatred. There was a feeling of betrayal. Gaia always sensed the betrayal, and was left with its bitter taste.

The morning came, and the wind and rain remained. The group ate, packed up and moved on, wasting no time. Freya headed out first, running down the ravine to check the route ahead, and make sure the dogs had gone. Gaia and Freya did not mention the dogs to the others. There was no need to alarm them any further. The young girls would not understand, Aran knew they were being hunted, it was only a matter of time. The dogs were just detail, and not one to dwell on.

Freya returned. The path was clear. They headed out of the cave and back into the biting weather. Though it was morning the sky was dark, and the cloud was thick and black. There was little sign of it clearing, or the rain easing. The group made their way down the ravine, over the rocks and boulders, slipping on the muddy ground. They reached the narrow path that headed up higher into the hills and forged on. The going was tough, their spirits sapped. Gaia stopped to check on Ruth and Mary, both shivered. The girls were weary, but neither spoke, their eyes lost as ever. Gaia looked at Ruth's face, as the raindrops trickled down the child's raw cheeks like tears. Gaia knew they were not tears, but wished they were. Tears were a sign of emotion, feeling, and life. Better the children cried than showed nothing, just stared. The girls had been through so much, and it was better they grieved. All emotion had been crushed and locked away inside the sisters. They had learnt to fear emotion, so buried it, maybe they did not even feel it anymore. The children were alive, but no longer lived.

Gaia and the others trudged on, slipping on the drenched earth, their boots caked in mud. They walked for hours seeing little and no-one. The only solace was each other, the only companion the weather which ebbed and flowed throughout the morning, but never let up. The group crossed some moorland, and struggled up the brow of a hill. The wind and rain were relentless and visibility was poor. The sky remained dark with a thin mist mingling with the moisture of the falling rain. In the distance on the edge of the moorland Gaia spotted something, a structure, but not something natural in shape. As the group neared Gaia saw it was made of wooden planks, stretched horizontal and vertical in the air with a bar across in support making a triangular shape.

They approached the wood structure and could see something hanging from the end of the outstretched horizontal beam. It was hooked to the end, and looked like a head in a metal frame. Gaia drew closer and could see it was not a real head, but a wooden one carved to look like that of a man's. She stared up at the macabre sight, and spoke.

'What is it?'

Aran replied without removing his eyes from the head as it twisted and turned in the wind.

'It's a gibbet. It's where they hanged the people they'd executed. They didn't kill them here, but they'd bring the dead bodies and display them on open moorland like this so people could see them. It was a warning to others. The bodies would rot and be taken away, but they'd leave the skulls in the metal frames as a reminder. They didn't mess about with criminals in those days.'

Gaia grabbed the girls and hugged them close, turning their heads away from the ghastly sight. Gaia's mind drifted back to the image of Rebecca hanging from the tree. Her limp, lifeless body swaying in the woods, just the day before. Freya noticed a wooden board at the base of the gibbet. She approached it, wiping it with the sleeve of her jacket, and read the words out to the others.

'There's some writing on here. It says, '*The body of William Winter was left here following his execution in Newcastle on August 10th, 1792 for the murder of Margaret Crozier. He was executed along with the sisters Jane and Eleanor Clark whose bodies were sent to a surgeon for dissection. William's body was brought here to Whiskershields Common where it was hung in chains until it was cut down and the bones scattered. It stood as a warning to all of the consequences of their crimes.'*

The words chilled Gaia. *The consequences of their crimes.* The others soaked up the words along with the pelting rain. Gaia thought of the year, 1792. She had no idea what year it was now, whether it was a long time ago or not. This was how people dealt with criminals in the days before. Their leaders killed them and hanged their bodies in chains on display. Gaia had been told the ways before were brutal, but this was worse than she imagined. It was primitive, and reminded her of the words in the red book. Those were words of terror and vengeance, clear and unequivocal. You reap what you sow. Gaia turned and addressed the others, the words spluttering through droplets of rain on her lips.

'1792. How long ago was that?'

Freya began to pace around the gibbet, studying and admiring it. She shouted in reply to Gaia.

'I've no idea. It can't be that old. It'd rot pretty quickly out here. It's only made of wood.'

Aran shook himself from a daze, a mixture of exhaustion and fascination at the grim discovery.

'I don't think it's been used for a long time. The board sounds like it was here for information.'

Freya was fascinated, but confused.

'What? Out here? Who's going to see anything out in the middle of nowhere?'

Aran shrugged his shoulders.

'It does seem strange, but why put a sign here? They obviously wanted people to read it.'

Freya continued to pace, circle and study the wooden structure. Gaia was lost, almost in a dream, her words came without thinking.

'It's the beauty.'

Freya stopped pacing as Gaia continued.

'People come here for the beauty. You must have seen it? This whole place is incredible. It's like Yann said, remember? People messed up the world, but the world is still a beautiful place. The mainland, this part of the world. It's magical.'

Aran thought about Gaia's words. He had not looked for beauty on the journey. The primary goal had been survival, watching for predators or threats, and whether the group were being followed. Aran's mind was always on other things. For Freya beauty was irrelevant. It was a raw, untamed world, a place you treat with caution. You respected nature, or it would take you. There was no room for romance in Freya's world. It was weakness. Gaia was different. She had thought about Yann's words. They had touched Gaia, and she had looked for the beauty on the rest of the journey. Even now, staring at the face of death she saw it.

'Yann saw the beauty in everything. That's why he always seemed so content, happy. We thought he was in another world, but he wasn't. He was in this one, but he saw it for what it is, what we can't see. We're too busy trying to survive. They've taken everything from us, even the beauty in the world, especially the beauty.'

Gaia held the two girls, as Freya sat against the gibbet and closed her eyes, the cold rain spitting against her frozen cheeks. Freya thought about what Gaia had said. Maybe she was right, but Freya had little time for such folly. Nature was heartless. The natural order was about balance. You survive first, then you live. If you were lucky you might get a chance to experience something special. Beauty was a luxury Freya could not afford. Aran surveyed the moorland around them. All of a sudden he stopped and plunged to the ground, crouching low on his knees. Aran hissed at the others.

'Get down.'

The others fell to the ground. Gaia looked in the direction of Aran's stare. In the distance, on the furthest visible edge of the darkness and hazy mist Gaia could see a shadowy figure. It was standing still, and appeared to be alone. Gaia moved her stare across the moorland and saw another person step into view. Facing forward, both of the figures were about ten metres apart. Both were just silhouettes, and Gaia could make out little. Her head moved in a panoramic sweep and more shadows appeared. Every ten metres or so there was another figure standing still, watching and waiting. The group were surrounded. Gaia waited, but there was still no movement or sound from the shadows. There were no dogs, just human silhouettes. Freya was crouched by the gibbet, the first of the group to speak, her voice quiet.

'We're surrounded. There's quite a few. There's no use making a run for it.'

Aran looked at Gaia, then Freya who slipped out her knife and continued.

'If we have to, we fight. How many are there?'

Aran's stare was locked on the silhouettes, whispering a reply.

'I count twelve, at least that's all I can see, but there could be more.'

Freya hissed a response.

'I don't hear or see any dogs. If they've got dogs we're done for. Do you think it's them? I mean the community we're looking for? Do you think they could have found us.'

Aran placed his hand on his knife and steadied himself, still crouching on the ground.

'I'm not sure, but let's not take any chances until we know.'

Gaia put her arms around the girls. They were crouched beside her, as she scanned the moorland again. The shadows were watching. Gaia noticed one of them moving forward. With slow, steady steps the figure edged towards them. Gaia pointed.

'One of them's coming!'

Gaia, Aran and Freya gripped their weapons, each remained spread out, low to the ground. The rain continued around them, the mist swirling in the wind. The dark shadow swept in and out of sight as it neared, sometimes the thick mist softened to reveal, then a grey blanket would return. As the figure neared the mist lightened and the shadow lifted becoming more real in form, no longer a haze. The figure was dressed in black wearing trousers, heavy boots, gloves, and a thick waxy jacket. This was not the standard issue clothing of the community. It was different, and not something Gaia had seen before. The face of the figure could not be seen as they wore a balaclava, mesh covering the eyes. Judging by the height, thick neck and build it was a man. Gaia noticed a belt with a small revolver attached.

The figure approached and stopped about ten feet away from Aran who was crouching furthest forward of the group. The figure waited, standing tall and erect, almost to attention. There was a bold, regimented air to his manner, a formality. His head pointed straight ahead, still and focused. The man spoke, his voice deep, firm, and commanding.

'You must be runners from the island. We aren't going to harm you.'

The group remained silent, each waiting for the others, hoping someone else would respond. The rain continued to lash down, and the bitter wind cut through them like the blade of a sword. Gaia pressed the two girls close to her chest as they all remained crouched on the ground. Aran and Freya were now on their feet, shoulders back, arms by their sides, poised for any sudden movements, or attack. The man spoke again.

'Let's assume you are. We've had others come to us before. It may be that you are looking for us as they were.'

Gaia, Aran, and Freya looked at each other all thinking the same thing. Gaia could feel a tingle of excitement mixed with a sweeping feeling of relief. She so wanted to believe it to be true, that their journey might now be at an end, hoping this was the moment. Gaia, Aran, and Freya had come so far, struggled through and lost so much. They had risked everything, but now it seemed as though it could be worthwhile. Aran edged forward, his voice louder and more commanding.

'We're from the island. We've come to find a community. Somewhere we'd heard about, but how can we be sure you are who you say you are?'

The man remained still, staring ahead, as though he were addressing some distant person or place beyond them. The air of regimented formality remained.

'You can't be sure. Perhaps you know of someone called Savas? Maybe he spoke of us?'

Gaia was filled with growing excitement. She looked at Aran, urging him to quiz further. Aran continued.

'I know of Savas. He showed me a letter sent from the hills. If you are from the community you'll know who signed it.'

There was a pause for a moment. Gaia was willing the man to answer. She still had doubts, part of her trusted no one. The others would have doubts, but the layers of uncertainty were being peeled back. This was the chance to confirm what they all wanted to be true. The man's voice was the same dry and lifeless tone.

'The letter was signed 'M'. It stands for Mater. She lives with us in the community.'

A wave of excitement and relief hit Gaia. Her chest tightened and pulse quickened. *Just head to the hills and we'll find you.'* That was the message. *'Come to the hills. It is true, the community is here. There is hope, and a better way.'* The group had pinned their hopes on the thinnest of promises, a whisper of a dream that seemed to be fading with each day. Gaia clutched the dream, had faith it was true. This had driven everyone on, got them this far. Now it looked as though the promise would be fulfilled, the dream might become real, their faith would be rewarded.

There was still something, some doubt, a part of Gaia that wrestled with her wave of excitement. The young had been programmed not to trust. The instinct was caution, and Gaia was still wary. Through the maelstrom of emotions that churned within lay a faint cry of logic and common sense. She had to be rational about this, but could see they had little choice but to go. Aran seemed much calmer, as he quizzed the man further.

'If we decide to come, where are we going?'

'I can't say. Put these on and hand over all your weapons. You won't be needing them.'

The man took out some masks and blindfolds from his pocket and held them to the side above his head. Freya's instinct had been to fight, but could see the group were out-numbered. It would be a risk to fight. In all likelihood the group would lose and be captured and taken, or worse. Freya said what Gaia and Aran were also thinking.

'Why do we need to wear them?'

The man continued to respond, his tone never changing.

'We need to conceal our location. It's for our own safety. We'll lead you there. You'll be safe. You've nothing to fear as long as you do as we say.'

Freya did not want to give up her weapons. It was different with Jack and the priest. They were old and offered little threat to the group. Freya felt vulnerable now, but realised that with or without weapons the three of them were no match for these people. Despite this Freya was defiant, wanted to make it clear to the man she had not agreed to anything. This would be her decision.

'And what if we choose not to?'

The man lowered his arm, placing the mask and blindfold back in his pocket. He pressed his gloves together.

'You don't have to come. You're free to stay out here and roam the moorlands. But be warned. There are others looking for you. Many others. We don't have much time. A confrontation wouldn't be good for any of us. If you don't come it's likely they'll find you soon. Like I said, the choice is yours.'

Gaia, Aran and Freya all looked at each other. Freya's face was awash with worry. Gaia could see the doubts. Freya's instinct for caution and mis-trust was deeper and more difficult to overcome. Freya was a

fighter and survivor. Every part of her was tuned to
avert risk, maximise the chance of survival. The
instinct was to strike, not negotiate or compromise,
but Freya was not stupid. She could weigh up the
chances, and knew it was best to go with the people
or face a bleaker alternative.

Aran seemed more relaxed, almost resigned to this.
Gaia thought he looked weary, and sick of running.
Perhaps, Aran was happy to take this risk, and
planned this outcome. The note to Savas had been
the spark of hope and the man knew of the note.
That was all Aran needed. Gaia was torn. There was
the elation of all this could be, and an alternative that
was too terrifying to contemplate. Gaia was tired,
wanted an end, and was prepared to make the leap of
faith. This had to end at some point.

Gaia nodded to her friends, took out her axe and
long dagger and hurled them on the ground in front
of the man. Aran did the same. Freya waited, the
others giving warning looks. Freya took out her
weapons and one by one thrust them onto the pile.
The man was impassive, head still staring forward as
he spoke.

'Are you sure that's all of them?'

The man turned his masked head to face Freya and
waited. It was the first time he had moved from the
stiff, formal position, the first time he had looked at
one of them. Freya scowled and lifted her trousers. A
small knife was in a pouch on the side of her right leg.
She removed the pouch and threw it with the other
weapons. The man took out the masks and blindfolds
and stepped forward, handing them one in turn. Gaia
helped the girls to put the masks on. The masks were
black, woolen balaclavas, the same as the one worn by
the man. Gaia stretched the blindfold over her head

and across her eyes. It was elasticated and tight, plunging her into a deep darkness. Gaia's mind rushed back to the cave. It was the same alternative world of sensory overload. Gaia's hearing sharpened, her smell and touch become more alive. All the other senses clicked back into place as they had the night before.

Gaia and the others waited. Gaia could hear the soft, squelching footsteps of others approaching. There were no words. Someone approached and took Gaia by the arm, lifting it and spinning her body round a couple of times. Gaia heard the voice of the man.

'This is so you don't sense the direction we're heading.'

Gaia laughed in her head. As if that would fool any of them. Giddy and disorientated, Gaia took a tentative step, then another, and another. One foot forward, the start of every journey, and this one nearing its end. As with the first steps on leaving the island this journey was beginning in darkness, a different kind of darkness. As with the escape Gaia did not know where this would lead, or what lay waiting. The group were at the mercy of hope and faith once more, their destiny was in the hands of others. Today would be their judgement day.

21

They moved at a steady pace. Gaia could feel the heavy, damp moorland beneath her feet. The rain continued to fall, lashing and stinging. The wind twisted and swirled, biting at their faces. Gaia could smell the damp air through the holes in the mask, taste it. Her face was no longer cold, wrapped in the protective veil of the balaclava. The mask gave no comfort though. It magnified her fear, reminded Gaia of how vulnerable the group were. They had escaped one web, only to land in another, a web of uncertainty.

Gaia listened to the world as they trudged on. It was a new and alien world. She was there, but was not there, passing through and knowing nothing of the place. All Gaia could hear was the soft, rhythmic crunch of their footsteps, the march, mixed with the rustle of clothing, and the odd weary sigh. She listened for the girls, but they were the quietest of all. The children drifted without a sound, floating, leaving no marks, but carrying many scars. The sisters were ghosts on the misty moorland. Ghosts guided by shadows.

They all came to a halt and Gaia was helped across what she was sure was a stile in a fence. On the other side the ground was different, the texture gnarled and uneven, the thorns of the thick undergrowth ripped and tugged at the trousers. The wind changed. It was less intense, but darted and whistled beside them, as though it were dancing through branches. Gaia could feel something around her. The rain had eased, but there were still droplets falling from above, less frequent and heavier. Something was breaking the raindrops fall, forcing them to gather, become larger and stronger. The group were in woodland, Gaia and the others being guided through trees, and round obstacles. Gaia tripped and lost her footing several times. The damp mist was now mixed with the musty smell of rotting mulch, and the faint, refreshing hint of pine needles.

They moved through the woods, stumbling in silence. Gaia heard the flutter of wings, some startled birds. It was heavy, clumsy flapping. There was the squawk of crows, many of them, a murder, a nesting site, a rookery. The crows sharp, shrill calls echoed through the trees more chilling than the biting weather, sounding like a warning, or threat.

The sense of being surrounded began to subside, as Gaia felt the wind pick up again. The rainfall began to prick and sting any glimmer of exposed flesh. The ground altered, as the clawing vines disappeared, the surface becoming heavier, grassy, and damp. The umbrella of trees had gone, and the group were open to the naked skies. Beyond the blindfolds the light had returned, but Gaia remained in darkness.

After a while the group were stopped and given water and food. There were nuts, berries, cheese and biscuits. Few words were spoken, only by the man who had addressed them before. They were functional, prosaic words, instructions and polite queries as to how they were, if they needed anything. There was only ever the minimum, nothing more than necessary.

They pressed on across the moorland, the rain never letting up. Gaia's clothes were wet through and heavy. The water had seeped through to her legs, with skin clinging to the material. Gaia was shivering and tired, her spirit waning. The will to survive had driven

Gaia on. The others needed her as she needed them. Together the group had to be strong, but now they were not leaders they were led. They were reliant on others, surrendering their freedom. Gaia was tired of the suffocating silence and felt the urge to speak.

'Do we have much further?'

'A few more miles.'

At first Gaia had a flash of relief soon replaced with a mixture of apprehension and excitement. What awaited the group when they arrived? What would the community be like? Who were these people? What did the future hold? Questions hurtled through Gaia's mind. Questions she could not and dared not answer. She tried to push them aside, wanted to concentrate on this moment, the last part of the journey. Gaia had to remain alert. The group were vulnerable, their lives in the hands of others. For the first time in days the group were not relying on themselves. Their captors had been polite, with no sign of threat, but Gaia knew the potential was there, simmering under the surface. The others knew that too, and Freya would feel it most like a caged animal waiting to spring. Gaia needed to be there for Freya, for all of them. The group had to stick together.

The ground became firm and even. They were on a road winding downwards, snaking their way north west. The spin had not confused Gaia. The sound and feel of the wind began to die, as something was blocking or diverting it, and shielding the group. The wind disappeared and Gaia and the others were brought to a stop. Gaia heard a scraping sound, something large and heavy was being dragged across the ground. A large wooden gate opened and they were ushered forward by the invisible hands. Gaia heard the sound again, this time from behind. They had been led into something, somewhere. The group were here. Finally, they had reached the journey's end.

As the rain poured down, Gaia sensed something different. Blind and in darkness, Gaia sensed more than ever. They were being watched, no longer alone. Their pace did not let up as Gaia and the others were urged on. The road was flat and even, Gaia's footsteps firm and loud. They pressed on for a short while and slowed to a standstill. Gaia heard the voice of the man again.

'Wait here.'

Freya's voice echoed in the silence. It was the first time she had spoken throughout the trek. Gaia could hear the hatred and resentment in her friend's tone.

'Can we take these masks off?'

'Not yet. We'll take you to rooms where you'll be met by someone. Your masks will be removed there. You'll then get showered and changed, and given a briefing. We need to clarify a few things. I'm sure you'll understand we need to be cautious. You're welcome here, but there are rules we must discuss. All will become clear soon.'

Gaia thought of the girls, how they must be feeling. She wanted to be with them, hold their hands, comfort them. Gaia quizzed the man further.

'Will we be kept together?'

The man answered.

'You'll be prepared and met separately.'

Gaia felt a rush of panic. She could not let the girls be on their own. They needed her. Gaia continued to press the man.

'I want to stay with the girls.'

'The girls will be taken care of. Now we'll take you all to freshen up. You must be exhausted after such a long journey. It'll take time to adjust, but try to be patient. We have rules and procedure to follow.'

Gaia was incensed, her voice was still controlled but her tone threatening.

'I don't care about your rules. I want to stay with the girls. Do you hear me?'

There was no response from the man. Gaia felt a firm grip take either arm. She began to kick and scream.

'Did you hear me? I'm not going anywhere without them.'

Gaia heard the man's voice. It was measured, firm and assertive.

'I suggest you calm down.'

Gaia stopped struggling, relaxed and took a few deep breaths. This would help none of them, least of all the girls. Gaia could hear Aran and Freya struggling and shouting too. She spoke again, her voice softer.

'Please. Can I have a few moments with the girls and my friends before we go?'

There was a pause and the grip on Gaia's arms loosened, as the man spoke again.

'You have a few minutes.'

Gaia was led forward, and could sense Freya and the others near. They had heard the response and had stopped fighting. Gaia waited, concentrated. Perhaps they were not alone? Someone could be nearby listening. Gaia felt sure they would be listening. Panic set in as her mind reached all around searching for sounds, a feeling, any sense that the people were there. All Gaia could hear was the patter of the rain, then she heard Freya whisper.

'There's something not right about this. I don't like it. They're splitting us for a reason, to weaken us. I don't trust them. Sit tight, and play their game. We'll wait till the time is right. We'll get through this. I'll come for you all.'

Gaia felt Aran take hold of her hand and squeezed. His soft voice whispered in her ear.

'Gaia. They'll say things to you, anything to break us. Don't listen to them. Don't believe anything they say. Do you hear me?'

'What do you mean?'

Aran did not respond, as Gaia felt him edge away. Time was slipping and Gaia needed to speak to the girls. Crouching low Gaia reached out her arms to them, grabbing at the air until she found them. She pressed them tight against her body, feeling their warmth despite the cold and drenched clothes. The children's soft, delicate hair brushed against Gaia's face, as she whispered to them, her voice calm and gentle.

'Girls, I know you're scared, but try to be strong. I'll come and find you as soon as I can and we'll make things right. Whatever happens I will find you.'

As Gaia spoke she felt one of the girls wrap her arms around her. The other child followed. It was the first moment of recognition, a moment of tenderness. All three knelt together, locked in each other's arms. Gaia felt the slow movement of the sister's breathing. The children were so delicate and fragile.

There was movement from behind, a sudden change in the mood and level of activity. Gaia was grabbed by two or three strong people and led away. There were scuffles and cries from Freya and Aran as they too were led away. Gaia could hear fighting, shouting and screaming. Freya's voice boomed from the darkness, her voice defiant.

'Be strong. I'll come for you. Do you hear me? I'll come for you.'

The cries became muffled and distant as the group were dragged in different directions. There was no sound from the girls. Gaia stopped kicking and struggling. It was futile as the people leading her were too strong. Gaia was masked, unarmed, and outnumbered and now separated from the others. It was clear the people wanted things done their way. Gaia had no choice now, do as the people wanted and see where it led. She needed to conserve her energy. Anything could happen now and Gaia had to be ready. She recalled what Aran had said. The words puzzled and alarmed her.

Gaia heard a door being opened as she was led inside. The guards sat her down and removed her shoes and socks. Gaia was led into a room. The surface of the floor was smooth, hard and cold. The guards forced Gaia to sit, something firm and wooden. The grip of the captors loosened, and some left the room. Gaia sat in silence, listening and waiting, sensing someone was still in the room, their eyes looking at her. There was a tug and the balaclava was removed.

Gaia's eyes struggled to adjust. Her vision was blurred and the light in the room stung. She rubbed them, blinked, as the pain subsided and her sight returned. Gaia was in a large bathroom, the light from the frosted windows dampened by wooden walls. She was sitting on a slatted, wooden bench. Beside her were some white pyjamas and a towel. A pair of tartan slippers were on the floor by her feet. In the opposite corner of the room stood a woman wearing the black clothes of the others. Her hair was short and black, and she wore dark glasses. Gaia looked for the woman's eyes, as always, but could not make them out. The female guard stood up straight, staring forward, back stiff. Her arms were folded, a blank expression on her face. Gaia looked at the shower. Despite all her fear and apprehension it looked inviting. Her bones were chilled through, her skin wrinkled with the cold and damp. Now Gaia had stopped moving she could feel her body beginning to shiver. The female guard spoke, her voice cold and without emotion.

'Remove your clothes and shower, please.'

Gaia struggled to her feet and peeled off her clothes. Shuffling into the shower, Gaia eased the chrome dial and waited as the water gushed out. She gazed at the ceiling, watching the steam begin to rise. The heat from the water and steam hit Gaia in the face, burning her lungs as she breathed. Gaia stepped into the cubicle and the sharp, hot needles stabbed her freezing skin. She shuddered with the sensation, closed the cubicle door and let the water envelope her. The water was comforting, caressing her, washing away her cold. Gaia remained wary and alert though, stealing sly looks checking the guard.

Gaia ran her fingers down the clean and smooth tiled cubicle. The sound of the rushing water comforted her. The water spiralled down the plughole, swirling to the start of its own long journey. It was on an endless cycle of change, river and rain, mist and moisture, ocean and sea. The sharp needles were restoring Gaia, washed over her aching body, and long, flowing red hair. As Gaia lifted her face toward the shower she let the sprinkles of water tickle her skin. The clouds of steam burst into the air and beyond into the room.

Gaia wanted to stay here forever, never wanted to lose the water's soothing touch, leave its warmth and protection. Her mind evaporated into the warm mist. Gaia was a child again, a baby, not yet born floating inside her mother's womb. It was dark and quiet with only a faint light seeping through her mother's skin. Gaia felt safe and happy floating in this strange chamber, a world within a world, knowing no harm would come to her. The water whispered, singing sweet, slow lullabies, caressing her body, comforting her. This was where it all began, the start of all journeys. Gaia was back at the beginning, inside the mother she had never known, had been denied. The mother who should have reared her, fed and sang, nursed and kissed Gaia. The mother the community had replaced. It all began in water, the birthplace of everything.

Gaia drifted back to the world, the one she wanted to flee from. Her dream faded. Turning the dial, Gaia waited as the flow of the water eased and trickled to an end. The tingling of the warm needles disappeared, and the cold of the room began to creep in. Gaia leant against the wall of the cubicle, staring at the floor, letting the water drip from her. She dried and dressed, the pyjamas were soft and light, too much so for the cold season. Gaia sat on the bench and looked at the guard who remained upright and alert, with no movement or expression. Gaia played with her long, red hair twirling the wet strands around her fingers. After a while Gaia broke the silence.

'Do you have a brush or a comb?'

Without any acknowledgement the guard moved across to the cupboard by Gaia. Inside there were shelves and drawers. The woman took a brush from one of the drawers and handed it to Gaia who thanked her and began to brush her hair. The ends were thick and matted, but soon she had moved through all the strands till it was smooth and shiny. The pyjamas had patches of wet where Gaia had been combing the water from each strand. She laid down the brush and stared back at the guard.

'You don't speak much.'

There was no response, as Gaia continued to press the woman.

'So what happens now? Do I just sit here?'

There was a long silence, then a sudden response from the guard. Gaia was startled.

'Someone will be along to collect you soon.'

There was a knock and the woman approached Gaia and picked up the balaclava.

'Put this back on. It's time for your briefing.'

Gaia looked up at the guard and down at the mask. There was a look of defiance on Gaia's face. The guard was quick to respond, her voice more commanding.

'Just do as I ask.'

Gaia placed the balaclava over her head and was plunged into darkness once more. She heard the door open and footsteps approach. Someone took her arm and led her from the bathroom along what seemed like a long narrow corridor. Gaia could feel the walls close by as the guard ushered her forward. They stopped, a door opened and Gaia was led inside. The guard sat Gaia in a chair. There was a sick odour, the thick smell of damp. It was familiar, her mind told Gaia she knew it, but struggled to place where. There was something ominous about the room, a feeling of danger. The smell had triggered something in her mind, lurking in the vault of her brain. Gaia associated the smell with fear and threat, with pain.

The door closed and Gaia sensed she was now alone with her thoughts. She wanted to cough, but could not. The foul air was beginning to burn the back of her throat. There were no sounds, and only the pitch black before her eyes. There was a long wait, seconds seemed like minutes. There was a sound, the door was opening, and a thud as it slammed shut. There were footsteps, slow and steady marching across the room. They stopped a few feet in front of Gaia. There was a long pause, and someone spoke. At first her brain struggled to process the voice, but Gaia knew it - the voice and smell. Gaia was still in darkness, but she saw the room in her head, and the image of a face staring back.

'Take off your mask.'

Gaia removed the balaclava. Her eyesight was fuzzy, blinking over and over. Things began to clear and the room appeared as the mist of confused colours took shape. Someone was there, standing behind a table, towering over Gaia. It was no longer a dream.

22

'Welcome back, thirty seven.'

The words sliced through Gaia like a sword of ice. Rage bubbled up inside like lava, as Gaia stretched her fingers and tensed feeling each muscle and every sinew. Her neck strained with the fury running through her. Kali watched and waited. The light from an oil lamp on the table lit the leader's tall, slender body, hanging over Gaia with the faintest of grins, mocking her. Kali's arms were folded in triumph, as Gaia struggled to quell the festering emotion inside, feeling the anger twitching, reaching for the switch, fighting to keep control. A small chamber in Gaia's brain, a voice of reason spoke, calming and reassuring her. Confrontation was foolish. Kali was strong, an unassailable opponent. Gaia was weary and unarmed. Whatever the outcome there were other leaders who would come. Gaia was trapped. The voice begged with Gaia to sit this out, not do anything foolish, play it through, find the right moment. Freya's final words were *'Play the game.'* It was always about waiting for the right moment, and this was not it. Where were Freya, Aran, and the girls? There was a stabbing pain in her chest.

Gaia listened, focused on the voice, tried to suppress the emotion. The twitching finger of her ire began to ease. Sweeping up all her emotion, she squeezed back into its box, pressed the lid shut, and smothered it. The pulse still raced, the breathing still frantic, but Gaia began to regain control. This was all about control.

Kali watched and waited, never moving, not even a twitch. There was all the time Kali needed. She was in command. This was a shock to Gaia who needed time to let it sink in, to settle and adjust. When her prisoner was ready Kali would explain everything and it would all become clear. Kali could see Gaia wrestling with her anger, fighting it. The training was coming good. The young one remembered. Kali waited for the right moment, then spoke, her voice assured.

'I know this will be a shock to you.'

Gaia bit her lip, vowing to remain silent, let Kali speak, let her explain. Gaia would not get drawn into conversation. Kali was clever, too clever. This needed thought. The anger had subsided, but the sting of disappointment began to seep through. The fury had snuffed out the pain, but flames of despair now flickered. Then came the questions. How could this be happening? After all the group had gone through, all they had suffered, how had it come to this? Gaia had travelled far only to be face to face again with her nemesis and darkest fear, the enemy. Gaia had run away to find herself, to find freedom, yet found herself staring into the eyes of all she had run from. How? Why? Everything lay shattered in pieces. The promise of something else, something better, was all gone.

Gaia's heart ached, the shards of shattered dreams, now splinters in her flesh. Anger was futile, fear was defeat. They could be controlled, but Gaia could not smother the bitter taste of her despair. Her eyes remained focused on Kali, not wanting to avert her gaze, determined, gripped in proxy combat. Inside Gaia was broken, wanted to let her head drop onto the table, her body crumble. She wanted to weep, collapse, surrender. But Gaia could not, and would not. It would be weakness, submission, defeat and there would be no surrender to Kali, never. Gaia had to stay strong, match her enemy, show her the spirit had not been destroyed. Gaia took a deep breath and prepared.

Gaia widened her focus to take in the room, the prison cell. It was familiar, as she had dreamt. It was dark and windowless, the only light from a lamp that stood on the table. The smell of damp was everywhere. Beyond Kali, the faint glow failed to reach into the corners. The room was a veil of shadows.

Kali was as before, still dressed in the standard issue green and navy, hair cropped, eyes cold crystal blue. Her light, almost translucent skin, rugged and scarred. Her body lean and strong, older but still fit and powerful. The leader's presence was imposing and intimidating. Kali spoke again in a clear and commanding tone. It was the voice of authority, someone who knew they were in control.

'What I'm about to tell you could be difficult to take in. You might struggle to accept it, but in time you will. You must if you are to have a future.'

Kali paused, lowered her arms, leant forward and placed them on the table. Her face was closer than ever, eyes still locked on Gaia, burning, laser sharp and precise. The leader was weighing her victim up, looking for a reaction, waiting for a response. Gaia stared back, holding her ground, refusing to be intimidated. Gaia said nothing. There was so much going on inside her head, so many conversations. The calm internal voice was wrestling and reasoning with the other frantic screaming of her emotions. Gaia was tormented, dizzy and confused, but refused to show Kali. The leader waited, continued to scan her captive for any hint of emotion or response, hoping for a reaction, but there was none. When Kali realised nothing would come, she spoke again. This time a more measured, calmer voice, almost reassuring and comforting.

'Your escape from the island, your journey here, you thought it was all some grand plan, your chance to be free. You were wrong.'

Kali paused, allowing the words to sink in, waiting for a response. Kali had realised Gaia's game, suppressing the emotion, giving little away. Gaia was attempting to remain in control, the training was working. This was good, very good. Kali was impressed. The leaders had programmed Gaia well. Kali continued.

'You see thirty seven, this whole charade was planned. Not by you, but by us, the leaders. The escape was a test.'

Gaia listened to the words, trying to process them. The words tumbled over in her head, one by one. Kali went on.

'We allowed you to escape. I allowed it, because that's what the community wanted. That's what I wanted.'

This was a trick, one of Kali's games. There was no way the community would have allowed this to happen, no way Kali could have planned this. Why would they? Why take the risk? Gaia was convinced Kali was toying with her. *Just let her speak, let the words wash away, ignore her. Let her think she was in control, let her play this* out. Gaia knew the truth, and could see through this pathetic little game. Kali grinned and kept pressing.

'I know what you're thinking, but it's true. This was all just a test, your final test. You see thirty seven you're one of the special few chosen. We've been watching you since you were born. We've always had big plans for you. We've been moulding you, shaping you. All of your education and training, it's all led to this point. We've programmed you to become a leader. That's what all your training has been about. Right from the beginning this was always going to be the end. The escape was a test to see if you're capable and worthy.'

Kali paused and smiled. Opening her arms up to the darkness, she almost sang out the words in glory.

'This is it thirty seven. This is your becoming.'

Gaia erupted inside. Lies! This was all lies! Kali was adding layer upon layer to make the story convincing, but Gaia smelt the desperation. Gaia began to process Kali's words, unpick and destroy them. The community could never admit to the escape. This would be too much for the egos of the leaders. They would have to save face, could not let escapees think they had succeeded. What better way to destroy the group's success than to concoct such a lie. The bigger the lie, the better. The leaders wanted to be in control, because they were always in control, could never lose it, but now they had. Gaia and the others had escaped, and humiliated the community. Now the leaders needed a story to destroy that.

Kali had plunged the blade of her words into Gaia's chest and began to twist them, the pleasure dripping from her face.

'You made it. You survived. All that training paid off. You've shown us your desire to survive at all costs. You've done what was needed. You've killed. Yes, you've killed, and will do anything to survive. That is what we need in a leader.'

Gaia remembered Hakan. The knife plunged inside his bloodied corpse. Not only had Gaia killed, but she had murdered a leader. The community would never let her get away with it. The leaders would make her pay for what she had done. Kali's voice dropped to a whisper, her face still pressed close to Gaia.

'We have concerns, grave concerns. There's always a risk with your type. You're the brilliant ones, the ones with the exceptional talents and skills. You're intelligent, the very brightest, but all that brilliance comes with an edge.'

Kali paused, standing back from the table.

'But you always want more, and think there's something out there that you deserve. Why? That's the problem. You know you're special and you want it all. But the biggest problem is that you want freedom. The community built you to be the best, but you think you're to good for us. You're wrong.'

Kali began to pace back and forward. Gaia could no longer see her face, only her body moving. The leader kept up the tirade, Gaia still trying to block out the words.

'The community needs you, and you need us. Despite the risk. I want to harness your brilliance. You and seventy three, you were my project. You were both given to me by the community. It was my job to make you what you've become. You've got so much to offer, more than you'll ever realise. I've always known it. I knew there'd be problems. There was bound to be with two as brilliant as you, but you've come through. You've both survived.'

Kali stepped forward, her face coming into view again. Her eyes were large, more intense, burning with passion and conviction. This was no longer an order, it was almost a plea to Gaia, a plea and a warning.

'I need to be sure that you're onside, that you'll commit. The community is the place you belong, the place you can realise everything you are and could become. But I have to be sure of that, if you're to pass the test and both join me.'

Gaia laughed inside, a laugh of disdain. Kali had changed tack now, moved to flattery in an attempt to disarm Gaia. It would not work. Kali thought she could swamp her victim in gushing praise, make her feel so very special and valued. Gaia knew these techniques so well. It was pathetic, almost insulting. The leader would have to do better than this. This was disappointing. Gaia would never fall for it. *Let her keep talking and digging, remain calm and silent, let the words pass by. They were only words, small, plain, and harmless words. They were empty and meaningless. They only had meaning and power if Gaia let them.* Gaia would not let them. Kali was not finished.

'I know you've got doubts about us, but this is where you belong. The community created you. Everything you are is because of us. You're only here in this room because we wanted it to happen. Everything that has led to this moment was because of us.'

Kali paused. The words echoed inside Gaia's head, still trying to push them out, expel them, but they twisted and turned refusing to leave. The words were laughing at Gaia, mocking her. Not content with this assault Kali kept up the attack.

'You think you chose this, but did you? What led you to make those choices? What made you the person who would make them? What gave you the courage to do what you did Ask yourself who made you what you are?'

Gaia tried to deflect the words. They were only words, and meant nothing unless she let them. Gaia was in control, not Kali. The words would not hurt her. Never! Kali continued to batter Gaia, trying to weaken her.

'I know you think there's something else, something better. There isn't. You've seen the world out there. You've walked through it, seen what it's become. It's a lawless place filled with nothing but chaos. There's no order or structure, no values. It's a world of death and destruction.'

The words were breaking through despite all Gaia's effort. The images of the journey flashed in her mind - the spiders, rats, the blood and slaughter. Kali was weakening her and they both knew it. The leader increased the pressure.

'Is that what you call freedom? That is chaos. That is survival, nothing more. Everyone and everything is out to destroy you. That's the reality of the world we've inherited, the world the fools of the past plunged us into. We're the future, and we're fighting back. The community offers something better. We create order and structure, provide freedom from harm, and suffering. You've got the freedom to be someone, to contribute, to be part of that new future, to help build something even better. The community's your best chance of that future and the freedom you want. The community is real. Out there is nothing. The other world you're looking for doesn't exist. If you stay with us you can make the world you want.'

Gaia tried to shut out the words, but it was pointless. They broke through and were disarming her. The different voices in her head were still fighting, at odds, but a new voice had emerged. This voice was telling Gaia to listen to Kali's words, maybe the enemy had a point. The voice reminded Gaia of the pain the group had endured on their journey, of the daily struggle to survive, the relentless fear and the loss. The voice spoke of the people they had met, and the creatures they had faced and run from.

Life in the community was oppressive and controlled. It had suffocated Gaia to the point where she had to break free, but life had been safer and more secure on the island. Gaia had a role, a purpose, and was part of a structure. Another internal voice spoke. What Gaia was looking for was not the chaos and disorder of the world outside, nor was it the oppression of the community. The world was as Kali described, but Gaia did not want to be part of it, or simply survive. She wanted something else - a new way of life, a different place, somewhere with order, structure, security, but something more. Gaia wanted to find who she was, not be moulded or shaped, a cog in a machine. She wanted to be Gaia not thirty seven, whoever Gaia really was.

Kali was on a roll, the blade deep and the wounds oozing blood. She just needed to keep twisting, one turn at a time, keep her victim wincing, increasing the pain.

'There are many amongst the leaders that think I've lost you, that you've already gone, that you can no longer be saved.'

Kali leant forward onto the table and pressed her face close. Gaia felt the heat of the leader's stale breath as she spat out the words.

'I'll save you. Whatever it takes I'll save you.'

Kali remained poised, the tension hanging over them. Stepping back, the leader stood up straight, stretched, and placed both hands together. Kali began to play with her fingers. There was a long pause, as she lowered the tone and pace of the assault. The words were getting through, working. Kali was winning, as she always did.

'You may be brilliant, but you can't see beyond your own ego. It tells you you're always right. How could you ever be wrong?'

Kali laughed. It was cold, heartless, chilling. Its waves and echoes cut through Gaia. Kali sneered out more words from the ashes of her laughter.

'There is no right or wrong anymore. In a world of order there's survival. Survival built on structure, safety and security. In a world of chaos there is pain. The only true escape is death. The freedom you want, the freedom of chaos only ever leads to pain and death. So, what's it going to be? Order or chaos? Pleasure or pain? Life or death? You choose.'

The voices inside Gaia wrestled. Her head was spinning with confusion. Every instinct was telling her not to trust Kali, that her enemy was manipulating and playing with her, trying to mould and shape her as the community had moulded and shaped her life. There was the voice of doubt, the one that heard the logic and reason in Kali's words. It saw the opportunity, and the potential for a way out. There was also the voice of hope, telling Gaia that Kali was wrong, there was another way, there had to be. This voice clung to the faintest glimmer of light, the tiny remaining fragment of faith that told her such a community existed somewhere. There was an alternative.

Kali removed the cold blade, leaving only the open wound, the icy pain inside. She stepped back and folded her arms, eyes staring down at Gaia, the cold blue pinning her victim to the chair. There was a pause. The leader continued, laying out her final offer, voice lowered to a whisper.

'I've persuaded the other leaders to give me time. I've told them I can save you, bring you back. There's still a chance for you. What I'm offering is this. I want you to become a leader. You've survived the test, proven yourself. You'll have responsibility, power, influence. You'll be able to support, shape and mould the lives of others. You'll be able to develop your brilliance, and skills. You'll be able to build that better world you seek. I'm offering you the chance to be somebody, be part of something. You'll work alongside me and seventy three. I'll train you both, help you develop. I'll give you all that I know.'

Kali paused again, wanted Gaia to soak up the words, understand them, think the offer through. This moment could make or break Gaia.

'I have to be convinced that you're with us. I've got to be sure that you're what you were always meant to be. I can save you, but only if you let me.'

Gaia listened to Kali's words as they burrowed into her. Each word twisted inside her like a hot knife, feeling the pain of their promise and loss. Here was a choice, a way back, an opportunity. This was a path, a certain future. What were the alternatives? What would happen if Gaia did not accept? What Kali was offering was not a real choice. This was the only real option. Kali wanted to save Gaia, but this was for Kali not Gaia. Freya and Gaia were Kali's project, and the leader did not want to see her project fail.

Gaia was tired, her body weary and aching all over. The battle in her mind had burnt her out, along with the struggle of the past few days. Everything had converged and was crushing Gaia. She needed rest and food. Gaia had heard Kali's pleas and held her resolve, not becoming locked in a row, or war of words. Gaia had listened and fought the onslaught, knew what was being offered. Now she just wanted to eat and rest.

'I'm hungry.'

'Of course, you must be. I'll get you some food.'

Kali left the room. Gaia was alone, and gazed around the room, unable to see much but shadows. The table was dark wood, old and stained. Some of the stains were a deep dark red. The surface was scratched, littered with graffiti and etchings. The lamp flickered and hissed, the faint smell of kerosene mixed with the rank odour of the damp. The silence and solitude let the sickly smell creep back into her consciousness. Gaia could not bear it, feeling sick, as though she might choke. She listened to the rumbles in her stomach echo, the bubbles rattling inside.

Kali returned with a plate of meat, bread, cheese and salad, and a plastic beaker of apple juice. Gaia ate and drank in silence, while Kali looked on. Kali took the plate and beaker and stood at the table opposite Gaia.

'I'm going to leave you to think about what I've said. When I return I want an answer.'

Kali left the room, locking the door behind her. Gaia laid her arms on the table and rested her head on them. She stared at the flickering flame of the lamp. After all they had been through it had come to this. Where were Aran, Freya, and the girls? Gaia pictured Aran's face and tried to feel the warmth of his lips, the delicate touch of his hand. Would she ever see Aran again?

Gaia's heart sank, the pain of loneliness and despair flooded through her. Alone with only her thoughts, Gaia realised she was weeping. Lost and lonely tears trickled down the side of her face. The light of the lamp hissed much louder, the flame flared, faded, and went out. Gaia was plunged into darkness, with her tears in the musty, foul stench of this cell. She had no idea where she was, or what the future held. There was a choice which was no choice at all, and time to think and dwell. How much time was not known. Gaia closed her eyes, fought back the tears, her eyelids trapping them. She drifted into a deep sleep. There were no dreams and no nightmares. There was only emptiness and darkness, and drowning in the depths of loneliness.

23

Gaia stirred. Her neck was sore, the side of her face and arms numb. The room was black and still reeked. There was a scratching noise in the far corner, a scuttling sound and silence. She sat up and waited. Thoughts swirled in her mind, the voices fought again. Gaia wanted to block them out, silence them, but they kept bombarding her. Her thoughts turned to Aran, Freya, and the girls again. Were they going through this too? Were they being given the same choice?

Kali's image and voice kept appearing, the smug grin, the mocking tone, the subtle sound of triumph. Gaia tried not to think of her. The poison of hatred would destroy. If it was allowed to pollute the mind the enemy had won. Gaia had to stay focused and in control. The options were few, but she would not surrender, or let Kali's victory be complete.

The dark, empty minutes seeped into hours, and there was nothing. Gaia was starving again after the sleep, her stomach churning knots of hunger. Her mouth was dry, a foul taste mixed with putrid air. Sleep had done little to satisfy the weariness. Her head ached, as the hours drifted by with no idea if it was night or day, her body and mind tricked by the darkness. Gaia fought back anger and frustration. This was all part of the game, to keep her waiting, to wear her out, crush her spirit to the point of desperation. Gaia was stronger than Kali imagined, resolve reinforced by a hatred of her enemy.

Gaia's mind raced, seeing the emptiness that lay before her. If what Kali said was true, and the other leaders had given up on her, Kali was all that was keeping her alive. The enemy had become the lifeline, Gaia's fate was at Kali's mercy. There was an urge to attack and bring everything to an end, but killing Kali would be near impossible. She was skilled and strong, and Gaia was weary. She would need a weapon and to strike when the leader was not expecting it. Even if she did succeed it would mean almost certain death. The guards would come. Revenge would be Gaia's final act. Her life was hanging by a delicate thread. It was fraying moment by moment as Gaia twisted and turned. What about Aran and Freya? What if they refused the offer? What if they did not want to become what Kali wanted? Would the leaders kill them? What about Ruth and Mary? Where did their future lie?

As the hours drifted by, the hunger grew, and the pain and anger evaporated into despair. Gaia lost all sense of where she was or what was happening. The darkness enveloped her, and she became delirious. Weird, distorted visions flashed through her mind. The rats chewed and began to devour her, their rabid, salivating jaws ripping at her flesh. Gaia tried to move, but could not get away. The spiders crawled over her, their thick, black hairs pricked, their bulbous eyes were staring. The creatures' rancid breath was upon her. There was the deformed body of the calf, calling out for her help, a frenzied, desperate plea as it was led to solitude, isolation, abandonment and death. Killed by its own. Rejected and murdered for being different.

Images haunted Gaia. They were fleeting, but macabre visions of all she had seen, her worst fears. Kali came to her with a twisted, demonic face. She was shouting, spitting in her face, pressing a knife against her throat. The priest appeared sneering and dripping thick white saliva from his lips. He was standing on his pulpit, spewing out words in a language Gaia did not understand. The church seats were filled with the bloodied corpses of little girls, all in rags, their eyes gorged out and lips sewn together. Image upon image, vision after vision, a wall of madness, crushing and breaking Gaia, suffocating her. Maybe she was dying. Maybe this was how it happened. If it was the end Gaia was ready, and would welcome and embrace death, anything to escape this torture.

When Gaia thought she had reached the end a light returned. The lamp on the table flickered into life. It burned her eyes, the ache in her head raged with fire. Rubbing her eyes, Gaia could barely see, only a blur and distorted images. The haziness cleared and Gaia saw Kali. She was not demonic, but real, beyond the table, arms folded, face awash with concern. Kali's voice was just above a whisper.

'How are you?'

Gaia tried to speak, but her lips and mouth were dry and stuck together. Kali reached down and picked something from the floor and put it on the table.

'Drink this.'

Gaia guided her arm towards the water bottle on the table, as though it was someone else's arm, another body, the mind disconnected and transmitting from afar. She managed to lift the bottle to her lips, and pulled open the stopper with her teeth. The water was cool and refreshing as each gulp rushed down her throat, bringing new life, triggering the fragments that remained. There was a sickness in the pit of her stomach. Gaia had drank too much. She leant to the side of the table and threw up on the floor. Kali spoke again, her voice gentle and reassuring, almost a tinge of sadness and pity.

'Take your time. Your body will need time.'

Gaia could taste the bile, saliva hung from her mouth and chin. She wiped them with her sleeve, and looked up at Kali, managing to force some words from her lips.

'Can I have something to eat?'

'Later. First we need to talk. You've had enough time to think. I want your answer.'

Gaia was not prepared to roll over, as the final scraps of defiance took over.

'I don't remember discussing anything. I just remember you spouting words.'

Kali smiled, a wry grin. Leaning forward, she rested her arms on the table. All the pity had gone from her voice, the commanding tone had returned.

'You heard what I said. There's a way back. All you have to do is accept my offer.'

'And if I don't?'

Kali stood up straight. Arms locked together, she twisted her neck, the head swaying back and forth. Kali stretched, her mouth open wide, twisting every muscle and sinew in her face. The leader continued to do this, her face contorted and mad, pondering her words.

'You're a murderer. People are dead because of you, one of them a leader. Do you think we could let you walk out of here? The other leaders want your blood. If you won't accept my offer there's nothing I can do. You'll be taken to the haven where you'll face justice.'

'What about the others?'

Kali took time before answering. She was cautious in her response.

'Seventy three was given the same offer. You come as a package. I won't let either of you go until I am sure. She has accepted, as you will. She's a survivor and knows what I'm capable of. The outsiders you brought with you, the two young girls, they've been dealt with.'

Gaia sat up, alarmed.

'What do you mean dealt with?'

'They don't belong here. They aren't pure. They aren't of the community. Their place is outside with the others, so we've handed them over to their own.'

Kali's voice was cold, no hint of emotion or remorse. The fury flared up in Gaia, what few ounces of energy she had left were plunged into her anger.

'You've what! You can't. You said yourself what it's like out there. They're just kids.'

Kali continued without expression, Gaia's words were empty to her. The girls meant nothing.

'They're not our problem. We only have a responsibility to our own. They're outsiders, so they can look after them, or they can fend for themselves. That's the law on the outside. You've seen how it works. If they are strong enough they'll survive.'

Gaia felt the tears welling up. Fighting them, she tried to stop her lip from trembling. The voices were rushing through her head again, but it was all babble, background noise. There was an image of the girls, lost and wandering on the moorland outside, drifting in the wilderness, without anyone to protect them. They would be at the mercy of this group of others, the elements, and the creatures. What would they do to them? Her anger fought her frustration. There was nothing Gaia could do to save them. Leaning forward onto the table, Gaia put her head down. The moments drifted by in near silence, with only the hiss of the burning lamp. Kali waited, said nothing. Gaia thought of Aran, and the words she feared. She needed to know.

'What about Aran? You haven't mentioned Aran.'

'He's fine. You needn't worry about him.'

They waited in silence again. Gaia sat, head bowed, as Kali stood over her. Gaia knew it was over, the only victory now could be Kali's. Would her victory be complete? Would Gaia surrender and let the enemy take total control? Kali broke the silence.

'You can fight this, and force me to break you. And I *will* break you. Or we can cut this short, you can see sense, accept my offer and join me and your friends.'

Gaia swallowed hard, summoning any remaining energy. Her body was running on the last few drops of anger.

'If I say yes, will you let Aran and Freya go?'

'There are no deals here. You're in no position to negotiate. Will you accept my offer?'

There was a long pause. The voices in Gaia's head in a frenzy, as she blocked them out and focused on the darkness. There was a tunnel, at the end a small dot of light. Gaia walked towards it. As she neared the light burned brighter, and her eyes stung at its heat. It was a pure light, white with a raging intensity. The answer came to her. In a moment of complete clarity amongst all the madness.

'Fuck you!'

Kali lunged onto the table and pressed her face into Gaia's. Her eyes were glowing with fury, spit splattering Gaia as Kali fired out the words. The stench of the leader's stale breath seared at Gaia's nostrils.

'This isn't over yet.'

Kali smashed the lamp against the wall and stormed from the room leaving Gaia in darkness. Gaia collapsed onto the floor, alive but all consciousness gone.

When Gaia came to she was back in the chair, hands tied behind her back. A new lamp was on the table, its light revealing Kali. There was a towel in her hand. Gaia sensed there was someone else in the room. Gaia was beyond exhaustion, the point of no longer caring. All that kept her going was the thought of Freya and Aran and the chance they were still alive. That and the anger and hatred for Kali. Passion and love kept Gaia clinging to life, but Kali was in no mood to waste time. The games were over.

Gaia felt her hair wrenched from behind, her head was thrust back. There was the face of the woman, the watcher in the shower standing over. The guard tugged at Gaia's hair, keeping her head steady, not letting Gaia move. Kali approached, pressing the muscles on Gaia's cheek, forcing her mouth open, shoving the towel in. Kali leant over and picked up a bucket of water, pouring it into Gaia's mouth. Gaia could feel the water running down her throat. She could not breath, gasping for air but there was only water. Her stomach filled and she felt a desperate urge to puke.

Everything began to slip away. Gaia's head was floating, as though in an ocean and underwater. The light of the sun shone above, as she tried to swim, to reach it. It was no good. The more Gaia reached for the light, the further away she seemed to be.

Gaia felt a sharp pain in her stomach, the towel dragged from her mouth. She vomited the water on the table and the floor. Grasping for air, still choking, but relieved as the oxygen reached her brain. Gaia was dripping wet, her breathing desperate, drifting in and out of consciousness. Kali stood over her, watched the suffering, waiting. Kali grabbed Gaia's hair and yanked her head back, leaning down, lips next to Gaia's cheek, snarling in her ear.

'Give in. The others are with me. They've accepted. Now it's your turn.'

Gaia heard her words. *The others are with me.* It had to be more lies. Aran and Freya would never give in, they would never accept, would both rather die. Kali dragged Gaia's head back again, pushed the towel into her victim's mouth and began to pour. Kali repeated it over and over. Each time Gaia was dragged to the point of suffocation, of drowning, all consciousness slipping away. The guard would punch Gaia, spewing the water everywhere. Kali continued the assault coupled with angry words, spitting bile in Gaia's face.

Kali ceased the torture, paced up and down in front of the table. Kali knelt in front of Gaia, lifting her face drenched in water. The leader spoke to her victim, lips pressed close, voice calm, the words slow and precise.

'It's time to accept your future. You're the only one now. You're all alone. Don't be a fool. You're smarter than that. You know you are.'

Gaia spat in Kali's face, jolting forward trying to free herself from the ties binding her to the chair. Gaia's body lurched against the table and bounced back, almost toppling over onto the floor.

'You're a liar! They'd never accept. '

'Have it your way.'

Kali moved behind Gaia, pushing her head forward towards the light, her eyeline looking across the table. Gaia's eyesight was fuzzy, but she noticed the boots. There was someone standing in the corner, just like the dream. Gaia knew the boots.

Kali spoke, her voice triumphant, almost delirious with anger and full of disdain.

'Your boyfriend, Aran as you call him. Did you really think he was with you? Did you think that it was real?'

Kali laughed, mocking her victim as she shook Gaia's head and leant close to her ear.

'Who approached you about the escape? Who suggested it? Who do you think we put up to this? He was ours all along. It was all part of my plan. The other boy, the dreamer, Yann. He was just extra baggage to make it look real. He was expendable. It's you and Freya I wanted all along. You're the special ones. I told you we were in control. I told you this was all just a test.'

It could not be true. This was the final lie, Kali's desperate attempt to break her. Gaia focused on the boots, concentrating with the remaining drops of energy. Gaia recognised the boots. The ones in the dream had been there all the time. Gaia could not see who was wearing them because she did not want to admit the truth.

The boots edged forward and into the light, and Gaia saw the face. In the dim light of the lamp she saw Aran, but his face was different. The beauty and perfect lines had gone. The eyes no longer held any sparkle, only despair and betrayal. Aran lowered his head and said nothing, stepping back into the shadows, hiding his face, the shame. All Gaia could see were the boots, the ones she knew but did not recognise, refused to. The woman guard took Aran by the arm and led him to the door. As they reached it Aran spoke.

'Gaia. I'm sorry. This isn't as it looks. They made me do it. I had no choice. What happened. It was real. I swear.'

Kali stood and shouted at the guard.

'Get him out of here and bring the other one in.'

Gaia plunged into the depths of darkness. Her heart felt as though it was being ripped from her chest. There was nothing left, everything had gone, the will to live was draining from her. She had been clinging to the precipice, the smallest fragments keeping her alive. Now there was only betrayal. The brief glimmers of love had all been a lie. The only time Gaia had opened her heart to someone, they had been a fraud. Aran had driven a stake through Gaia. Kali pressed her lips against Gaia's ear. Gaia could hear her breathing. She could feel it. Kali whispered to her.

'You can't run forever. There comes a time when we all have to stop running from others, from ourselves. If you run you're alone and you'll always be alone. Start to live, become somebody. We dream alone, but live when we're together, when we work together, play together, love together. That's what I'm offering. Become what you really are.'

The door opened and the guard led Freya in, her face swollen and caked in dried blood. The guard took Freya's weight, as she struggled to walk. Gaia winced as she looked at her friend's face, saw the pain. It was the first time Freya had looked vulnerable, broken. The guard let go and Freya flopped in a heap. Kali nodded and the guard left. Freya lay slumped on the floor, her arm covering her face. The only sign of life, the sounds of laboured breathing. Kali stood over Freya, looked down at the crumpled body, then turned to face Gaia.

'Everyone has a breaking point. She accepted my offer, didn't you?'

Kali kicked Freya who let out a scream of pain.

'Yes. I accepted.'

Kali grinned at Gaia.

'Like I said. Everyone has their breaking point. Even your sister.'

At first the word did not register. It began to break through the weariness, a look of shock spread on Gaia's face. Kali laughed.

'Neither of you realised, did you? I said you came as a package and were both special. You don't realise how special you are. That's why I need you together and you will accept.'

Gaia was slipping in and out of a dream. In it she saw Freya, heard her voice standing over her, pleading, *'Sit tight. Play the game. We'll get through this. Our moment will come again.'* Gaia focused on Freya's lips, as the words echoed in her head. She heard Kali's voice again, felt the heat of her breath as she spoke.

'It's over. Just give in. Accept or I'll kill you.'

Freya pounced, leaping to her feet and stabbing something into Kali's neck. Kali grabbed at her throat as she fell to the floor. Freya was jabbing the neck with her fist, blood spurting from the wound. The door burst open and three guards ran in lunging at Freya, dragging her kicking and screaming away from Kali. Gaia stared down at Kali, covered in blood still clutching her neck, eyes bulging in pain and terror.

The voices in Gaia's head fell silent. The whispers died, as her body went limp, all energy evaporating from exhausted limbs. Gaia lay slumped on the table, the colour draining, her chest moving with the faintest of breaths. Her heart still moved, tapping out a silent beat, lips locked in a grin.

24

Gaia focused on the gentle wind as it whistled through the trees. Staring at the snow at her feet, watching as flakes melted together. The patterns etched in white, she tried to pick out each individual shape as they formed, always changing. Everything around dissolved, only the myriad of icy patterns remained. Gaia emptied her mind, as the pain eased.

Winter was upon them, the cruelest for many years. Clean, crisp snow enveloped the village, a prison of ice. The snow had fallen for days with no let up. Sometimes it was gentle and delicate, would slow and threaten to end. Soon dark clouds would move in and the brutal blizzard would return. Every morning Gaia would wake hoping for a glimmer of warmth, the start of the thaw, but the thick white blanket remained. Sometimes shafts of sunlight would break through the clouds, smiling with golden rays of hope. They were a false dawn, severed by blades of ice, and the bitter arctic air sucking every fragment of heat.

It was a misty morning, Gaia the only glimmer of life in the white desolation. She sat on a wooden bench overlooking a stream, wrapped in layers of thick woollen clothing and a large ill fitting overcoat. Her body shivered in the icy air, as the cold nipped at her cheeks. Gaia loved it here. The spot was secluded, protected by trees and bushes. It was a place to be alone, and the bitter weather made her feel alive again. Gaia gazed into the frozen water, a thick sheet of ice encasing what trickled below. Icicles hung from bare branches that draped the stream, glistening in the light, daggers in the sky, poised to fall.

The gentle sound of the water comforted and soothed Gaia. In the days that had passed the capture she still dreamt of her ordeal, of the torture and drowning. There were visions of Kali in the dark, musty room, the smell of damp in Gaia's nostrils. She could almost taste the kerosene from the lamp, mixed with her own blood. Gaia would wake in the night in cold sweats gasping for air, the image of Kali's body in her head, covered in blood, clinging to life. There was Freya, being dragged from the room.

Freya and Kali were gone, both taken to the haven, one to face justice, the other clinging to life. Freya had tried to kill Kali and may have succeeded. The haven was Kali's only hope of survival. There had been no news since they left. Aran remained in the village. Gaia caught occasional fleeting glimpses from the window of her bedroom. He had avoided Gaia since the capture, still hiding in the shadows with his betrayal and shame. The stream had become Gaia's refuge, her attempt to cleanse herself, and clear her head. There were important decisions to be made. Gaia had to make them soon. She would stare at the water, imagining she was a single drop within its icy flow, invisible, but there, locked within the flurry of the stream. She would let herself drift away, silent and unseen, rushing towards the sea, forever free.

Gaia would be taken to the haven. The leaders were waiting for the moment. They would not tell Gaia when, but it would happen. Every part of Gaia's life had been shaped by others, every part betrayed. For a moment, Gaia had believed the future was hers, she had escaped the island to find and make it. The truth was the future had belonged to the community, those that made her. Gaia was left with the ashes of her love for Aran, the feelings she thought were real, but had been used to trap her. All she felt was hatred, the desire for revenge. Ruth and Mary were lost, cast into the wilderness, given to strangers, roaming the hills. Freya was gone, the sister Gaia never knew she had. The sister who had saved Gaia's life, but in doing so may have sacrificed her own. *All is not what it seems. Seek the truth.* Words once filled with so much hope.

Gaia heard footsteps behind, the crunching of boots on crisp, fresh snow. She turned, peering at the bushes draped in flecks of white. There was a rustle, the branches parted and one of the leaders appeared.

'It's time. Pack your things tonight. We leave at first light tomorrow.'

ACKNOWLEDGMENTS

I would like to thank family, friends, and my copy editor Victoria Watson. You all believed and gave me the wings.

ABOUT THE AUTHOR

Chris is a married father of four boys. After graduating in the early 90s he became an English language teacher living in Turkey, Portugal, India and traveling beyond. He returned to the UK to study an MA in International Politics and worked at Warwick University. He then moved into policy research and implementation.

Chris is a musician involved in a range of musical projects. He plays solo horn for Jayess Newbiggin Brass Band, the village where he grew up. Chris loves running and in addition to a couple of marathons has run many half marathons and 10Ks. He currently lives in Monkseaton, near Newcastle upon Tyne.

Chris' dream was always to write a novel, and his writing journey began in August 2015 when he took voluntary redundancy from his role in education policy. 'Becoming' is his debut publication.

Chris is editing a mystery set in mid-nineteenth century Northumberland which he hopes to publish in 2017. He is also writing the follow-up to 'Becoming' which is titled 'Awakening.'

Further information on Chris and his work can be found at:
http://chrisord.wixsite.com/chrisord
or on Facebook at:
https://www.facebook.com/chrisordauthor/

Printed in Great Britain
by Amazon